ALWAYS A RUNNER

BRUCE BLIZARD

CHRISTIAN BOOKS WITH AN EDGE

PROLOGUE

THE SHOUTING STOPPED. Something crashed, as if someone had thrown a bottle and smashed it against a wall, then the front door slammed shut. Mike got out of bed, made his way down the hall and out onto the front porch. He stood there and watched his mother march north along the right shoulder of the Mountain Loop Highway.

Mike went back into the house.

"Dad?" he called.

There was no answer, so he rushed to his room and pulled his faded sneakers onto his bare feet. He grabbed a sweatshirt from the floor and followed his mother. He was certain she knew he was following her, but she never looked back.

She reached the bridge above Silver Falls, a noisy series of foamy cataracts at the end of the last wild stretch of the Silver River. A pickup he thought he recognized stopped. The driver reached across the seat to open the passenger-side door and asked if she needed a ride. Mike stepped onto the side of the road, crouched between two old trees and watched as she climbed into the seat.

"I need to get to Abel," he heard her say.

Mike jumped up and ran toward the pickup.

Through the open window, his mother looked at him and said, "Go home, Mike."

The driver's green eyes flashed when he looked at Mike's mom and then darkened when he glanced past her at Mike. "Hey, I know you. You're Bobby's wife."

Mike used the back of his hand to wipe tears from his cheeks and then cursed both his parents as the taillights disappeared across the bridge.

1

MIKE BECK HAD RUN 2,177 days in a row, and he wondered about things when he ran. He wondered if his mother would ever come back and if his father would stay. If his only friend, Joyce, would go to heaven and if James, the local tough guy and top jock, would go to hell.

He also wondered if he'd ever find out how hard and how fast he could run.

Mike ran every day and won every time he raced, and he didn't mind that no one seemed to notice. But by age sixteen, he had absorbed the two most important lessons kids learned as they grew up. One, what teenagers wanted for themselves was seldom what grownups wanted for them. And two, if adults believed their own crap, they'd act differently.

Mike knew adults didn't like him because he was belligerent and disrespectful, and he refused to listen to their advice. The official version arrived at by Doctor Linda Lasch, who had long, straight hair and a soft voice and who had tested and questioned Mike every day after school for two weeks, was that Mike had become belligerent and disrespectful after his pious mother left. His pious mother left because his father, Robert, smacked her around when he drank. Yet, when Robert stopped drinking for good, Mike's mother did not come back, so he suspected Doctor Linda Lasch might be wrong.

Still, the doctor reported her "findings" to school officials as stone truth, and the officials reported the doctor's diagnosis to Robert as stone truth, and that was that. The doctor gave Mike's "condition" a name and a set of capitalized initials. She prescribed drugs, which Mike would not take, and recommended counseling, which he refused to attend. Then, at the end of their last session, Dr. Linda Lasch had given Mike a minute or two to explain his situation in *his own words*.

Mike did not have to think about what he would say because he'd thought about little else since the night his mother left.

"I live alone most of the time because my mom left when I was twelve, and my old man is on the road four or five days a week. What kid wouldn't be screwed up?"

"There's more to it than that." Dr. Linda Lasch leaned forward and put her hand on Mike's knee. "These situations are complex. Interpersonal relationships are complicated."

Mike didn't believe in complications, and despite what he'd just said, he did not believe he was screwed up.

"Nope," he said and pushed the doctor's hand away. "It's easy. Mom prayed, and Dad drank, and I came along before they figured out drinking don't mix with praying."

The doctor told Mike and the adults at school she did not believe his situation was irretrievable and that some significant event or person might intervene, and he'd be okay, but Mike suspected she didn't actually believe what she'd said. And the adults at school had just nodded and gone on about their business.

So, while he ran on the logging roads and hiking trails near the tiny Cascade Mountain town of Silverton, Washington, Mike wondered about these things. He ran through the old-growth forests soaring out of the lush underbrush, and he ran past vast acres of faded stumps hunkering in neat rows alongside tender saplings. By the end of eleventh grade, he was running ten or twelve times a week. The weather didn't matter. The time of year didn't matter. How he felt didn't matter. He ran sick. He ran hurt. He ran when he was happy, which was rare, and when he was angry, which was normal.

And on what would have been the last Friday morning of the eleventh grade had he not been suspended for fighting with James again, Mike stood at the bedroom window in the house he sometimes shared with his father, stared out at the dense drizzle, and wondered if he'd drown.

The black clouds that brought rain to the foothills of the Cascade Mountains lingered at the treetops, obscured the green hillsides, and perfectly reflected Mike's gloomy morning mood. The perpetually gray skies had been blamed for high rates of depression and suicide in the Pacific Northwest, and Mike thought his dark moods might be something else to wonder about because they seemed to be occurring more often and lasting longer.

Like many sullen boys, Mike was not actually depressed, but he'd never taken the opportunity to become habitually happy either. So, he continued to stare out the window, and rain or no rain, he would run, like always.

Mike left his bedroom, headed toward the back door through the kitchen, and was surprised to see Robert sitting at the kitchen table, gripping a porcelain coffee mug with both hands.

"Son?" Robert said without looking up or turning around.

Son? Mike's father never called him that.

"There's coffee made."

Mike took a step toward the old-fashioned percolator on the stove.

"I've been to see your mother."

Mike walked to the kitchen sink, leaned forward on his hands to stretch his shoulders, and stared into the drain. He took a deep breath and held it. Then, after a moment, he responded to Robert's first statement. "You made coffee. Congratulations."

Robert sighed, and Mike thought about leaving his father at the table and running out into the rain. But, instead, he took a coffee mug from the drying rack, filled it from the percolator, leaned against the counter next to the sink, and stared at Robert's back.

"I don't know what to say." Robert slumped forward in his chair and continued to stare into his mug. "Your mother's been gone a long time. I know you blame me."

"Yeah. A *long* time. And you're right. I blame you. And her." Mike sipped his coffee, held the mug against his lips, and waited for Robert to look at him.

"She's right up the road, you know." Robert finally looked up and turned halfway toward Mike. "She's been living in Abel, where she grew up." He turned back and continued to examine the contents of his mug. "What should I tell her?"

"I know where she's been, and I don't care."

"You don't *care*? Is that what you want me to tell your mother—that you don't care?"

"I'm sorry, *Dad*."

Mike had always called his father Robert. "I. Don't. Give a damn. Tell her whatever you want. It's nothing to do with me."

Mike was taller than Robert, and they had the same brown eyes. But he had his mother's long legs and narrow hips. A year earlier, Mike had appeared frail, and although he was still thin, the long muscles in his arms and legs seemed to ripple below the taut surface of his skin. Mike waited for his father to speak with one heel off the ground and his knees bent, as if he was about to dash off toward some indistinct, invisible, and faraway finish line.

"School's out, right?" Robert said. "Got plans with your friends?"

"Don't got any," Mike said, tapping the rim of his coffee mug.

"Friends or plans?"

"Don't need friends and don't make plans. There's a party at Junior's place tonight. Maybe I'll go. Maybe not."

Mike waited for his father to say something parental, but Robert merely nodded and continued to spin his mug slowly with his fingertips.

"I guess I won't be here when you get home." Robert chewed on his lower lip. "I got to be in Bellingham...um, work. Not sure when I'll be back."

"Whatever. I'll be fine." Mike shrugged. "Is she coming home?"

Robert stopped spinning his mug and looked up at Mike.

"No, son. It's gotten complicated." Robert stared into the porcelain mug again. "Your mother does want to see you, though. Maybe you could, you know, grow up a little and let it go. Otherwise, I don't know what you're going to do."

"Like she *let it go*? Like you've done?" Mike took a deep breath and held it for a second. "Fine. I'll let it go."

Robert stood and took a half step toward Mike. Mike stiffened and then escaped through the back door into the rain. He jogged between the house and the garage and picked up speed when he turned north onto the highway toward the mountains. In less than a mile, the rain had soaked his running shoes, and cold water squished between his toes.

By the time Mike reached the gravel road that led past the Sportsman's Club and the shingle mill, the steady rain had become a deluge. His T-shirt was soon wetter than his shoes, and he shivered a little for the first mile. He crossed the bridge above Silver Falls and continued up the highway away from town. Warm tears mixed with the cold June rain that ran down his face and dripped off his chin.

* * *

When Mike returned from his morning run, the rain had stopped, his father was gone, and the back door was still open. Rainwater had blown under the brief awning above the back porch and puddled on the fading linoleum just inside the door. Robert might be back sometime, but his mother was gone all the time. He'd told Robert he did not care, but he thought about the night his mother had left every time he ran.

Mike had begun running when he was twelve. Robert drank heavily in those days, and Mike's mother, Janine, went to church all the time. Sometimes, Mike went with her, but Robert never did. The official, gossipy version was that Janine got tired of Robert's boozing and getting slapped around and had high-tailed it back to Abel, where she'd grown up. There was some truth to that, but the official version of most things was not any more accurate than the gossipy version. Janine didn't pack up and run off with Mike to some shelter or to a relative.

She just ran off.

Without him.

Mike was twelve, and when you're twelve, you don't think about your mom leaving your dad. Your mom leaves *you*. Later, Dr. Linda Lasch explained that Mike withdrew from his friends and acted out in school because he blamed himself.

But he'd never blamed himself.

Never.

He blamed her.

Robert had found Janine *just up the road* in Abel the same night she left. He'd come home drunk later that night and told Mike he'd found Janine but that she wasn't coming back. Mike had retreated to his room, and Robert had begun to sob, deep, desperate sobs that sounded damp through the thin wall separating Mike's room from what had been his parents' room.

Robert had never blamed Janine.

Never.

He blamed himself.

Mike hadn't been able to sleep that night, and sometime before midnight, he'd heard bottles crashing in the kitchen. Then Robert had come into Mike's room.

"I'm sorry, Mikey. I'm done drinking. I promise."

Then he'd said he had to go to work, and he didn't know how long he'd be gone. Mike hadn't known what to do when his father left. It had been dark out, and he had been only twelve.

So, he'd run.

He'd run out the front door, a half-mile toward town and onto the grass track behind the high school. A single street-light in the parking lot illuminated one end of the track. He'd run around and around the track, harder and harder. After a long time, he'd stopped. His forearms had tingled, and his legs had wobbled. He'd staggered onto the football field, and when he had not collapsed, he'd realized he could have run farther and harder.

But he had decided to stop. *He* had decided to stop.

His mother had made a choice. She'd left. His father had made a choice. He'd checked out. Mike had also made a choice. He stayed, and he'd run.

Mike's mother had been gone 2,177 days.

2

"A WHOLE 'NOTHER YEAR UNTIL GRADUATION," James said. "I don't think I can make it a whole 'nother year."

He would have preferred to be suspended for the last two weeks of school, but all he'd received after his latest altercation with Mike was another reprimand, which he answered with an insincere and repetitive promise to do better. On the last day of the school year, James and his two-man posse, Tall Paul and Pork, were spending the lunch hour in the locker room beneath Silverton High's decrepit gym. Only the intermittent thudding of basketballs bouncing off the saggy gym floor upstairs interrupted their post-lunch stupor. James lay on the cool concrete with his feet resting on a wooden bench. A nasty odor wafted out of the far end of the locker room, where Pork was sifting through a canvas tub filled with dirty shorts and T-shirts, looking for anything labeled XXXL. James grabbed his nose.

"Jesus, Pork," James blurted. "What've you been eatin', son?"

"It ain't me. These dirty shorts and socks ain't been

washed for a coupla weeks, and there's dirty towels in here, too."

"No way, man." Tall Paul was stretched out on the floor with a damp towel beneath his head. "You farted, Pork. Unless sweaty socks and jocks all of a sudden smell like fart."

"They could if they been farted on." Pork's head was still buried in the tub.

James had been the biggest kid in town since the seventh grade. He still had the same beefy build that had made him a football terror in junior high, and he still had the size and imposing demeanor that had gained him enough notice to be named an all-state tackle the previous fall. He had always been big enough to get by on the football field without working out, but he'd begun to soften around the middle and spread out in the rear. The cheeks of Pork's extensive rear end and the crack of his ample backside were exposed when he bent over. *Am I starting to look like that?* James wondered.

"I don't think I can make it another year," he said. He started to sit up but had to take his feet off the bench and turn sideways so he could use his arms to get to his feet.

"At least we got the summer first..." Tall Paul said. "To party."

Tall Paul and Pork each shared a single physical attribute with James. Tall Paul was well named because he was the only kid in Silverton taller than James, and Pork was the only kid in town who was as heavy. Tall Paul was long-limbed and awkward, and Pork was just fat. James's status as a local hero was ironic, considering the fear he inspired in younger, smaller kids. Tall Paul and Pork misinterpreted that fear as respect and were happy to enjoy it by default. James had begun to notice a difference, though—and not just in the way he looked. Kids who used to move out of his way in the halls didn't retreat quite as fast anymore. As a result, he'd begun to wonder if he could maintain his place as the tough guy at the top of Silverton High's food chain when school started in the fall.

When the bell signaling the end of lunch rattled, Tall Paul was stretched out on the locker room floor on the edge of dozing off, and Pork was still rummaging through the lost-and-found tub.

"Two pointless, crappy periods left," James said. "Let's go, peckerwoods."

James and the boys ambled up the stairs. When they reached the crowded hallway, Tall Paul turned left toward another failed attempt at practical math. James and Pork turned right toward the boredom and irrelevance of Mr. Sorenson's history class.

Despite his top-jock status, James hated everything about school. He hated the teachers, even though several accorded him a certain amount of cautious deference based on his reputation and the fact he could play football. He hated the principal, Mr. Thompson, who had gone to Silverton High School with James's father, Ollie. But the principal refused to be impressed by James or accord him the proper respect and deference. But more than anything, James hated the desks.

"I haven't fit into one of these damn torture-device desks since fifth grade," he told Pork, who had his own problems trying to squeeze into the downsized furnishings. "Every year, it's harder to squeeze my ass into one of these chairs."

Pork nodded, and James continued, expecting his friend to be riveted by the coming monologue.

"I hate this town." James tried to stand, but he'd already squeezed himself into the chair with his knees jammed tight against the underside of the desk. "I hate the trees and the mountains and the rain." He wiggled to the side so his left butt cheek was hanging off the seat and tried to stand up again. "There are no jobs. The girls flirt and tease and then clamp their knees together."

James slid back onto the seat, and Pork made kissing sounds at James.

"They're all a bunch of tight asses. And these desks get smaller every year," James said.

Pork leaned back and laughed, but when he did, his desk nearly tipped over with him still stuck in the seat.

"At least you got football, man," Pork said.

At least I got football, James told himself. He knew everyone thought he was big and bad and a hardass because he was good at football. But James hated to practice, and he didn't like the coach very much. And the games were boring.

"Coach says football will get me out of here," James said, as much to himself as to Pork, who was still squirming around in the desk. *But I don't guess I need football to get out. Maybe I won't play next year at all.*

"But, hey, Porker, I'm leaving no matter what. School ends in a year, and then I'm gone."

"Yeah, whatever," Pork said. "Hey, where's Mike been?"

Pork had stopped squirming and was examining a brown, waxy clump he'd dug out of his ear with his pinky. "He ain't been to school for a coupla weeks." He rolled the clump around on the desktop and then squished it with his forefinger.

"I told you I got him kicked outta school."

"Man, I really hate that guy," Pork said. "Remember how we used to kick his ass in junior high? Now he tries to be the hero all the time just 'cause everyone knows he used to be a pussy."

Mike had once been the smallest and most-picked-on kid in Silverton, but he'd outgrown that vulnerability, which created a problem for James, who was only a little larger in the eleventh grade than he'd been in junior high. On the morning of his most recent confrontation with Mike, Tall Paul had a puny little waste of a freshman everyone called *Little Georgie* in a headlock. James was in the process of yanking Georgie's threadbare jeans off his spindly hips. Georgie had learned the encounter would go better if he didn't resist, but dignity required that he cling to the front of his pants while James jerked on them from behind. Georgie was about to lose his grip when Mike came striding down the hall with Joyce close behind.

"Beck took a swing at me with a book when I tried to pants that little faggot, Georgie." James paused to watch Pork play with the clump of earwax. "Then Sorenson comes running out of his room, and Joyce is trying to tell him how I started it, but he drags Beck off to Thompson's office anyway."

"*Drags*" was an exaggeration. Whenever he got caught breaking some pointless rule, Mike would smirk at the accusing teacher and then strut to the principal's office on his own while the teacher trotted along behind. That attitude was the only thing James admired about Mike.

"He still needs an ass-kicking," Pork said. "And he's going to get one. We got plans for Mike Beck. Right, James?"

"If you say so, Porker," James said. "Sure. We got plans."

3

WITH MIKE SUSPENDED, Joyce Summers spent the last day of school mostly by herself.

The heavy rain had become a persistent western Washington drizzle by the time the final bell rang. But the gloomy weather did nothing to dampen the enthusiasm of the one hundred and fifty students anxious to celebrate their three-month emancipation. Kids loitered in antsy clumps, and the metallic clang of each locker slamming shut for the last time served as a series of ardent and defiant declarations of temporary independence. Joyce Summers did not slam her locker shut, and she was in no hurry to leave the building. She clutched an old-fashioned Bible to her chest, the forefinger of her left hand marking the page she had been reading in the back of her English class when the final bell had rung. School was easy for Joyce, and Matthew 24:11 seemed appropriate for leaving on the last day: *And many false prophets shall rise and shall deceive many.*

She walked down the center of the chaotic hallway slowly, but she did not linger. Joyce never lingered. Behind her, James and his boys followed closely enough to make sure she was aware of their presence. But instead of ambling down the hallway as usual, slow and cool, certain dozens of anxious and admiring eyes were scrutinizing their every move, they seemed different. James seemed to slump more and strut less, and his girth appeared to be sliding from his shoulders and chest into his waist and backside. James's t-shirts always seemed a size too small, probably to show off his muscular chest and gaudy biceps, which would swell impressively against the fabric. But lately, it was the fabric of his jeans across his expanding backside that seemed under the most stress. Joyce shrugged. It didn't matter; she'd never been impressed by James, anyway.

So, Joyce walked calmly down the hallway, as always determined to ignore James and the boys.

But then Little Georgie came running down the hall in their direction.

"Hey, Joyce."

Georgie waved as he sprinted past Joyce, and she turned her head to follow his progress. Pork threw his hip into the smaller boy, launching him across the hall and into a row of lockers locker. Joyce stopped and headed back in the direction of James and his friends.

"Hey, Georgie. Bam! Sorry, man," Pork said. "That looked like it hurt. You need to watch where you're going."

Georgie slumped to the floor, and Mr. Sorenson, a timid history teacher with an authoritarian mean streak, craned his bald head out the doorway of his classroom and smirked. James turned toward Mr. Sorenson and flashed a wicked grin, and Joyce shook her head in resignation. The history teacher disappeared back into his classroom and closed the door. No adult help was coming.

"Leave him alone." Joyce's voice was insistent.

"Ain't none of your business, Joyce," James said.

She stepped around James and helped Georgie off the floor, and they headed down the hall together, with James and the boys following a step or two closer this time.

"She pretends to be so pure." Pork huffed, loud enough for Joyce and anyone else in the vicinity to hear. "But I'll bet Mike Beck's screwing her. They ain't got any other friends."

"Nice. Pure. Church girl," Tall Paul said with a nod. "Yeah, he's screwing her."

The principal, Mr. Thompson, was approaching from the opposite direction, so Joyce stopped and raised her hand to get his attention.

"Mr. Thompson," she said.

But he continued on down the hallway without even glancing in her direction.

Joyce turned to follow Mr. Thompson, but James stepped in front of her, put both arms around her waist, and squeezed her butt with both hands.

"You like that, doncha, Joyce? You make sure to tell Mike what big, bad James did to you?"

Georgie grabbed James's arm and tried to pull him away.

"Let go of my arm before I paint the wall with you," James said, but he released Joyce and stepped back.

"Go home, James," Joyce said.

"Only if you come with me." He sneered.

James gave Georgie one more half-hearted shove and stalked off down the hallway with Pork waddling and Tall Paul stumbling along next to him.

James and Pork turned right at the end of the hall and disappeared into the giggling and shouting and rubber-burning confusion of the parking lot, but Joyce was still worried they might be lurking nearby to make another pathetic run at Georgie.

She steered Georgie to the left toward the main entrance

and away from the parking lot behind the building. "How do you normally get home, Georgie?"

The persistent drizzle had stopped, but water had puddled on the sidewalks, and the half dozen elm trees standing in a neat row in front of the building dripped and drooped. When Joyce was little, she'd felt bad for the trees because she thought they must be cold. These days, she admired their fortitude.

By the time Joyce and Georgie emerged from the building, the sun was beginning to peek through the dark clouds, and wisps of steam were already rising from the damp sidewalk and sodden lawn.

"I always walk home," Georgie said. "It's not far. I know you walk home every day, too. I seen you. You don't hang around after school much, do you?"

"I don't like being at school all that much."

"Me, neither. But you're good at it."

"I don't think you have to like everything you're good at." Her mind wandered to Mike. *Did he really like to run as much as it seemed?*

"Maybe. But my dad says if I don't do better in school, I'll end up working in the woods, like him."

The only thing Joyce knew about Georgie's family was that his father was a logger, which meant little money coming in for much of the year.

"Is that so bad?" she said. "Working in the woods?"

"He's awful tired all the time."

They reached the sidewalk, and Georgie looked back toward the building and then both directions up and down the street.

"Why don't I walk home with you?" Joyce said.

"James and Pork won't do nothin' now. No reason to. No one's around to see. But I always watch out anyway, just in case."

"I'm sorry they're so...that they are the way they are."

They turned left and headed toward town. Georgie stepped around to walk on Joyce's right, nearest the street, and she smiled.

"They've never really hurt me," he said. "My dad says they won't 'cause that would mean they'd be in real trouble, and they're afraid to be in real trouble."

"Can't your parents do something, get the principal or someone else to make James stop?"

"My dad says I got to either take it, or I got to stand up to them."

"But they're bigger than you, older."

"Yeah. But Dad says they won't always be bigger, and then... Well, they won't always be bigger. That's all."

"So, you have a plan for James?" Joyce caught herself before she laughed at Georgie's implied threat.

She didn't want him to think she was mocking him, but she did smile, and Georgie noticed.

"It's okay, Joyce. My mom says I'm a late bloomer. My dad is a big guy, and my uncles are all almost as big as James. And I'm gonna get a summer job setting chokers when I turn sixteen. That's as good as lifting weights."

Joyce was impressed that Georgie seemed determined to stand up to James. She thought back and realized Georgie wasn't much smaller than Mike had been in the ninth grade. And even though James still talked big, he didn't bother Mike much anymore."

They crossed Main Street and turned left on Sixth. After two or three blocks, they passed in front of the two-story frame house where James lived with his mother. A battered pickup with a cracked windshield was parked in front of the house.

"Looks like Mrs. Olsen has a friend over," Georgie said. "My mom says she has lots of friends over because James's dad doesn't live there anymore.

Joyce wondered whether Georgie had recognized the irony in the polite reference to Mrs. Olson's *friends*, considering what everyone in town seemed to know about her.

"Mom says we should be nice to her anyway."

Three blocks past James's house, Joyce and Georgie crossed the street and stopped in front of the church Joyce had attended until just after the previous Christmas.

She had not attended church since.

"I live next door to the church on the other side," Georgie said. "My dad's not home, but Mom is. She's doesn't have a job. She helps out with the little kids at church, though. Sometimes, she plays the piano."

"I didn't know Mrs. Cleary was your mom." Joyce glanced away. How could she have gone so long without knowing Georgie's last name? "I don't think I've ever seen you at church."

"Me and Dad sit way in the back. We usually come late and leave right away when it's over."

Joyce thought she knew everyone who went to the church she no longer attended. But she hadn't recognized the connection between Georgie and his mom. What else didn't she know?

"Come on," she said. "I'll walk you the rest of the way home."

They went around to the back of the church to a clapboard house badly in need of paint. The dirt yard showed no signs of ever having been a lawn, and the lot was strewn with old tires, odds and ends of car parts, and scraps of metal, most of which Joyce could not identify.

The only vehicle on the lot was a new-looking pickup

parked in the hard-packed dirt. The newish truck seemed out of place among the automotive detritus scattered about the yard.

"Your dad must be home," Joyce said, indicating the truck.

"That's not Dad's truck. There's people in town who like him to work on their cars and trucks. He's pretty good at it. I am, too."

Again, Joyce suppressed a laugh. Like everyone else at school—adults and kids alike—she had assumed Georgie was just, well...*Little Georgie*, an apt object of either derision or pity. It hadn't occurred to her he might be *good* at anything.

"We worked on your dad's new truck a couple of weeks ago. Adjusted the timing belt. He paid us a hundred bucks, and I got ten of it."

Joyce started to put her hand on Georgie's shoulder, but his mother appeared in the doorway, and he turned and jogged through the clutter toward the house.

"Bye, Joyce," he said with a wave.

She remained on the cracked sidewalk in front of the house until Georgie was inside. Then she turned away, walked past the church she no longer attended, and then home.

4

Pork didn't fit into the front seat of his rusty Volkswagen any better than he'd fit into the cramped desk in Mr. Sorenson's classroom. He wiggled in behind the steering wheel with his flabby left arm hanging out the window. James's newish truck was parked next to Pork's pathetic VW.

"I'll bring Tall Paul to your place, and we can leave for the party around eight," Pork said. He turned the key, and the old car groaned to life. Sparks flew from under the faded-yellow bug when it bottomed out over a speed bump.

James fit just fine behind the wheel of his four-door pickup. His father had bought the truck when James made the all-state football team. It wasn't new, but it had four-wheel drive, and James liked to brag about its big-ass back seat. He eased through the parking lot in first gear and drove home slowly enough for all the losers to get a good look at him and his rig.

The house James shared with his mother was the same color as Pork's sad car, but James had plans to repaint the old place now that school was out. Despite the frequent rain, the grass was brown in places, but James kept it cut. He even trimmed the edges along the concrete walkway that ran from the sidewalk to the front porch.

James's mother, JoAnn, and his father, Ollie, had not lived together for years but were still married. Ollie was supposed to take care of the place, but he worked long hours at his mechanic's shop, repairing everything from lawnmowers to logging trucks and heavy machinery.

"But he don't do much around here," James would tell anyone who asked. "He goes home to his place every night and drinks beer until he falls asleep. He used to smack me around, but I got bigger'n him, and now it takes too much effort unless he's really pissed and been drinkin'. Mostly, he just buys me stuff and smacks Mom around when she won't screw him."

When James got home from school, he pulled in behind a strange pickup truck parked along the curb out front. His mother would be upstairs with her latest *boyfriend*. They would spend most of the night at the Spar Tree Tavern and then come back to the house and go upstairs again. And tomorrow, the boyfriend would leave a few bucks on the kitchen table when he left.

The dishes hadn't been done for a couple of days, and the kitchen was a mess. James liked things to be neat and clean, so he washed the dishes, tidied the kitchen, and then spent a couple of hours working in the garage.

Everyone at school knew James wasn't very smart, so Coach Wahl nagged him about his schoolwork.

"If you want to play football in college, you got to get better grades," the coach reminded him.

"Don't matter how hard I try; it don't make no difference. I'm good with my hands, though, and I like to make things."

"I know, son, but that's not enough."

James shook his head. In his view, it should be enough.

His current project was a box made from some cedar he'd found in the scrap pile at Morton Shingle. It had a snug lid and neat, brass hinges. The joints and corners all fit together, with no nails or screws. No glue. No spaces. Tight. Perfect.

He ran his fingers over the box and nodded with satisfaction at how well the joints and corners fit. The box would come apart if the joints weren't perfect, if there were gaps. He put the box on a shelf above the workbench in the shop behind the house where no one would find it and then went to his room to change his shirt for Junior's end-of-the-school-year party.

An hour later, James headed out the front door to meet up with his boys. Pork had parked his tiny car across the street from James's house. He and Tall Paul exchanged crude jokes as they drove away from town in James's truck, but James was thinking about the cedar box. He'd work on the box for a while tomorrow. *Make sure all the joints are sanded smooth and the lid fits snug.*

A loud fart from Pork in the back seat interrupted James's meditation.

"We got all summer, then one hundred and seventy-five school days until graduation!" James shouted. He pounded the steering wheel. "I don't know how I'm going to make it."

5

THE OCCASION WAS Junior Hooker's annual, last-day-of-school keg party, held at a remote cabin at the end of a rutted dirt road about twelve miles from town. But Dahlia had been bored because Mike and Jake, a kid he'd paid five dollars for gas and a ride, arrived late.

Junior was well known as the go-to guy for underage kids and opportunistic twenty-somethings willing to pay for booze or pot or sex. He charged high school boys ten bucks for all the beer they could drink. Drugs were extra. Girls didn't have to pay because Junior and his lecherous cadre assumed the combination of alcohol and teenage girls held promise. In the weedy yard, on the narrow porch, and in the crowded front room, several dozen kids and a handful of twenty-something opportunists lounged in various stages of intoxication and undress.

"There will be plenty of free booze, so the girls will be easy," Junior bragged to his friends. "Twenty bucks."

The party started out rowdy—someone even fired loud gunshots into the old-growth forest behind the house. But as the booze, drugs, and immature passion had their inevitable and desired effect, the evening became more subdued. Dahlia was a year older than Mike, but everyone knew they were an on-again, off-again weekend hookup. Graduation had been held a week before school ended for everyone else, and Dahlia had escaped Silverton High with a generously granted diploma. But she hadn't seen Mike since.

"Where ya been, Mikey?"

As Mike came through the front door, Dahlia put both arms around his neck and danced him backward toward the kitchen.

Dahlia had small breasts, a round backside, and brown hair that reached stylishly below her ear on one side of her head and all the way to her shoulder on the other side. Though no great beauty, she had a perpetual, I'm-up-for-anything smirk that boys and young men in Silverton found if not irresistible, then at least intriguing. Dahlia's small dark-brown eyes seemed to enlarge and grow dull when she drank. The smirk was the single physical trait she shared with Mike, except his smirk denoted something less amicable than Dahlia's well-practiced eagerness for a good time.

"I got suspended for the last two weeks of school, Dal. You know that. You could've come by the house."

Mike took two bottles of beer from one of three refrigerators in Junior's kitchen and gave one to Dahlia, who reached in and took another for herself.

Mike opened his beer. "I've been at home."

"Your old man might've been there. I don't want to come around when he's there."

"Whatever." Mike took a sip of beer, then guided Dahlia to the wall opposite the three refrigerators and pulled her onto his lap as he slid to the floor. "The old man ain't been around much."

Dahlia began a long pull on her beer, and by the time they were settled on the floor, it was half gone.

"I didn't think you'd be here tonight," she said, and then she'd burped. "Thought you'd be off running somewhere this weekend."

"Season's over. I got kicked outta school before the state meet anyway."

"Season's over" was a term Mike was familiar with because he had never managed to stay out of trouble long enough to complete an entire season. His small high school didn't provide the best competition, so Mike had never lost a race. He was so good he'd have won a half dozen small-school state championships if he'd been able to stay on the butt-kissing side of the Silverton High authorities.

"Well, screw 'em." Dahlia burped again.

"That's what I told Sorenson. That big, football tub-o-lard, James, had his hands on Little Georgie in the hall, so I hit him upside the head with my history book. He finally let Georgie go and turned around, so I hit him in the nose with the book. He would've cried if I'd hit him again, but Sorenson came out of his room and grabbed me."

"Sorenson's about a hunnert years old. Why's he care?"

Even though Dahlia was still sitting on Mike's lap, she'd begun to sway, first to one side, then backward. Mike caught her arm so she wouldn't fall over.

"You okay, Dal?"

"Screw you." She smiled and tried—and failed—to suppress another burp.

"James was about to start blubbering," Mike said, "and Joyce was there, trying to explain to Sorenson what happened. Sorenson pushed me up against the wall and said, 'What do you have to say about James's nose?'"

"And you said, 'Screw you'?"

"Yeah. Probably not very smart."

"And when Mr. Thompson took you to his office—"

"I told him, 'Screw you'."

Dahlia drained the rest of her first beer and threw the bottle toward a trash can in the corner. She missed, and the bottle rattled off the wall and rolled back against Mike's shoe. She took a long pull on the second beer and began to sway again, back and forth this time. Mike took a short sip of his beer and looked toward the ceiling.

"I think you like that Joyce, doncha, Mikey?" Dahlia said.

"Not that way. She's not that kinda girl."

"What kinda girl is she, Mike? And what kinda girl do you think I am?"

"We both know what kinda girl you are, so don't act all jealous. You don't give a rat's ass about Joyce. It's just...she's always been nice to me. When I was younger, when my mom left, kids made fun of me, but she was nice. Like she understood. Like a friend."

Dahlia bent down, placed her mouth next to Mike's ear, and whispered, "I don't think your nice friend Joyce will do what I'm going to do for you. I'm a *nice* girl, too." Dahlia took another long pull on her beer. "You'd better get started. You're way behind."

Mike put his barely touched beer on the floor. He stared at the ceiling and sucked in a deep breath of stale air.

"I wanted to run," he said.

"Huh?"

"The state meet. The mile and the two-mile..."

"Well, screw 'em." Dahlia giggled. "Let's get drunk anyway."

Mike picked up his beer again and took another negligible sip. Dahlia finished hers in a single guzzle.

"I'm deally runk," she said.

She started to put her arms around Mike's neck, but she missed and slumped forward. She caught herself with one hand on the wall and the other on Mike's shoulder. Twisting toward Mike, she bent down and gave him a sloppy kiss just before she passed out.

Jake came into the kitchen and glanced at Mike and Dahlia as he headed for the fridge. "Jesus, Mike. Get a room. No one wants to see that." Jake laughed. He pointed at Dahlia's inert body and set a single bottle of beer on the floor next to Mike. "Looks like you could use another, but I think your girlfriend's done for the night."

Mike took a long time to finish his first beer and left the bottle from Jake sitting unopened on the floor. By 10:30, Mike still hadn't touched the second beer. Dahlia was still passed out across his legs, and Mike felt like he might melt into the floor.

"I would've won," Mike said to himself. "I swear, I would've won."

He put his hand on Dahlia's ample butt and squeezed. When she didn't respond, he rolled her body down to his ankles and started to stand up. Dahlia sighed and then rolled the rest of the way off Mike's legs. He left her on the floor, but he had trouble straightening his stiff legs as he stood up and shuffled to the door that separated the kitchen from the dark front room.

In the front room, the red tips of a half-dozen joints flared up, one by one, and then faded. A girl coughed. Mike leaned against the door jamb and stared into the darkness. A girl moaned, and a couple of guys laughed. The acrid aroma of marijuana smoke, combined with the sour odor of adolescent sweat mixed with booze, reminded Mike of the way he felt at the end of a hard run.

"I would've won," he muttered.

Mike pushed himself off the door jam and returned to where Dahlia was still passed out on the kitchen floor. He never drank much, but he felt a vague burning sensation in his gut whenever he did. For a moment, he thought he might throw up, but the commotion in his stomach passed. He watched Dahlia sleep, listened to her snore softly, and was reminded of those nights before his mother left when his father grunted and snored and farted in a drunken slumber on their old couch. He bent down and nudged her shoulder, but Dahlia rolled away and folded herself into a tight fetal position. It struck Mike that in some strange way, Dahlia looked safe. But then he wondered if *safety* had anything to do with why it was his devout mother who'd left and his drunken father who'd stayed.

6

THERE WERE sixty-six books in the Bible, almost a thousand pages. Sometime in the sixth grade, Joyce decided she should read at least one chapter of one book of the Bible every night. Then, about the time her interest in Mike began to shift from a chaste concern for his well-being to an interest in, well, *him*, Joyce started to blackout while reading the Bible. She'd look up and brush her hair out of her eyes, and it would be two or three in the morning. The lights in her room would still be on, and she'd discover scribbling in the margins, sometimes right across the text, often covering two or three pages. Notes. Awkward poetry. Rudimentary drawings. Joyce had very neat handwriting. She'd even won a prize in sixth grade, and she was a capable artist. But the scribbling and the drawings in her Bible were messy and frenetic. She had just turned sixteen when the scribbling and the sleeplessness began.

When she was still going to church, Joyce would dress up on Sunday, but her everyday appearance was uncommon because she intended to appear *common*. She was taller than average, but she never slouched. She wasn't exactly thin, but she had long legs and slender hips. She would have been attractive to the boys in Silverton, except she always wore her clothes—dark greens and browns, never black—a size or two too large. Every Sunday, she'd sat in the first or second pew, a pair of demure white gloves an ironic counterpoint to her dour, day-to-day apparel.

But things Joyce had heard in church often kept her awake at night. A common snippet of doctrine that seemed odd. An unremarkable homily that didn't sit quite right. A particular passage that contradicted some other particular passage. She was aware of a connection between her ecclesiastical confusion and the change in how she felt about Mike —from worry to wanton—but Joyce was not sure what the connection might be.

After more than a year of sleepless nights, Joyce realized insomnia was not fatal. She would occupy the deep hours by reading until her eyes began to feel scratchy and heavy. When sleep still did not come, Joyce would lie on her back on the floor of her neat room and stare at the luminescent stars her father had glued to the ceiling, a contrived galaxy of constellations, patterns, and spirals. On warm summer nights, she'd take her pillow and a blanket to the family's back yard, and with the green pungency of the forest and the cinnamon memory of some homemade dessert filling her nostrils, she'd stare into the real heavens and marvel at the disconnect between her father's luminous plastic stars and the vastness of genuine creation and find it curious to be awed by both.

At the beginning of her insomniac period, she'd toss and turn and fidget until the sky beyond her thin curtains began to turn red. Then she'd doze for an hour until her mother knocked on her door.

"Get up, Joyce. School."

Joyce would refuse to open her eyes at first. She'd groan and stretch and eventually stumble into the shower across the hall. But by the time she was dressed and walking to school, she felt normal. Her family's modest house sat on three acres shaded by two dozen fir and cedar trees just outside the city limits and a mile from the high school. Joyce could have ridden the school bus, but the solitude of the twenty-minute walk had become a spiritual counterpoint to the cluttered and boisterous school day.

The only time she felt tired was during the first few minutes after she woke up. On the nights she did sleep, she slept heavy and dreamless. Oddly enough, walking to school was much harder after a full night's sleep than when some carnal stirring or theological disturbance kept her awake.

Joyce's disordered sleeping habits were not the result of the same anxieties that disturbed the sleep of other girls her age. She was unconcerned with the rituals and chaos of female adolescence—hair, makeup, clothes, gossip, boys, and for some, even schoolwork. Her lack of interest in these things had seemed strange to Joyce in the weeks before she entered high school. The one concession she made to normal female adolescence was an ongoing and growing interest in Mike. When she saw him, even from a distance, she felt a disturbance behind her navel and a delicate stirring somewhere lower. Whether these stirrings were sinister or sacred, she could not tell.

Joyce had been so frightened the first time she discovered the scribbling in her Bible, she'd slammed the book shut and flung it away. The Bible had bounced off the wall with a crash so loud she'd been afraid it had awakened her mother and father. Joyce had slid off the chair beneath the only window in her room and cowered against the wall.

She'd stared at the Bible, which had fallen open on the floor in a dim circle of moonlight, and then she'd crept across the room on her hands and knees to retrieve it.

She'd sat on the floor with her legs crossed in the circle of moonlight and stared at the open pages. She'd studied the scribbling in the margin. The letters formed themselves into what seemed like a random string of words, but then she had recognized an un-punctuated sentence: *I've planned a plan to stand a man with no purpose damned.*

"Did I write this?"

At the top of the same page was a crude drawing of someone running up a hill. Next to the running figure, written in easy-to-read, block letters was a single word. *Mike.*

Joyce had studied the drawing. "Mike?"

A passage down the page was underlined. Isiah 14:24. She had run her fingers across the page as she read the underlined paragraph. *The Lord of Hosts has sworn, saying, Surely as I have thought, so shall it come to pass; and as I have purposed, so shall it stand.* Joyce had gone to her bookcase and had retrieved a more modern translation. She knew the order and sequence of the Biblical books by heart, so she found Isiah 14:24 at once. *The Lord of Hosts has sworn, as I have planned, so shall it be, and as I have purposed, so shall it stand.*

Come to pass? Planned? Purposed? Stand? Joyce was confused.

The verse that came before Isaiah 14:24 said something about sweeping away Babylon. The next verse said something about removing a yoke.

She knew about Babylon, but she had wanted to be certain about the various nuances of *yoke.*

Back to her bookcase. She'd grabbed a dictionary and looked up *yoke.* The first three definitions had to do with draft animals. That didn't seem right. Then a reference to carrying buckets. Probably not.

Then definition number five: *an agency of oppression, subjection, servitude.* And number six: *an emblem or symbol of subjection, servitude, slavery.* Number seven was a little different: *something that couples or binds together; a bond or tie.*

"I've planned a plan to stand a man with no purpose damned."

Joyce had thought hard about the passage and the single line of messy verse. Someone was under a yoke. A plan? A purpose?

Joyce did not pray in the self-conscious manner of many young Christians. That night, she had slid on her butt across the floor, pushed the little chair aside, leaned against the wall beneath the window, and prayed. She had closed her eyes and waited until the sky above the foothills began to glow, and the darkness began to fade.

"Yoke?" she had said, just as the first light of the morning sun filled her room.

"Mike." Joyce was sure she'd gotten it right. She also had a strong feeling about what *a plan* and *a purpose* referred to. But she'd been astonished by that realization in the same way she had been astonished by the scribbling in her Bible and in the same way she was astonished by the stirring below her navel when she was with Mike.

Now she was afraid the scribbling would stop if she did not read her Bible every day. She didn't know many people who had read the entire Bible. Joyce's Christian acquaintances spent most of their time worrying about the same things her non-Christian friends worried about. Schoolwork. Who's "dating" whom. Sports. Cheering for sports. Grades. Clothes. Gossip. The artificial rituals and sacraments of adolescence didn't leave much time for reading the Bible or anything else.

"If you start the day with your Bible," the youth pastor Kevin Good told the kids in his Wednesday night young adult group, "the temptations of the world will have a harder time getting a hold on you."

Pastor Kevin was a nice guy. But his advice seemed shallow to Joyce, like it came from a textbook rather than from the heart or from some deeper place. So, she ignored the youth pastor's admonition and read her Bible at night, realizing Mike was in "the world", and that fact complicated her own battle against temptation.

By the time Joyce stopped going to church, she had read the Bible from Genesis to Revelations three or four times. That seemed like a lot, but it was only about twenty pages a week. At first, she poured over every line and every verse, searching for profundity, hidden meanings, and sacred secrets. Later, she skimmed over most passages.

"A lot of the Bible is pretty boring," Joyce had told Mike. "But you have to read the rest again and again."

Mike had laughed at that and had started to tease her about her Bible-reading routine. He called it an *obsession*.

"So, why do you run *every* day?" she'd asked.

Her question had shut Mike up.

Participating in the perfect rhythm of sunset and the certainty of sunrise became a sacramental habit that Joyce retained long after she stopped going to church.

Mike was on Joyce's mind as she sat at the window in her little chair late at night on the last day of the eleventh grade. She had opened her Bible and had begun to read. After a time, she closed her eyes, and when she opened them, she'd noticed something new scribbled across the top of the first page of Genesis. *This is easy. The important stuff is easy. Everyone wants to argue about the hard stuff.*

And underlined below the scribble, she read: *In the beginning, God created the heaven and the earth. And the earth was without form and void; and darkness was upon the face of the deep.*

"First things first," she said. "First things...first."

Then the phone next to her bed rang. Joyce picked up on the first ring.

"It's after eleven. Who is this?"

"It's Mike. I need a ride."

Joyce did not say anything.

"Please, Joyce?

7

MIKE HUNG up the phone and maneuvered over several unconscious bodies strewn across the room. He went outside and leaned on the porch rail for a long time. Then, somewhere off to the right, he heard a gunshot, a shrill female scream, and then screechy, girlish laughter.

Mike returned to the kitchen, where Dahlia was still passed out. The beer he'd left on the floor was gone, so he stepped over Dahlia and went to the refrigerator. He opened the door and was glad to find one beer left, but when he reached for it, James shouldered him out of the way and grabbed the last beer.

"You've had enough, Mikey." James turned and pointed at Dahlia snoring on the floor. "Hey, look—Mikey's girl is wasted." Then he pointed at Mike and sneered. "What's she doing with you anyway, Mikey? Now *that's* a waste."

James shook his head as he left the kitchen. Mike started to go after him, but even though he hadn't had much to drink, he suddenly felt lightheaded. He staggered a little against the wall and then let himself slide down to sit on the floor next to Dahlia. He looked down at Dahlia's inert form

and sighed. "Why did I call Joyce? She doesn't even drive."
He leaned his head back against the wall and closed his
eyes.

Mike must have fallen asleep because when he opened
his eyes, it was after midnight, the kitchen was empty, and
Dahlia was gone. He thought he should go find her, but
when he tried to get up, he only got as far as his hands and
knees with his forehead on the floor. He rolled over onto his
back, took several shallow breaths, and then sat up with his
hands pressing down on the floor. He pushed himself back
against the wall and closed his eyes.

He felt stiff and weak, so getting to his feet took some
effort. He had a clear path through the living room because
the few people who remained were either passed out or
semiconscious. Dahlia was not among them, so when Mike
reached the front door, he grabbed another boy by the arm
to steady himself and to get the other boy's attention. The
boy was holding a square, clear glass bottle by the neck. The
translucent-brown liquid sloshing around inside the bottle
reminded Mike he might need to throw up.

"Hey, where'd Dahlia go?" Mike asked him.

The boy with the bottle shrugged, pulled his arm away,
and stumbled down the steps.

Mike hadn't had much to drink, just a single beer, but
something in the air violated all his senses and made him
feel sick again. Some combination of the mumble of intoxication, punctuated by explosions of insincere laughter; the
sight of inebriated couples, long past the ability or desire to
feel or express anything but mutual disgust; the rancid
stench of vomit, the heady sweetness of pot smoke, and the
sour aroma of spilled booze.

He had to put his head down with his hands on his
knees to steady himself.

I need to get out of here.

He bumped into another boy who dropped to his knees and threw up over the edge of the porch. A girl wearing expensive-looking jeans and no bra under her unbuttoned shirt tried to help the boy to his feet.

"Come on, Jacky," she slurred. "We ain't done nothin' yet."

The boy did not move.

"Drunk jerk." The girl backed away and turned toward Mike. She stumbled into him and said, "How 'bout you, cowboy? You too drunk to...?" The rest of her question dissolved into the alcohol-soaked fog in her brain, and she stumbled back to the sick boy whose head hung over the edge of the porch.

Mike was trying to see where Dahlia might have gone when he saw James had someone pushed up against the fat fender of his truck.

"Dahlia?" Mike called out. He stumbled down the steps and ran stiff-legged toward James's truck.

Before Mike reached James, a female voice called Mike's name. He turned. Dahlia stood on the porch with Jake. Mike turned back. James had *Joyce* pinned against the truck.

"James! Goddammit!" Mike shouted. "What are you doing?"

James had opened the rear door of his truck and appeared to be trying to force Joyce into the back seat. Mike grabbed James by the belt and tried to pull him away, but he was too heavy. James turned and lunged at Mike. At the same moment, Joyce shoved James as hard as she could in the back. Mike got a hold of James's shirt, and with Joyce still pushing, Mike leaned back and pulled James down. Mike landed hard on his back with James on top of him.

Mike still had a hold of James's shirt when the sound of

two gunshots drew his attention to the cabin. Junior sprinted across the yard in his underwear. With a very young and half-naked girl tugging on his arm, the shooter stopped on the porch, took careless aim, and fired one last shot. The bullet grazed Junior's head above his left ear just as he crashed into James and Mike. The shooter stumbled off the porch and flung the pistol. The gun landed near Junior, who lay semiconscious on top of Mike. Mike couldn't see much, but James said, "Dang!" and the sound of cars starting, more screaming, and running footsteps quickly filled the air.

Mike dragged himself out from under Junior, struggled to his feet, and craned his neck in Joyce's direction. Still standing next to the truck, she pointed at James, who was on his knees a few feet away, breathing hard with the gun in his hand. He stood, raised the gun, and pointed it in Mike's direction.

8

JOYCE SCREAMED, "MIKE!" Terrified, James dropped his arm, ran to his truck, pushed Joyce out of the way, and clambered in behind the wheel.

Tall Paul was already in the front passenger seat. Pork was leaning forward in the back seat with his fatty forearms on the seatback between James and Tall Paul. James tossed the gun to Tall Paul, who turned and flipped it toward the back seat. Pork slapped the gun onto the floor just as James fumbled with the key. Then when he tried to jam the truck into first, he neglected to engage the clutch and the gears ground.

"The clutch," Pork screamed from the back seat.

"Shut the hell up," James said. Finally, he slammed his foot down on the clutch and slammed the truck into gear. The truck jerked forward and nearly hit two girls running down the dirt road away from the house. James was able to gain enough control to join the panicky, alcohol-deranged convoy bouncing along the dirt road back toward the highway.

When he reached the main road, James swerved around several cars and trucks as he raced toward town. He arrived at the gravel parking strip in front of his mother's house and slammed on the brakes to keep from crashing into the same pickup parked there when he'd gotten home from school.

"See ya," Tall Paul said as he leaped from the front seat and bolted across the street to where Pork's VW was parked.

James could feel Pork squirming around in the backseat, and when he turned to see what his fat friend was doing, Pork tossed the gun onto the front seat next to James.

"Jesus, Pork. I don't want the damn gun."

But Pork had already wiggled himself out the door, releasing a damp fart when his feet hit the ground.

"Sorry," he said. Pork pushed the door closed, trapping the foul odor inside, and then waddled off to his car.

James watched while Pork wiggled his bulk in behind the steering wheel. Tall Paul was already in the passenger seat with his knees jammed up against the dashboard.

Pork's sad little VW wouldn't start on the first two tries and made a wheezing racket as the engine finally turned over on the third crank. When the wheezing stopped, James watched as the ugly yellow bug pulled into the street and disappeared around the corner at the end of the block.

Still in the driver's seat of his truck, James glanced toward the second-floor window of his mother's room, but the house remained dark. James shifted in his seat, and his hand brushed the gun. He jerked away, pushed the door open with his shoulder, and stepped out of the truck. His heart began to race as he backed two or three steps into the street and stared at the gun in the weak glow of the dome light.

Like every other boy in Silverton, James wasn't bothered

by the presence of a gun in his truck. He knew what guns were for. He knew how to use a gun. Guns didn't scare him. He recognized the pistol as a short-barreled .22. Any proud dad in Silverton might have given his son such a weapon on his ninth or tenth birthday. The gun rested inert on the seat, like the coiled serpent of original sin, and James was afraid to touch it.

"Crap," he said. "That's the murder weapon." He had seen the blood from Junior's head wound and concluded Junior must be dead.

He approached the open door of his truck one slow step at a time while the storyline of every bad cop show replayed in his brain: He had the murder weapon. Someone might have seen him with it. The deputy sheriff would think James was the shooter.

James took one tentative step back toward the open door of his truck. Then another. And then one more until he was close enough to retrieve the gun. He rubbed his chin and looked up and down the street. He glanced over his shoulder to make sure no light shone from nosy Mrs. Stamp's house across the road.

Satisfied no one was watching, he reached into the truck for the gun, but when his fingers closed around the plastic grip, a shrill siren out on Main Street blared like the voice of perdition, and James jerked his hand away and jumped back. The gun remained on the seat, and the siren faded into the distance, to the north, away from town. James took a deep breath and checked the street in both directions again. He glanced over his shoulder toward Mrs. Stamp's house one more time and then reached into the truck and grabbed the gun.

He climbed back into the cab, closed the door, and

placed the gun back on the seat. His mind kept rehashing the moments before the shots were fired. Before he was aware of the blood on Junior's head. Before the pistol landed at his feet. Before he and the boys raced back into town, swerving in and out of the young-and-drunk convoy. Before guilt or fear or both prevented him from deciding what to do with the gun. The guilt and fear confused him, but after a few seconds, his mind cleared. He knew he hadn't shot Junior, and he figured there must be people who could say who had.

Then the guilt returned. Or was it doubt? He did take the gun. Should he have left it or waited for the sheriff? His mind raced backward over the flurry of events. *The race away from junior's cabin. The gun at his feet. Junior's head wound. Someone firing from the porch. Mike pulling him away from...Joyce.*

More guilt. And then more doubt.

Joyce knows I have the gun.

James picked up the gun and tried to thrust it into his waistband, but he had to loosen his belt so it would fit. He snuck around the back of the house and went into the garage. He turned on a light and retrieved the cedar box from the shelf above the workbench. He wrapped the gun in a soft rag and placed it inside the box. He turned off the light and sat on an old kitchen chair next to the door, the box with the gun inside resting on his lap.

After several minutes, James cradled the box against his chest, left the shop, and went into the house. He crept through the kitchen to the bottom of the stairs near the front door, climbed four steps to the first landing where the stairs turned right, and then stopped and listened. The upstairs hallway was dark, except for a dim light escaping from under his mother's closed door. A slurred male voice sounded from behind the door, followed by a womanish giggle and a snort. James thought about the gun in the box. He put one foot on the first step above the landing, but before he could gather himself to spring up the stairs, he changed his mind.

9

WHILE HE WAITED to be interviewed by a familiar deputy sheriff, Mike sat next to Joyce on the front porch of Junior's cabin. He rocked slowly back and forth and massaged his thighs, leaning in with his shoulders to press his fingertips and the heels of his hands deep into the muscles.

The deputy was interviewing scared kids one at a time at the kitchen table inside the cabin. Earlier, Joyce had talked to a tall female deputy who was now leaning against the rickety railing with her eyes nearly shut. A nametag above her badge read Deputy Dori Woods. She was dressed in the same woodsy brown and green uniform as the other half dozen deputies milling about, except she had a discreet silver cross pinned to her uniform shirt above the badge. She appeared bored. Apparently, babysitting the desolate collection of anxious teens who had failed to escape was not tough duty. An ambulance sat parked in front of the house with its lights off and the back doors open.

Joyce looked at Mike. "What's the name of the guy who got shot?"

"Junior."

"The boy who owns this place?"

"I don't know who owns it," Mike said, still rubbing his legs. "Junior has parties out here a few times a year. This is the biggest. End of school."

Mike stopped rubbing his legs and fingered a bloody spot on his shirt.

Joyce noticed. "Sweet Jesus, Mike. Were you hit?"

"No. Almost. I guess? It's Junior's blood, I guess."

When he removed his finger from the tear, his hands were shaking. He leaned forward and resumed rubbing his thighs with the heels of his hands.

"Mike? You're shaking."

"No. I'm not." He stopped rubbing. "It's no big deal. I must be getting cold."

"That's nonsense. Gunfire, Mike. And all these drunken kids. This is a big deal, so you might as well say so. Don't pretend."

Joyce had wrapped her arms around her knees and leaned over. Her shoulder touched Mike's upper arm, and the gesture had a calming effect on Mike. After a few minutes, he began to feel something like normal and was glad Joyce had come.

"How did you get here?"

"With Mark, a guy I know from church. And don't change the subject."

"So, where is he?" Mike made an exaggerated show of looking around for Joyce's friend.

Joyce crossed her arms and set her jaw. "Don't be an ass."

Mike forced a laugh because he had never heard Joyce use any kind of profanity.

"The jerk left when the shooting started," Joyce said. "Along with everyone else who could climb into a car or truck."

Mike pulled his knees up to match hers and rested his forehead on his folded arms. Joyce stretched her legs out straight.

"I called you because I needed to get out of here." Mike turned his head away and squeezed his eyes shut. When he turned back, he said, "I don't know anyone else's phone number."

"I wish you'd called sooner. Maybe we'd have missed all this."

Mike and Joyce waited with several others who were either too drunk or too sick to leave. A few feet to Mike's right, the girl who'd been braless had her shirt buttoned and was standing with her back against the wall, teetering from side to side. She was barefoot and wrapped in a dirty green blanket, staring at a fresh yellowish stain just above the knees of her unbuttoned jeans. The girl flopped onto her hands and knees and crawled to the edge of the porch.

Mike made a face and shifted to his left until he bumped Joyce's shoulder. The girl let the blanket slide off her back while she hung her head over the edge of the porch to puke. When the sick girl was done throwing up, she sat up and leaned forward to rest her head on the floorboards. Joyce started to get up to help, but Deputy Woods motioned for her to stay where she was. The deputy helped the girl to her feet, wrapped the blanket around her shoulders, and guided her off the porch and into one of the sheriff's cars parked next to the ambulance.

Mike leaned his head back against the wall. "What now? No one who's still here has a car."

Joyce sucked in a deep, loud breath, held it, pursed her lips, and exhaled through her nose. "I called for a ride when the lady deputy took me into the house. The sheriffs are having everyone call home."

"You called your old man?" Mike shook his head. "Great. He'll want me dead."

"No, he won't. I'm a good girl. Remember? Anyway, I didn't call home. I called Coach Tyler. He'll think of something."

10

AFTER SEVERAL MINUTES, a slender deputy sheriff tapped Mike on the top of the head and made a "come with me" gesture with his forefinger. Mike struggled to his feet and followed the deputy through the front room into Junior's kitchen. The deputy pointed to a chair at the kitchen table and sat down across from Mike.

"I'm Deputy Dodge."

Mike responded with a scornful laugh. *Deputy Dodge* sounded like a cartoon character.

"You okay?" Dodge said. "The others are either drunk or sick, or they didn't see anything."

"What about Junior? He fell on top of me. Is he—?"

"Well, that's what I want to talk to you about. But first, I have to say that you don't have to talk to me." Dodge paused before adding, "But I'm not looking to get anyone in trouble, just trying to get a handle on what happened here."

"A party happened," Mike explained. He began to tap his feet and drum his fingers on the table. "Someone had a gun, and Junior got shot. Pretty simple."

Dodge waited, and Mike relaxed. Then, when Mike

didn't say any more, Dodge continued.

"You say Junior fell on top of you. What were you doing? What did you see?"

Mike thought a moment. Should he say anything at all? He had no idea who shot Junior. He hadn't even known anyone had been shot until Junior fell on top of him. While Mike sorted through everything, he suddenly remembered James and the gun. Why hadn't Dodge asked about the gun? Mike came to a quick decision. He wouldn't say anything about James and the gun or about Joyce and James. And he would make his own plans for James.

"I know your name's Mike. Mike Beck, right? You need to call someone to come get you?"

"There's no one home. But I know a girl here. She called someone."

"So, an adult is coming for you?"

"Um...you said I don't have to talk to you. So, does that mean I can leave anytime I want?"

"You're not leaving here by yourself or with another kid, okay? A responsible adult needs to see you get home."

"A responsible adult. Yeah, right."

"Look, Mike. You're not guilty of anything much—minor in possession and illegal consumption, maybe. But given the circumstances and the fact the others have left you high and dry, I'm going to let that slide." Deputy Dodge paused and leaned back. "Besides, being a stupid kid is still not a crime. Although, around here, being a stupid kid sometimes seems like an inherited obligation. No one thinks you shot Junior. But from what I hear, you're in the wrong place at the wrong time a lot. Answer my questions, and you can get out of here when your ride shows up."

"I don't want to get anyone in trouble." Mike had begun drumming his fingers again. "I didn't see much anyway."

"What did you hear?"

Mike paused for a moment. "A gunshot. No, two, maybe three gunshots. And people running and yelling. I think a girl screamed."

"One shot right after the other, or was there some time in between shots?"

"I don't remember…"

Deputy Dodge had been calm, but now he sat forward and raised his voice. "Gunshots at a party aren't that easy to forget."

Mike squirmed uncomfortably in the hard chair, and his finger drumming stopped.

Dodge leaned back again and lowered his voice. "Think about it, Mike."

"There were two shots close together, then another shot a few seconds later."

"Good. Then what?"

The deputy sat up, slowly this time, and folded his hands on the table.

"Okay. We'll let you leave when someone comes for you. Are you going to need help dealing with this? You saw your friend shot. The other kids are very upset, scared. But you just seem, I don't know, nervous."

Mike looked away. When he turned back, Dodge leaned in closer and waited for Mike to speak.

"Junior's not my friend. He's got this cabin, and kids pay him for a place to drink, and…you know, connect."

Dodge tapped his lower lip with his forefinger. "But when Junior got shot, weren't you scared? Why didn't you run away like the others?"

"I don't really care about Junior. And I'm *not* scared. And my friend Joyce was still here."

"Yeah. We've already talked to Joyce." Dodge sat back

again and placed his hands behind his head. "What were you doing right before Junior fell on you?"

Mike put his hands flat on the table and spread his fingers. Images of what James had tried to do to Joyce flashed in Mike's mind. What might James do with the gun? Mike thought about what needed to happen to James and what the sheriff might do or not do.

"You said I don't have to say anything if I don't want to."

"That's right, Mike. You don't."

"Well, I don't want to say nothin' more."

The deputy began to chew on his lower lip. Mike watched and then smirked and looked away.

Dodge folded his hands on the table. "Mike, I'm a little troubled that you aren't more distraught by what happened here."

Mike began to tap his feet, but his hand remained still.

Dodge continued. "Doesn't this incident upset you, at least a little?"

Mike didn't trust adults who could make him do what they wanted. His father was gone most of the time, and he didn't bother Mike when he was home. And Mike thought most teachers were fools. Coach Tyler was a special case. Most kids didn't like Tyler because he made them run in PE, but running was easy for Mike, so he didn't mind. Mike would retreat to some private place when confronted by inquisitive adults. They made him feel on edge and out of place until the questioning was done, and he was able to run away into the mountains. Now Dodge, with a gun and a badge and handcuffs, and the whole force of the law behind him, could make Mike do anything he wanted. But apparently, he wasn't going to.

"You can wait outside on the porch, Mike. But I need to talk to whoever comes to get you. An adult is coming, right?"

Mike thought about what to say. "I was trying to pull a pig off the girl who came to take me home. He was trying to, uh, you know, *connect* with her. We fell onto the ground, and when I tried to get up, Junior fell on me." Mike pulled his T-shirt away from his body to show the deputy a small smear of Junior's dried blood.

Dodge scratched his head and nodded. "Your ride, Mike?"

"I called a girl I know—before all this happened. I don't know anyone else's number. Then the guy who brought her left when the shooting started, and she called someone else to come get us. I don't know who, but she said someone would come." Mike took a deep breath, and his senses were assaulted by the generational reek of stale beer, spent pot, and fresh vomit.

"Mike, either you are one tough sucker, or you're a heartless bastard. I'm not sure which."

"Is there a third choice?"

Dodge put both hands on the table and pushed himself to a standing position. "This time of night, with a bunch of sick kids and a shooting victim waiting in the ambulance? No. Those are the only two choices." The deputy gestured toward the door. "You can wait outside with your friend, but remember, I need to talk to an adult before I can let you go."

Mike left the table, but he stopped and turned around to face Dodge when he got to the door between the kitchen and the front room. "Do you know who shot Junior?"

Dodge cleared his throat and said in his best TV-cop voice, "I can't comment on an ongoing investigation."

Mike smirked. "Yeah, right."

When Mike returned to the porch after being interviewed by Deputy Dodge, the other kids had left. All except Joyce, who was still sitting on the steps, waiting. The sheriff's vehicles were still there, but the ambulance had left with its emergency lights off. Mike figured Junior must be in the ambulance, and he felt a twinge above his stomach. But the sensation passed.

Mike looked back through the cabin door. Dodge stood at the door to the kitchen, talking to Deputy Woods. Woods turned to look at Mike and then turned away again. Mike sat on the cabin steps next to Joyce, pulled off his running shoes, and removed his jeans. He always wore running shorts under his clothes.

Mike pulled off his socks and put his running shoes back on. He stood and stared out beyond the overgrown yard into the greenish void the forest became at night. The scent of cedar and fir on the mountain air had diluted the indoor odor of vomit and alcohol, and he sucked in two deep, cleansing breaths. He could make out the forms of individual trees along the road, but just barely. He knew at least half a dozen trails that led back to town, some overused and some forgotten.

"I'm going to run home." Mike tossed his jeans to Joyce and then shrugged to stretch the tightness out of his shoulders.

"You're leaving me here?" Joyce said. "Jeez, Mike."

"You said Tyler was coming. Don't worry. The cops will make sure you get home."

He still felt sluggish, but whether from the beer or some malaise, maybe brought about by his father's revelation about his mother, he couldn't tell. It didn't matter anyway. He left his socks on the steps and walked through the ankle-high grass in the yard and past the sheriff's vehicles to the road. He ran about two hundred yards through the dark and then onto a narrow path that angled to the right, away from the gravel road.

11

JOYCE WATCHED Mike run slowly away from the cabin and disappear into the darkness. By the time the deputies noticed he was gone, Mike would have covered most of a mile.

Dodge came out of the house and approached Joyce. "Where's Mike?"

Holding Mike's jeans in one hand, Joyce pointed with her free hand into the darkness toward the mountains. "He left." She folded Mike's jeans and draped them over her forearm.

"With who?"

Joyce shook her head and brushed a bit of dirt off Mike's pant leg.

"Do we need to look for him?" Woods asked Joyce. "He shouldn't be on the road if he's been drinking."

"He's not driving," Joyce said. "Besides, he usually doesn't drink much."

"He's relatively sober compared to the other kids," Dodge said, staring toward the road. He turned toward

Joyce. "He said a ride was coming for the two of you. Is someone coming for you or not?"

"Maybe Mike's ride will see him on the road," the female deputy said.

As they talked, Joyce's father's newish, three-quarter-ton pickup rolled across the yard past the sheriff's vehicles and stopped a few feet from the porch. Joyce's dad got out of the truck on the driver's side. Don—he'd been "Donald" as a child and "Donny" at Silverton High—had spent his entire life in Silverton, except for three years in the Army, most of that time in Vietnam.

Before the Army, he'd spent two hazardous summers working in the woods, where there were too many ways to get injured, or worse. Falling trees. Heavy equipment. Axes and chainsaws. Bad roads. Boredom and fatigue. He'd known two young men from Silverton who had been killed working in those woods—one more than the little town had lost in Vietnam. After the Army, he'd returned to his old job, but for the past ten years, he'd driven a log truck. He was reticent by nature, but people sometimes paid attention when he spoke.

Coach Tyler waited a few seconds and then stepped down out of the truck on the passenger side. Tyler had moved to Silverton after four years near the front of the pack at the University of Oregon and a single season racing in Europe. No one was quite sure what had brought Tyler to Silverton.

"Hello, Donny," Dodge said. "Been a long time."

The two men shook hands.

"We're here to pick up a couple of these dumb-ass kids," Joyce's father said.

"Mike Beck," Tyler said.

"And my daughter." Don nodded in Joyce's direction.

"She called Coach Tyler. Told him the boy was in trouble. And the coach called me."

"Not much trouble," Dodge said. "There was a shooting, but no one was hurt bad, and the boy wasn't directly involved. He may have seen something, though. Apparently, he was trying to protect a girl."

Joyce stepped down off the porch and stood a few feet in front of her father. Her dad gave her a stern look.

Dodge glanced at Joyce. "Mike said the girl was having some trouble with another boy." He continued looking at Joyce. "Mike didn't say who the girl or other boy was."

"James," Joyce said, gazing straight ahead.

Joyce's father took a step toward her. "I know James. And you know his old man, Dodge."

Dodge nodded. "Yeah. Joyce, do you know who James was bothering?" he asked again.

Joyce didn't answer.

Tyler put his hands in his pockets. "What are you even doing here, Joyce? This isn't—"

"Mike called me...he wanted to go home. I came with Mark from church, but Mark left me here. I was trying to help."

Joyce's father frowned but nodded. "Later," he said. "We'll talk about this later."

"I don't think Joyce has been drinking," Deputy Woods offered.

"I know she hasn't been drinking," her dad said sharply.

"Anyway," Dodge went on, "someone may want to talk to Mike about how he spends his weekends, but he's not in any real trouble with us. We may have a few more questions about what went on here, but that'll be later. I told him to wait for his ride, but he disappeared."

"He's running," Tyler and Joyce said at the same time.

"He'll get home in an hour or so," Tyler added.

Dodge looked surprised. "Are you sure? Gotta be nine or ten miles back to town on the road."

"Yes," Tyler and Joyce replied in unison again.

"And you are—?" Dodge nodded at Tyler.

"Peter Tyler. I'm Mike's coach. I teach PE at the high school." Tyler paused, then added, "He won't be running on the highway, though. He knows the logging roads and hiking trails as well as anyone. And he's a pretty good runner."

"He's Bobby Beck's kid, isn't he?" Dodge nodded as if knowing Mike's parentage solved a riddle. "Bobby's probably out of town, but I'd like an adult to be there when the boy gets home. Are you sure we don't need to find him?"

Tyler turned to Joyce's father. "You can drop me at Mike's. I'll stay with him."

"That would make me feel better," Dodge said. "We're going to need to check on some of the other kids."

Joyce, Tyler, and her father climbed into her dad's truck and headed back toward town in silence.

About half a mile from Mike's house, Joyce leaned forward from the back seat and said, "I'm going to wait for Mike."

Her father glanced at her in the rearview mirror, and for a moment she feared he'd say no.

"Please, Dad," she said, injecting a solid note of urgency into her tone.

"Your mother will not like that."

"Tell her—"

Joyce's father held up his hand. "I'll take care of it."

12

MIKE HAD BECOME adept at running in the dark. If he didn't hurry and was careful where he put his feet, he could feel his way through the trees without needing to see the ground. He knew he'd be able to speed up when the trail spilled onto a well-maintained logging road, so he remained patient.

After about six hundred yards, though, he tripped on an invisible tree root and stumbled. He managed to lunge forward and catch himself before he fell, a skill perfected by running hundreds of miles on hazardous trails. He stopped for a moment, made a quick check of his body parts to make sure he hadn't hurt himself, and then started to run again. But after about a dozen steps, he felt sick to his stomach, and his head began to pound. He could not tell whether he was sick from the small amount of alcohol he'd consumed or the shock of having Junior's body fall on top of him, but the cramping and the pounding forced him onto his hands and knees. He vomited in the middle of the trail and then rolled onto his back away from the pungent mess and closed his eyes.

When his head stopped pounding, he struggled to his feet and began to jog up the trail. He felt clumsy and tired until the trail made a long, swooping bend to the left and then switched back and forth toward the top of the first of several hills he'd have to climb before he got home. As the trail ascended, he welcomed the familiar heaviness in his thighs. Running uphill in the dark was safer than running downhill, so he pressed the pace for a few steps. The heavy sensation became a dull ache after a couple of minutes, and Mike pushed harder. By the time he completed the three-quarter-mile climb to the top of the first ridge, he was breathing hard, and the annoying ache in his thighs had become a satisfying burn.

At the top, the trail opened onto a logging road that wandered down through a clear-cut dotted with new saplings but no trees tall enough to block the welcome light of the three-quarter moon. With the pain in his head gone and the odorous puddle of puke a guilty memory, Mike pushed hard out of the trees and onto the logging road. He nudged his shoulders forward, and with each stride, reached as far down the hill as he could. He let the combination of gravity and the thrill of being able to move unencumbered by the darkness of the trail propel him down the gravel road.

As he ran, a vague fear rose in the back of his mind, something to do with what had happened to Junior and what had almost happened to Joyce. But familiarity with the surface of the logging road and the discomfort of the effort made him feel safe. He almost lost control around a sharp bend to the left and had to scramble to regain his footing in the loose gravel. Then he ran hard for a mile up a gentle grade, then slowed on another wooded trail that led to another stretch of logging road and then another trail and so on and so on.

On the final hill, he was breathing hard, but he continued to press the pace with his eyes down, the moonlight casting vague shadows across the ascending surface of the road. The burning sensation returned, and he shortened his stride when his feet began to slip in the gravel. Near the top, he pumped his arms and increased the pressure of his feet on the roadway.

The tree stumps in the clear-cut receded not only from his vision but also from his consciousness. He was unaware of the gravel road now, sensible of nothing but the effort. Junior and Joyce disappeared from his mind. His mother and Robert and being suspended from school. All gone. Nothing from the past. Nothing in the future. Nothing but the present, step-after-step moment occupied by profound exertion.

Then, as he neared the top, he felt the familiar, liberating acceleration that was always there at the end of a race or a hard run. He was exhausted, but Mike welcomed the discomfort and pushed harder against it, testing his tolerance for pain and calling on the one inescapable fact in which he had absolute faith.

His own will.

Mike reached the top of the hill, slowed to a jog, and finally stopped. He leaned forward for a few seconds, then stood erect and spread his arms. He tilted his face to the sky as the moon receded behind a cloud leaving the clear-cut hilltop utterly dark. And he screamed—a guttural, primal howl of frustration.

He'd come close, but he still didn't know how much he could take or how far he could go.

Mike waited for his breathing to stabilize. The clear-cut

ended at the top of the hill, and the old-growth timber lining the road in front of Mike was still and silent. The faint smell of damp ash drifted up from a shallow valley. He took in a deep breath through his nose and jogged down the hill toward another opening in the trail. He ran through the trees and sped up on the logging roads until he emerged from the woods behind the high school, bone-tired and cleansed.

13

JAMES STARTED his truck and slammed the accelerator to the floor. The engine roared, and he made the tires squeal as he pulled away from the house he shared with his mother. He braked hard at the end of the block and made the tires squeal again when he turned left and headed away from town on Scout Lake Road.

James slowed his truck as he approached Joyce's house. The place was dark, but there was a car he didn't recognize parked in the circular drive. He turned into the driveway and stopped. The headlights reached all the way to the house, but there were no lights on, and Joyce's father's new truck was not parked in the carport.

James backed out of the driveway and turned back toward town. He drove past the high school and slowed again when he reached Mike's house. Mike's old pickup was parked in its usual spot to the right of the house.

He drove about fifty yards up the highway, pulled off, and parked, hidden at the back of a gravel lot between two empty log trucks. James could see Mike's house, so he turned off the engine, rolled down the window, and settled into the seat.

The night air was warm in June, but the damp promise of rain and the faint aroma of cedar mingled with fir was always present. Alone and in the dark, James relaxed. He felt more at home in the front seat of his truck than in his own room, which was separated from his mother's bedroom by nothing but a thin, uninsulated wall. In the years since his father had moved out, James had learned that the amplitude of his mother's squeaky bedsprings increased when she was not sleeping alone.

James's favorite time of day was between midnight and dawn. The dark, quiet hours. Great things were predicted for someone as big and as bad as James, so he had a reputation to live up to. He was a tough guy. A badass. The Man. He was expected to behave accordingly, and he did, but more out of habit than commitment.

At this time of night, everyone who feared or admired or loathed James was asleep or otherwise occupied. So, he could sit alone alongside the highway, hidden by idle log trucks, and breathe in the warm air. He thought about the cedar box—about the neat corners and the imperfections in the wood. In the dark and alone, he could relax and let his guard down, so he hoped no one would show up at Mike's house for a long time. He even began to wonder if Pork's plans for Mike and Joyce would be worth the effort.

After a time, Don's new pickup passed on the highway and turned into the short driveway in front of Mike's house. Joyce got out of the truck first, then Don, and then someone James did not recognize until the man walked around the back of the truck and said something to Joyce.

Coach Tyler. *What is he doing here? And where is Mike?*

James waited and watched. But when Mike did not show

up, he put his truck in gear and pulled back onto the high-way. Joyce glanced across the road as he drove by.

When James reached the high school, he saw Mike jogging toward the road between the main building and the library. He pulled off the street, parked, and turned his headlights off. He took the gun from the cedar box and dangled it between his knees with the barrel pointed toward the floor. Mike jogged by but gave no indication he'd seen James.

James waited until Mike was out of sight then continued toward home.

14

JOYCE WAS SITTING on the steps next to Tyler when Mike jogged up to the house and stopped a few feet from the porch. Joyce's father was sitting in a kitchen chair and leaning back against the house with his eyes closed.

"Are you surprised, Mike?" Joyce said. She turned and glanced at her father.

Don let the chair tilt forward and stood up.

Mike remained standing in the yard but took a careful step back.

"Well, son, I guess you survived your little adventure," Don said. He walked to the top of the steps and looked down at Tyler. "I can drive you back to our place to get your car, or you can wait here. I don't think Deputy Dodge is going to check on Mike tonight." Don stepped down and put his hand on his daughter's shoulder.

Joyce touched his sleeve, stood up, and smiled at her father.

Then they approached Mike together.

"Son, you confuse me. Seems you're a lot like the rest of

those peckerwoods back there, but I never heard of anyone running through these hills, especially not in the dark."

Mike remained silent. Joyce's father put his hand on Mike's shoulder, the same as he'd done to Joyce, and left it there.

"What about Joyce?" Tyler called out from the steps.

Joyce's father still had his hand on Mike's shoulder and said, "She'll be all right. Won't she, Mike?"

"Yes, sir."

Joyce put her hand over her mouth to hide a smile because she had never heard Mike call anyone, *sir*. Then she blushed because she could not remember the last time she'd giggled.

"You take care, son." Don looked back and motioned for Tyler to follow. "Let's go, Coach."

The tires of Don's new pickup spun in the gravel, and rubber squealed when the truck reached the blacktop. Joyce shook her head.

She returned to the porch and stood on the bottom step so she could look down at Mike. She had been thinking about what she would say, but... *Ephesians 4:29. Let no evil talk come out of your mouth.* She had heard that Biblical principle preached from the time she was old enough to sit up in a pew. As if the most important doctrinal principle for young Christians, except for maybe the appearance of chastity, was sanitary language. But...*only such that is good for edifying, as fits the occasion, that it may impart grace to those who hear.* Joyce had never, at least within anyone's hearing, uttered the kind of language she flung at Mike that night. But Ephesians 4:29...*as fits the occasion*...was clear.

"What the frack, Mike? What happened back there at that cabin? Why'd you leave me there?" she asked.

"Nice language for a church girl,"

Joyce had not been a *church girl* for a while. *Can you be a Christian and not be a church girl, as fits the occasion?*

"Go to hell, Mike. I haven't been to church for months. It's all nonsense anyway."

"Jesus, Joyce. What the—?"

"Don't *Jesus* me. You call me up in the middle of the night and beg for a ride home. You know I don't have a car. Have you ever seen me drive a car?" Joyce plopped down onto the step at his feet. "Why'd you call me?"

Joyce looked up at Mike, and he turned his head away.

"I make it a point not to care about much," he said. "And there aren't many people who owe me any favors."

"And you think I owe you a favor?"

"No." Mike paused. "But I thought you might...be able to help me."

"You knew I'd find a way...to help you."

"Yeah. I knew. Or I hoped you would...maybe."

"Despite evidence to the contrary?"

"I had *faith*."

"Don't be smug. I hate smug."

"I can't help it."

"Yes. You can, Mike. 'I can't help it' is just an excuse."

Joyce patted the space on the step next to her. Mike hesitated and then sat down. The mountain air was cold and damp. Joyce wrapped her arms around herself and leaned forward. Beside her, Mike shivered. The sweaty heat of his run must have begun to wear off, so she leaned in closer and savored the delicate warmth where their shoulders touched. She inched closer still and put her hand on his knee. Mike started to put his arm around Joyce's shoulders, but she pulled her hand away...

"I never imagined Junior's parties could be as bad as I've heard," Joyce said. "Are they always that bad?"

"Whatever. A lot of kids go to those parties, so they must be good for something."

Joyce leaned away. "Good for what? It's fracking Sodom and Gomorrah. Did you see that girl? Half-naked, and she'd already puked on herself. How is that *good*? A guy got shot. He could have been killed. You were nearly hit."

"But you came for me anyway. You called Mark, and you came."

"Mark's a good friend. He kind of likes me, so I told him I'd owe him a favor."

"A favor?" Mike laughed.

"He's not like that."

"Yeah, he is. I know Mark. Christians like to screw, too."

Joyce's first inclination was to slap Mike and leave, but then, without thinking, she said, "Sweet Jesus, Mike. You. Are. Better. Than this."

"Better than what?"

"Than this. Better than this cynical 'I don't give a crap' jackass who pretends to do whatever he wants, no matter what. That's not who you are."

Mike stood and stumbled down off the steps. "You don't know," he said with his back to Joyce. "No one does."

"No one?"

"No. One."

Mike turned back around. Joyce had moved to stand on the ground in front of him, less than an arm's length away. She folded her hands at the waist.

"I know you've run every day since your mother left," she said.

"Those two things have nothing to do with each other."

"Okay, fine. But I also know you've never had sex with Dahlia, even though everyone thinks you guys do it all the time."

"How would you or any of your churchy friends know anything about screwing?"

"Well, to paraphrase the sexual sage of Silverton," Joyce said, "Church kids like to screw, too. Besides, I asked Dahlia, and she told me she would, but you won't."

"Dahlia is full of crap."

"She's messed up, and she's lonely. And she seems to think the secret to happiness is between her legs. She will do anything for anyone who makes her feel less alone."

"What does that have to do with me?"

"Dahlia isn't connected to anything, so she grabs on to you. But you are better than that, so you won't, uh...*connect* the way she thinks she wants you to."

Mike's T-shirt was still damp from his run, and he had begun to shiver. Joyce reached out and touched his bare arm above the elbow, and he flinched a little.

"I need to take a shower before I take you home," he said. "I don't want to get sick."

"So, what if you get sick? Why does it matter?"

"I need to run tomorrow."

"Yes," Joyce agreed. "You do." She applied a soft pressure to Mike's arm and nudged him toward the house.

Joyce waited on the couch while Mike took less than ten minutes to shower and put on dry clothes. She had begun to nod off when he came back into the front room. She shook herself awake and followed Mike toward the front door. He went through the door and turned to face her before she could step out of the house.

"I'm not going to see Dahlia anymore," he announced.

15

Joyce leaned against the passenger side door and watched Mike drive. She thought about his trouble at school and remembered something a teacher—Mr. Sorenson, probably—had said about Mike: "What is the matter with that kid?" In her mind, she thumbed through the New Testament and settled on several verses: Romans 12:6 (*Having gifts...let us use them*), Matthew 25:4 (*Take heed that no one lead you astray*), James 1:17 (*Every good endowment and every perfect gift is from above*). All spoke of divine gifts. Or talent. Or purpose.

None said anything about, *What is the matter?*

The porch light was on when Mike parked in front of Joyce's house. Coach Tyler's car was parked a little farther around the circular driveway. When Mike's pickup lurched to a stop, Joyce noticed a flutter at the window of her parents' room, and then the dim reading light on her father's side of the bed went out. The brighter light at the top of the stairs remained lit.

"Do you think Junior's okay?" Mike said.

"The ambulance left kind of slow, so he's probably not hurt all that bad. But he's not okay, Mike."

Mike hunched over the steering wheel and closed his eyes. Joyce inched a little closer. Mike's chest rose and fell, and she slid across the seat until she was almost touching him. She tried again to put her hand on his knee but stopped and pulled it back when he stirred and sat up. He turned toward Joyce and leaned back against the driver's side door.

"I'm not going back to school," he said. "As soon as I'm eighteen, I'm getting out. Maybe join the Army or the Marines or something."

"What are you talking about?"

"There's no reason for me to stay here. No one would much care if I left."

"No one, Mike?"

"Everyone thinks I'm a screw-up. No. That's not quite right." Mike looked at Joyce and fell silent.

Did he expect her to tell him what he'd said was not true?

"Well, that's because you are a...whatever," she said. "But that's what you want, isn't it? That's what you want people to think."

"It doesn't matter what I want or what anyone thinks. It's who I am." Mike put both hands on the steering wheel and pushed. "I don't mind."

Joyce thought about what to say next. When nothing came to her, she slid the last few inches across the seat until her left leg touched Mike's right leg, and she felt again the comforting warmth she'd experienced earlier when their shoulders touched.

The front door of the house opened, and Tyler came out and sat on the steps. Mike and Joyce both got out of the truck on the driver's side, and Mike leaned against the front fender nearest the house. Joyce hesitated and then sat next to Tyler.

Tyler turned to Joyce. "Everything okay?"

She looked at Mike and replied, "Everything's fine."

Mike placed both hands in his pockets.

Joyce said, "What are you doing here, Coach?"

"Mike saw a man get shot. Then he disappeared into the woods in the middle of the night after a deputy sheriff told him to stay put. I thought he might need something. Bail, maybe."

"I didn't see Junior get shot," Mike said. He folded his arms as he continued to lean against the front fender of his truck. "He fell on me after. I'm fine. But James—"

16

TYLER STOOD up from his place on the porch next to Joyce and approached Mike.

"Look, Mike, I'm usually willing to ignore what the grownups consider a kid's shortcomings. But it's early in the morning, and I'm tired. The school year has ended, and the most talented runner I've ever seen didn't finish another season because he couldn't keep his self-indulgent temper in check. So just forget about James."

Mike looked back and forth between Tyler and Joyce, thinking about his answer.

"James is a jerk," Mike said after a moment. "You didn't see what he was trying to do to Joyce."

"Forget about James," Joyce said.

"Forget about all of them," Tyler said. "Forget about everything except what you have at stake."

"So, what's at stake? College? A scholarship? That's what everyone at school keeps telling me. 'Stay out of trouble. You'll get a scholarship'. The same crap all the time. I don't need it." Mike started to speak again, but the words that formed in his mind got caught in his chest.

"Mike, this isn't about college or about what anyone at school or anyone in town thinks. It's not even about winning races or setting records. It's about finding out how fast you can run."

Mike wasn't sure what Tyler was getting at. "I run all the time. I've never lost a race. What do you want from me?"

"To have my curiosity satisfied. I want an answer to the question that's been nagging me since that first day in ninth-grade P.E."

* * *

During his very first class on the very first day of school, Tyler had everyone line up on the school's grass track to walk or jog four laps. He figured he might as well find out how out of shape the kids were. Every other kid in the class had whined about the task and had stopped to walk before they'd completed four laps. All except Mike. Not only had he not needed to walk during the one-mile test, but he'd also finished in less than five minutes, running barefoot and wearing baggy jeans with holes in the knees.

"Wow," Tyler remembered saying aloud. "Wow."

Tyler had run at the University of Oregon, but he had not broken five minutes in the mile until the end of his sophomore year in high school.

He took Mike aside after class. "What's your name?"

"Mike Beck." Mike had stared at the ground and had shifted nervously from one bare foot to the other.

"Do you know how good you are, Mike?"

"I know I like to run."

"But do you know how *good* you are?"

"I never thought about it."

"Well, think about it."

And that's how Tyler became Mike's coach. Many small schools didn't have cross-country teams in the early 1990s, so Tyler came by Mike's house every morning for a run before school. Mike already knew the best places to run around Silverton. And Tyler learned about Mike's habit of disappearing for hours at a time, running in the hills and the woods around town, unconcerned with time or distance.

Once a week, Tyler would drive Mike away from town for a long run on the logging roads and hiking trails in the mountains. To Tyler's amazement, no run was too long, no hill too steep. Tyler would sometimes increase the pace to test Mike, but the boy would just accelerate and keep going. One Saturday near the end of that first school year, Tyler and Mike came off a steep trail onto a flat, mile-long stretch of gravel road winding through a clear-cut at the base of Sauk Mountain. Deciding to push Mike, Tyler sped up to what he thought was a pace the boy could not sustain when they hit the gravel road. Tyler was feeling the effort and figured Mike must be struggling, also. After half a mile, Tyler looked over at Mike. The kid was breathing harder but running with no other signs of fatigue.

When they arrived back at his car, Tyler stopped and bent forward with his hands on his knees. Mike turned back in the direction they had come and sprinted full out for a quarter of a mile and then jogged back toward Tyler.

"I still don't know what you want." Mike thought about climbing back into his truck and driving away. "I've done everything you've told me to do."

"I want the same thing you should want—to satisfy that curiosity. I want to know how fast you can run. Not how far. Not how many miles. Anyone can pile up miles. We need to know how fast you can run four laps. But unless you play by the rules, unless you forget guys like James, and unless you get far enough outside yourself to see what's inside, you'll never know. I'll never know. No one will ever know, and all that talent will go to waste. There will be no point."

Mike was stunned.

The coach continued. "You say you've done everything I've told you to do, but that's not entirely true."

Mike was silent. He thought about his run through the dark woods to get home. And he thought about his feeling unsatisfied at the top of the hill.

"Okay. What else can I do?"

"Stay out of trouble. No fights. No skipping school. No backtalking teachers. No parties. For the next twelve months, you'll run and obey every pointless rule the grownups can think up."

No one spoke for a long time.

"You have no choice, Mike," Joyce said. "You're blessed. Don't you know that?"

"Me? Blessed? Right..."

"No. That's not what I mean. Well, yes, it is what I mean, but not the way you think. Tyler is right. You're better at this than anyone else. Anyone. Some people are jealous because no one in this town has ever been as good at anything as you are at running."

"I don't care what they—"

"No. You don't care. But you should. But *you* should." Joyce was in an emphatic mood, but she softened her tone. "You have a responsibility."

Joyce paused, and Mike waited for her to continue.

"This is no accident, Mike. This is not random. You

didn't win some genetic lottery. It's a gift. And you have more of this gift than anyone else. You have to...share it."

"That sounds like churchy crap. Are you gonna preach a sermon now about how God has a plan for my life and how I should run to glorify or praise or honor *Him*? I heard all that churchy crap from my mother."

"I'm not churchy. I'm never churchy. But I try to be a Christian."

All three were silent for a long moment, then Tyler chimed in.

"Mike, I think what Joyce is trying to say—"

"No...you don't know what I'm trying to say. But Mike does." She looked at Mike. "It's a gift, and you have more than you need, so you have to share it. You have to let everyone see what's possible, what can be done."

Tyler leaned back to lie on the porch with his feet on the top step. Joyce got up from the steps and walked over to the truck. She leaned on the fender next to Mike.

"What I meant when I said you have a responsibility—"

"You don't have to say anything. I kind of wondered why you never tried to talk to me about the God and Jesus stuff before. I know what you believe. It's the same stuff my mom believed."

Joyce shook her head. "I don't think you do. I'm nothing like your...it's nothing like what your mother believes."

"It doesn't matter. I don't have any other friends. Don't really want any. I think most people are full of crap."

The dark line above the hills was turning red. Joyce turned toward the sunrise. "I don't go to church anymore," she said. "I haven't for a while."

"I thought—"

"Not since sometime last year, about New Year's, maybe. It didn't all seem true anymore."

Mike huffed. "That's because most of it isn't."

"No, *most* of it is. But that's not the point."

The rosy glow deepened above the hills, and a chilly breeze filled the morning air with the scent of cedar and fir. Mike turned toward Joyce, and there was a new look in her eyes, something mysterious and far away. Intimate, but unlike the look he'd seen in Dahlia's eyes.

Without looking away from the sunrise, Joyce said, "I don't know what it is, but you're fast for a reason."

Mike was silent. Until now, everyone talked about how his running could pay off—scholarships, championships, records, recognition, and prestige for the town and the school. But when Mike ran, none of that occurred to him. There was nothing except movement and effort. How far? How fast? How hard? How deep could he go?

"To the roots," Tyler had said once. "When you can go to the roots, then you'll know."

"Talent is no accident," Joyce said. "But it's wasted if no one sees what it can do."

Tyler sat up and rubbed his eyes. "Is that the sun?" He got up and walked a circle all the way around Mike's truck, frowning. "Maybe I should follow you home. This rig's on its last leg."

"How fast? If I do what you say—kiss their butts, take crap from James, go to class—how fast can I go?"

Tyler did not hesitate. "If we get your training organized. If you eat better. No more parties. A regular schedule. Early to bed every night. If you play their game—"

"How fast?"

"You'll win the state title in cross-country in November. No one in the small-school division will be within a minute of you over three miles. Then, if we can get you in the right race next spring, maybe at Shelton or Pasco, against the big school studs—"

"How fast?"

"Fast, Mike. Damn fast."

"*How* fast?"

"At least 4:10," Tyler said.

Four-ten didn't mean much to Mike. It sounded fast, but until that moment, nothing but running hard and winning had mattered. He had never really cared about the time if he was spent at the end of a race and in first place.

"I don't know…" Mike hesitated. "I'm a screw-up. No one's going to believe I've changed just so I can run fast. What if I don't do it?"

"You don't have to be a screw-up," Joyce said. "And no one cares if you change or not. They only pretend to care because they don't know what matters to you. So, do what Tyler says, and forget everyone else."

"If you don't run that fast," Tyler added, "it won't be because you can't, or you won't. It will be because you didn't."

17

JOYCE ENTERED the house and went up the stairs to her room. As soon as she was inside, the porch light went out, but the hall light at the top of the stairs remained lit. She sat on the edge of the bed with the door open. The light from the hall spilled across the floor and mingled with the red glow of the spreading dawn. She waited until the sunlight overcame the light from the hall and then opened her hard-backed King James Bible to the first of two passages she had marked earlier. She hadn't been certain why she had marked them, but now she knew.

But they that wait upon the LORD shall renew their strength; they shall mount up with wings as eagles; they shall run, and not be weary; and they shall walk, and not faint (Isiah 40:31).

And then...

And so he that had received five talents came and brought other five talents, saying, Lord, thou deliveredst unto me five talents: behold, I have gained beside them five talents more (Matthew 25:20).

"Maybe it's that easy." Joyce kicked off her shoes and lay back on her bed.

Mike has to do what Tyler said.

She closed her Bible and held it to her chest as she fell asleep, uncovered. Her legs dangled off the edge, and the toes of her shoes scuffed against the floor. She either dreamed of or imagined what could have happened at Junior's party.

A suffocating weight pinned her against the back seat of James's truck. Her eyes were open, but the inside of the truck was dark. She tried to push the weight away, but her hands disappeared into something soft. Then the weight engulfed her, and she felt as if her heart stopped. Next, there was a flash and a bang, and she was standing on the ground outside the truck. In the flickering, spinning red-and-white halo created by a dozen sets of receding headlights and taillights, she saw James standing a few feet away with the gun in his hands. Mike's inert body was on the ground in a puddle of blood.

Joyce bolted upright and gasped. The Bible was still on her lap, a red pen clutched in her hand. She took a deep breath, flopped back onto the bed, and settled into a tenuous sleep.

She stared at the Bible, but the pages were blank. She began to fill in the blank pages, but when the pen touched the paper, the red ink pooled and dripped off the page, forming a puddle on the floor.

Still on her back, Joyce opened her eyes. Like the back seat of James's truck in her dream, the room was dark except for the fabricated glow of the artificial stars her father had glued to the ceiling. She closed her eyes and fell into a deep, dreamless sleep.

18

────────

BY THE TIME Mike got home, he was exhausted, but less from his run through the mountains than by everything else that had happened. He shuffled to his room and was about to tumble onto the bed when he found a note from his father pinned to his pillow.

Your mother called again. I have to go. Have a good life.

Mike was too tired to think about what the note meant. His legs ached. He was sticky with sweat. His stomach hurt. He needed a shower. He folded the note and tossed it onto the floor. He plopped down onto the bed, half expecting the cryptic note to keep him awake, but he fell asleep just as his face hit the pillow.

While he slept, sunlight streamed through the window, and warmth spread like a blanket across the bed. By the time he woke up, the soreness and fatigue were mere memories, like the tug of guilt on an unredeemed conscience. So, when loud knocking on the front door woke him, Mike felt reborn.

The path to redemption is not a straight line, but the destination always appears in the palpable distance once the sincere penitent sets out. In those mystical moments before Mike was fully awake, he was aware of a voice agreeing with Tyler. Mike would deal with James and the adults at school later.

First things first, he told himself.

Mike climbed out of bed, went downstairs, and opened the door.

"Put on your running shoes," the coach said.

* * *

Long after the sun was up, Joyce woke briefly when her mother, Molly, came into her room. She removed Joyce's shoes, lifted her legs onto the bed, and covered her with an afghan from the closet. Joyce turned over and curled up with her Bible clutched to her chest. Molly opened the curtains, and light flooded the room. She patted Joyce's shoulder and then leaned over and gave her a kiss on the cheek. Molly noticed a red pen on the floor. The pen would not write, so she tossed it into the small trash can next to the desk.

* * *

When Joyce woke up sometime later, she was still caressing her open Bible. Mike's name had been scribbled in red next to a running stick figure at the top of the page. At the bottom of the page was a crude drawing of a pickup and two more stick figures, a frowning girl with straight hair and eyes formed by two tiny punctures. The boy had no face, just an oversized circle for a head.

Luke 19:10 was underlined: *For the Son of Man came to seek and to save the lost.* She read the passage a second time and then a third.

"Seek *and* save? Who?"

She closed the Bible, fell back onto the bed, covered her eyes with her forearm, and prayed. A knock at the door startled her.

"Joyce, sweetie," her mother called out. "You're going to sleep the day away."

Joyce's mother was a good Christian woman. Joyce had never seen or heard anything to make her believe Molly was anything but a good Christian woman. Joyce also wanted to be a good Christian woman, just not anything like her mother. Joyce opened the door, and her mother was standing a little to one side. Molly reached up and moved a strand of hair off Joyce's face.

"Are you okay, Joyce? You were out late. That's not like you."

Joyce thought, *Maybe it is like me.* "I've been reading. Did Dad say anything about last night?"

"He told me a story. I'm sure most of it is true."

Joyce could not remember a single occasion when her mother had been angry because of something Joyce had done. And only once, when Joyce was in middle school, did she remember her mother being angry with her father.

"Mom, what would it take for you to get mad at me?"

"Have you done something that should make me mad?"

"No. It's just like...like when I stopped going to church."

"Well, sweetheart, you'll come back to church."

"Mom..." An uncharacteristic unease rose in Joyce. "I'm not as good as—"

"No one is, Joyce."

* * *

James woke to the sounds of a squeaky bed and a man's heavy boots clomping on the floor in the next room. He opened the door of his room, just as a man he did not recognize came out of his mother's room. The man was shirtless with a hard-fat gut hanging over the waist of unbuttoned work pants held up by heavy suspenders. He carried a dirty denim shirt in one hand and a wool coat in the other. His heavy logger boots were untied. He stopped when he saw James and gave a thumbs-up with the hand carrying the shirt.

"Hey, kid. Your old lady's great." The man flashed a sinister smile and headed down the stairs.

James gave the man the finger as he watched him walk away. When the man had disappeared down the stairs, James turned and leaned on the doorframe to watch his mother sleep. JoAnn snoozed with her naked back to James, a single blanket covering the lower half of her body. Normally, he would have retrieved another blanket from the hall closet to cover his mother, but this time he didn't.

19

Tyler drove away from Mike's house, across the bridge with the Silver Falls gurgling far below, and into the mountains. Mike scrunched down in the passenger seat and watched the sky flicker through the treetops.

After two or three miles, he sat up and turned toward Tyler.

"How do you know so much about all this stuff," he said. "Running is just running. Nothing to think much about."

"Is that what you like? You don't have to think. Just run."

"Never thought about it at all. I just started running one day and never stopped."

"But now I want you to think about it. Is that a problem?"

Mike turned his head and watched more of the forest slide by. From the road, the woods appeared impenetrable except to anyone who knew where the narrow trails and primitive roads began, passages, often hidden, that allowed a runner or hiker to breach the green wall and escape.

"Look, Mike, anyone can run that way, without thinking

or planning. But runners who get to be fast, I mean really fast, have someone to get them organized."

"Is that how you started? Someone got you organized?"

"Sort of, I guess. I'd been an average runner back home in Tacoma. I started in junior high school. Never won a race. Not once. But I did like to run.

"Then in high school, I read a newspaper article about Gerry Lindgren and some other guys in Spokane, over in eastern Washington, almost to Idaho. In those days, I thought all an ambitious high school kid had to do was pound away as many miles as his body would tolerate and then show up for the races. Sound familiar?"

Mike was staring out the windshield, watching the black ribbon of the Mountain Loop Highway unfold and unwind. He thought about what Joyce had said the night before.

"So, just running a lot didn't work for you?"

"It did. To a point. But Lindgren and Rick Riley were setting national records. Lindgren came close to becoming the first high school boy to break four minutes in the mile, and he ran in the Olympics the summer he graduated from high school."

Four minutes for the mile didn't mean much to Mike, but he figured it must be fast, or Tyler would not have mentioned it.

"At first, I was satisfied to run as much as I could. But when I read about the Spokane guys, I became so obsessed with running fast that I'd drive three hundred miles several times a year so I could train with those guys and see what they were doing that I wasn't."

Mike was intrigued, but he continued to stare at the trees leaning off the hillsides to form a greenish tunnel above the roadway.

"So," he said. "What were they doing that you weren't?"

"I thought I was running a lot, but in Spokane, I learned that if I wanted to run fast, I had to run a lot more. And be a lot more organized about it."

"I need to run a lot more, then, right?"

"Not more. More organized. More purposeful."

So, while he drove Mike farther into the mountains, Tyler explained the plan for the next three months.

"There are about a hundred days before your first cross-country meet," he said. "We're not going to change much for now, except to get your training week organized."

Mike had never noticed before that Tyler drew a distinction between training and running.

"I already run every day," Mike said.

"Yes," Tyler said. "But we need to organize what you do to make your training as effective as possible.

"Two longer runs every week. Ten to twelve miles on Wednesday. Fifteen or more on Sunday. Two runs on the other days. Steady, but not too hard, with lots of hills. Maybe up to 100 miles a week."

As with *four minutes*, one hundred miles a week meant nothing to Mike.

"Mike, it's been years since I've seen a kid who could do this much running for more than a week or two. I only knew one or two guys in college who could handle it. It may be too much."

Mike continued to watch the crowded forest go by in a green-brown blur. Every so often, some unique feature of a single tree—a gnarled trunk that had sagged halfway into the barrow pit or a collection of laden branches that seemed to tickle the ground—would draw his attention for an instant and then disappear.

"From a distance, the trees all look the same," he said.

"What?"

"Up close, though, they're each different."

Tyler glanced over at Mike but said nothing.

Mike turned toward the front of the car, slid his butt forward, and leaned back against the seat. He tapped his lower lip with his index finger.

"It's not too much."

"What?

"The running. It's not too much."

Ten miles from Silverton, the two-lane highway was narrow enough that an inattentive driver might have to swerve toward the shoulder to avoid a loaded log truck crowding the centerline. But on Saturday afternoons, most log trucks were parked at the Scott Paper lot in town, so the only distractions were the mountains and the forest. The woods were old-growth near the highway, gnarly fir, prickly with deep-green needles, and immense swaths of cedar with softer, leaf-like fronds that looked almost gray from a distance.

Tyler drove slowly. The warm breeze drifting through the open windows carried the ever-shifting aroma of cedar and fir mingling with the vegetative rot of the loamy forest floor.

Once they passed the ranger station at Verlot, eleven miles out of town, the shoulder shrank, and the trees leaned out over the roadway to form an intermittent green tunnel. A mile past the Abel turnoff, Tyler pulled off the highway onto a narrow, gravel parking strip at the Snow Lake trailhead. They could run two unrelenting miles up to Snow Lake, or they could stay on the lower trail and run the flat path parallel to the highway for four miles and then come back on the other side along the Silver River.

After his run the night before, Mike preferred the flat option.

20

ON THEIR PREVIOUS training runs together, Tyler would usually set the pace for the first few miles, and Mike would take over when they reached the halfway point. Then one or the other would push the pace in the last mile or two. But this time, Tyler let Mike lead from the start. He stayed back a few yards on the narrow trail and watched Mike's footfalls.

Tyler had run behind some of the best runners in the world. And he'd learned a lot by watching the way their feet came off the ground. When Tyler ran, he worked the ground with his feet, digging in and pushing off. When he began to suffer late in a race, he felt as if he was fighting gravity and friction. His legs got heavy, and his feet seemed to stick to the earth. Pulling his spiked shoes out of the ground required a desperate act of willpower, repeated over and over until he arrived at the finish line. But the best runners' feet barely touched the ground, even in the final, tortuous stages of a hard race. So Tyler studied Mike as he glided along the trail, dancing over rocks and roots and bounding over the low spots before surging away in the final two miles.

Mike was leaning against the car and drinking a soda from the ice chest in the back seat by the time Tyler finished.

"You're going to have to put something healthy in that ice chest from now on," Mike said.

Tyler jogged across the highway to the car. He reached through the open back window and pulled a soda out of the chest. "You don't have to drink it."

Mike crumpled the can, tossed it through the window onto the floor, and then opened the door and settled into the passenger seat. Tyler looked a little stiff when he sat down behind the wheel.

"I think I should talk to your dad," Tyler said. "He should know what you're up to."

"Bobby don't care. It hasn't mattered for a long time."

"I think he cares, Mike. Some parents just don't—"

"You don't know," Mike said, shaking his head. For the first time, Tyler sounded like one of those teachers who thought Mike would change if he'd just listen and do what he was told. "Until yesterday morning, he hasn't said two words to me about school or sex or drinking or anything else, much less running." Mike was not angry at Tyler, but he was a little disappointed.

"I'm sorry, Mike." Tyler started to put the car in gear.

"Wait," Mike said. He pulled the note from his father, crumpled and damp with sweat, out of the waistband of his running shorts. "I found this when I got home last night." He handed the note to Tyler.

"You want me to read this?"

"No, Coach. Just hold it in your hand while you drive."

Tyler unfolded the nearly sodden note carefully and stared at the three abrupt sentences.

Your mother called again. I have to go. Have a good life.

"This is from your father? He doesn't say where he's going or when he's coming back. Is that normal?"

"That's what I mean about him not caring what I do. He leaves every Monday morning and doesn't come back until Thursday or Friday."

"And your mother?" Tyler asked. "What does he mean your mother called again?"

Mike did not want to answer.

"Mike, I can't help if I don't know what's going on."

Mike clenched his fists to keep his hands from shaking. His eyes felt hot, and his jaw began to tremble, so he turned away and stared into the woods. He could not see more than ten or twenty yards through the underbrush. *The view is always cluttered,* he thought.

Tyler waited.

Still staring into the woods, Mike said, "You can't help." He inhaled, and his breath caught high in his throat. "And I don't know what's going on." Mike turned back and rubbed the bridge of his nose with his thumb and forefinger. "Let's go. There's no point."

Tyler nodded. He made a tight U-turn across the highway and headed back toward town.

After about a mile, a road sign caught Mike's eye. *Abel, next left.*

21

"CAN WE MAYBE DRIVE THROUGH ABEL?" Mike said, pointing to the sign. "My mom is from there, but I've never been."

Tyler gave Mike a strange look but then nodded.

Like everyone else in Silverton, everything Mike knew about Abel was based on rumor and legend. According to what Mike had heard from the grownups, kids in Abel didn't go to school at all. Mr. Sorenson claimed to know a lot about Abel because, well, because he was Mr. Sorenson.

The kids barely learn to read.

The state is up there all the time.

They claim freedom of religion or some such, so no one can do nothin' about those kids.

And the girls? The girls learn real young...well, you know.

Rumors and legends.

Mike's mother had left Abel to marry his father, and Robert had once told Mike that Janine had escaped from Abel. Mike had thought *escaped* was a strange word to use.

He did not know the whole story of his conception, but Mike recalled a comment one his teachers had once made concerning Janine's young age. Though Mike was only twelve when she left, he remembered Janine as a woman who had become anxious, nervous, and dissatisfied. Still, until she was gone, Janine never gave Mike reason to believe her anxiety or dissatisfaction had anything to do with him.

Tyler took the left turn toward Abel, and Mike was surprised that the dirt road remained flat. There was a wide turnout less than a quarter of a mile from the highway, but there was no other sign of human activity for the next two miles. The road curled along the narrow valley floor, and Mike could see and hear signs of a stream that ran parallel to the road on the right. Much of the road was open to the blue sky, but the aromatic mountain air cooled when the car passed through the canopy of old-growth cedar.

Tyler pointed to a hand-painted sign. *Entering Abel. Private. Visitors report to the community store.* There was no shoulder, and Tyler pulled as far to the left side of the road as he could and stopped.

"Here we are, but there's no one here," he said.

They saw no sign of human activity except for the sign, and the dirt road had changed to gravel.

"There must be something because there's a sign," Mike said. "Drive on a little farther."

"Maybe not. That sign didn't look too friendly."

"Whatever. It's a town, isn't it?"

"I'm not so sure." Tyler pulled back into the center of the road.

The road bent to the left, and there it was—a log building with another hand-painted sign above a covered porch. *Community Store.* Tyler stopped the car in the middle of the road. On the other side of the road stood another log building, a larger version of the store with another sign, this one hanging between two stout poles. *Community Meeting Hall.*

Mike started to get out of the car, but Tyler put his hand on Mike's shoulder and pointed with his chin at a man coming out of the store. The man was clean-shaven and had close-cropped hair. He wore a neat khaki shirt and new denim jeans. He had his right hand on the butt of a heavy pistol in a holster hanging from a leather belt. Tyler kept his hand on Mike's shoulder and watched in the rearview mirror as the man copied the license plate number onto a small pad. The man then approached the driver's side window. He put both hands on the windowsill and leaned in.

"This is private property. Unless you have pre-arranged business with someone here, you need to turn your car around and leave."

"We're just looking around," Tyler explained. "We wanted to see where the road goes."

"The road ends here." The man stood up and put his hand back on the pistol.

Tyler looked over at Mike, but Mike didn't respond. Instead, he glanced over at the meeting hall.

Tyler nodded. "No problem. Sorry if we're trespassing."

"It's Forest Service road until you get to the sign, and the dirt changes to gravel. After that, it's private. Pull your car forward and turn around in the lot next to the meeting hall."

Tyler did as he was told. Next to the meeting hall was a large gravel parking lot, but only one vehicle, a blue-and-white pickup, was parked in the lot. As he turned his car around in the lot and started back toward the highway, Tyler noticed about a dozen small houses tucked into snug lots among the trees.

Mike stared straight ahead.

"So, that's Abel," Tyler said, rolling up his window. "I

wonder what goes on in a place like that. Maybe the stories are true..."

"That was Robert's truck parked next to the meeting hall. My old man is here.

Tyler did not react.

When they reached the highway, Tyler stopped the car. When Mike did not say anything, he turned left and drove slowly back toward town.

"I've heard rumors about Abel, Mike."

Mike glanced at Tyler and then looked away out the window again.

"And rumors about your mother."

"So, you think you know about all that?"

"People at school talk. You know, about why she left. And why she's never come back."

"None of their business."

Mike waited for Tyler to offer still another unsolicited adult version of his situation. But Tyler said nothing.

"Just rumors," Mike said.

"Yeah. Not usually accurate, are they?"

Mike had never told anyone except Joyce about the night his mother left. But the image of the last time he saw his mother was vivid and immediate. She'd climbed into that strange pickup, and then the truck had disappeared across the bridge.

Tyler had been driving slowly. Mike remained silent for several minutes. Tyler slowed even more until Mike could see the tangled underbrush come into focus.

"My old man used to drink," he said. "A lot. I never knew why." He turned in the seat, leaned against the passenger door, and spoke directly to Tyler. "I guess my mom could tell you why."

"You remember all this?"

"It's not so long ago."

"Look, Mike, you don't have to tell me anything you don't want me to know."

Then Mike lied.

"I've never talked about this with anyone."

He had told Joyce. He thought adults would have made excuses for his parents or worse, would have blamed one or both.

Tyler might be different. So, he continued.

"I know she left twice before she left for good. The first two times, I think I was too young to understand what she was doing. Then one night, when I was twelve, I heard the front door slam. I got out of bed and stood on the porch. She walked away along the shoulder of the highway and got into a pickup. That was the last I saw of her.

"I ran all the way back to the house, but I didn't stop. I kept going until I got to the high school. I ran around the track for an hour. I got really tired. But I didn't stop."

"And you've run every day since."

"Every day. Whether I felt like it or not."

The car sped up, and Mike turned away and watched the tangled underbrush become a blur again.

22

JOYCE WALKED to the church she no longer attended and sat on the steps. From inside came the discordant plinking of someone learning the piano. Mrs. Clem, the pastor's wife, had a new student. A lawnmower sputtered off to her left. Someone had volunteered to cut the narrow strip of grass between the building and the parking lot.

The piano music stopped after a few minutes, and Joyce heard one of the double doors behind her open. Mrs. Clem was holding the door when she turned to look, and a thin girl with frizzy red curls emerged. The girl danced down the stairs and ran off toward the sound of the mower. Her father was cutting the grass to pay for the piano lessons.

"Why, hello, Joyce," Mrs. Clem said. "I haven't seen you for a while."

Joyce smiled and turned away. Mrs. Clem went back inside the church, but she left the door open. Joyce waited a few minutes, then went inside, closing the door behind her. She sat in the first pew on the left side of the center aisle and stared straight ahead. The mower outside had been turned off, and Joyce felt swaddled by the silence of the sanctuary. An array of stained-glass windows depicted scenes from the Gospels along one wall—the manger, the boy Jesus in the temple, the Sermon on the Mount, the Crucifixion; and visions from the Old Testament—the Garden of Eden, Noah's Ark, Abraham and Isaac, the Ten Commandments—along the other. Joyce loved the images because they required no explanation or commentary. The church was all brown wood and gray stone, except for the eight stained-glass windows, which were canted, so the refracted light coalesced to cast a purplish glow on the rough-hewn and unvarnished wooden cross above the altar. In the purple light and heavy silence beneath the unadorned cross, Joyce was content.

* * *

Half an hour later, Joyce stepped out of the church. James's truck sat parked on the street out front. Joyce stood on the steps for a few seconds and thought about what to do. James stared straight ahead with his left arm dangling out the open window. Joyce stepped down onto the cement walkway, stopped four or five feet from the truck, and waited.

"What?" James said.

Joyce waited some more.

"Look...about what happened...about what I did at the cabin. I'd been drinkin'. I wasn't myself." He started to apologize but then stopped short.

Joyce wanted to say, "*You were yourself. That is who you are,*" but the image of purplish light on the wooden cross was still on her mind, as was Luke 19:10...*to seek and to save.* So, she waited some more.

"What do you want me to say?" James was still not apologizing. "It's the way things are."

Joyce took a step forward so she could see inside the cab. A cedar box sat beside him on the seat. James leaned a few inches away from the window, pulled his arm back inside the truck, and pressed down on the lid of the cedar box with his right hand.

"This is not the way it has to be, James. It's the way *you* are. You don't have to be such a jerk, and you don't need to push people around." Joyce was pretty sure James knew he was a jerk and a bully because everyone said so.

"Jesus Christ, Joyce. You want me to apologize? I'll apologize."

"I don't want you to say anything. Just stop. That's all. Stop. And leave Mike alone."

"You know my old man." James pumped his fist in a gesture of mock enthusiasm. "I was born for this."

"No one was born for this. And you scared me, James."

James stared at her for a few seconds, and Joyce thought she saw moisture forming in the corners of his eyes. Then he rolled up his window and drove away slowly. Joyce stood silent and watched James's truck.

"It's doesn't have to be like this," she said. "Don't you know that, James?"

Then, as the truck turned right at the end of the block and disappeared, she realized James probably did not know.

Luke 19:10 crossed her mind again. *To seek and to save.*

Mike?

Or James?

23

MIKE WAS ABOUT to shower after his run with Tyler when he heard a soft knock on the front door. He went to the door shirtless, carrying one limp sock with a bloody spot on the toe in one hand and a muddy running shoe in the other. He still had his right shoe on, so he listed to the left.

He opened the door, and a youngish man wearing a cross, just large enough to be obvious around his neck, was running his fingers through his hair. Mike reached down and pulled off the other shoe but did not remove the sock.

"Are you Mike? Joyce's friend?"

"Yeah. I guess."

"I'd like to talk to you about Joyce."

"What about Joyce?" Mike stepped back but not to the side.

The youngish man stepped through the door, turning so he could get by, and then stood in the middle of the living room. Mike looked out the door, expecting someone he knew to be with the intruder, then he tossed his shoes and sock to one side and leaned against the doorjamb.

"Is your father home, Mike? I heard he works out of town during the week."

Mike shook his head.

"Can we talk?"

Mike raised both his hands, palms up in a *"whatever"* gesture. "Who are you?"

"Oh. It's a small town. I thought everybody knew everybody."

"I guess not."

"I'm Pastor Kevin." He put his hands in his back pockets. "I'm the youth pastor at Joyce's church."

"Joyce doesn't go to church."

"I know that. And I know you and Joyce have become close of late, and I thought we should have a talk."

"About church? I don't go to church, either."

"No. Not about church, per se. About...Joyce. Your relationship with Joyce."

Now Mike understood. Other adults were also curious about their *relationship*. Coach Tyler asked about it once, and even Mr. Thompson had brought it up.

"Look, Mike. Joyce is a good kid. Makes good choices. If she's your best friend, then there's hope for you." Kevin stifled a laugh. "Are you friendly with Joyce?"

Interesting word—*friendly*, not *friends*, Mike thought. "What do you mean, 'friendly'?"

Kevin sighed. Before he could speak, Mike stepped away from the doorjamb.

"I'll be right back."

Mike left the room and returned in less than a minute, wearing a faded orange-and-black sweatshirt with "Silverton Athletics" stenciled below the face of a fierce-looking tiger. Kevin was seated on the couch, so Mike crossed the front room and sat in the chair in the corner.

"So, what do you think you need to know about us, me and Joyce?"

"Did you just get done running?" Kevin asked, changing the subject.

Mike glanced over at the pile of wet shoes and socks by the door. *What was your first clue, genius?*

"Yeah, I did," he said with a slight nod.

"Do you run every day?"

"Yeah. Every day."

"How far?"

"Ten, twelve miles most days. Sometimes more."

"Really? And you do that every day?"

Mike didn't like to talk about his running, especially with someone like Kevin. "I haven't missed a day since I was twelve."

"Wow. That's impressive." Mike noticed a hint of sarcasm in Kevin's tone.

He doesn't believe me.

"Whatever," Mike said, tapping the arm of the chair. "What about Joyce? I saw her last night. She seemed fine."

"Look, Mike, I hear you're a good kid. But Joyce hasn't been coming to church, and she hasn't told anyone why."

"So?"

"The only thing that's changed is that Joyce has started to spend time with you."

Joyce had been Mike's friend since sixth grade, but he didn't want to tell Kevin anything about her.

"Mike, I think it would be best if Joyce didn't spend any more time with you and your crowd."

There's no crowd. Just me and Joyce.

Mike gave Kevin a blank look.

"Well?" Kevin said.

Mike didn't answer.

Kevin studied Mike. "Will you stop seeing her, Mike?"

Mike stood.

Kevin continued. "Maybe...maybe you...could..." Kevin stopped speaking and rubbed his chin. "Maybe you could come to church and bring Joyce back with you."

Mike walked to the front door and motioned for Kevin to leave. "I don't tell Joyce what to do," he said. "I don't think anyone does."

With a running shoe in one hand and both socks in the other, Mike left the door open and strode through the kitchen toward the back of the house, leaving Kevin standing in the front room.

24

AFTER JOYCE LEFT James sitting in his truck in front of the church, she walked toward home, but at the intersection where Pioneer Street became Scout Lake Road, she turned left without thinking and headed north past the faded-yellowish edifice that housed Silverton High School. Joyce stayed on the right shoulder of the highway, even though her mother's admonition to always walk facing traffic played back in her memory as a vexatious hiss. Joyce took some satisfaction in the danger, but she still felt guilty about the rebelliousness of violating the first of her mother's many safety rules.

The front door was standing open when Joyce arrived at Mike's house. She stepped onto the porch and went into the front room without knocking. One of Mike's running shoes looked tired and abandoned on the floor just inside the door.

"Mike?"

No answer. Joyce went into the kitchen. Mike's other shoe and both socks had been tossed into a haphazard pile near the back door.

"It's Joyce, Mike." She peered down the hallway that led from the kitchen. "Mike? Why's the front door open?"

Joyce waited, but after a few seconds, her stomach began to flutter, and she wondered if she should even be there. The single door on the left side of the hallway opened, and Mike came out. Joyce took a half step back before she could collect herself.

Mike came into the kitchen with nothing on except his running shorts. Joyce was either relieved or disappointed, she wasn't sure which, when she noticed he had a clean T-shirt in one hand. At that moment, she realized she had never seen Mike shirtless. She was familiar with boys at school or at church who never missed an opportunity to remove their shirts in the presence of girls eager to be impressed. Joyce had no particular objection to boys removing their shirts, but until that moment, she had seen nothing that had impressed her.

The muscles in Mike's chiseled torso and long arms matched his hips and legs. Joyce sorted through her vocabulary to come up with a word to describe what she was seeing. *Strength* came to mind first. Sure, but without the awkward bulk coveted by other boys. *Sinewy?* No. A cliché. *Substance?* That was it. Yes. And *pleasing*. She blushed and waited for the familiar church-lady voice in her head to sound a warning about boys and what they all wanted, but the voice was silent.

"What do you want?"

Mike's lack of inflection led Joyce to believe he was not happy to see her.

"James was waiting for me outside the church."

"The church, huh? I thought you didn't go to church anymore." Mike pulled out a chair at the kitchen table but didn't sit.

"I don't. I went for a walk and ended up there. I sat alone in the sanctuary for a while. Then I left, but I ended up here, Mike."

"That sounds like going to church. Pastor Kevin was here. Did you see him at church?"

"The youth pastor? Here?"

"You didn't know? He's all worried about our *relationship*. He thinks we're way more than friends, and he doesn't like it much."

"He said that?" Joyce glanced at the chair across the table from Mike, but she remained standing.

"Yeah. Good thing he doesn't know as much as he thinks he does."

Joyce felt a phantom pressure behind her heart, like a soft weight pushing out rather than down. Weren't she and Mike way more than friends?

"I didn't know. I didn't... Maybe my mother... No, she doesn't even like Pastor Kevin."

Mike put on his shirt, and Joyce relaxed.

"He shouldn't have come, Mike. I'm sorry. I promise I didn't send him." Joyce moved a step closer. "I don't like him, either. He thinks he's cool. I've never cared much for cool."

Mike turned the chair and sat sideways to the table, facing the back door. Joyce sat in the chair across from him and folded her hands on the table.

"It don't matter. I've heard it all before, one way or another." He was still staring at the door. "He said what he thinks he needed to say, so he don't need to come around anymore."

Joyce stretched her hand halfway across the table, but Mike did not look at her, his attention riveted on the door. After a few seconds, she got up and left the kitchen.

Joyce walked back into the front room and slammed the

door. When she returned to the kitchen with Mike's other shoe in her hand, Mike was halfway out of his chair. She strode past the table and propped the back door open with both shoes. She returned to her chair and sat with her hands folded as she had before. She waited until Mike sat back down, facing her this time.

The cedar scent of the summer forest drifted in through the back door and overwhelmed the sour reek from Mike's shoes and dirty socks. Mike glanced out the open door, and Joyce thought he might run. Instead, he reached a little more than halfway across the table with an uncertain hand. Joyce did not move.

But then she smiled just a little when Mike's face reddened. He again glanced at the open door, so she reached out across the table and took his hand.

"Mike?"

"Yeah."

He gently pulled his hand away, got up from the table, moved his shoes, and closed the back door. Then he went down the hall and into his room. When he returned, he slid a piece of crumpled paper across the table.

Joyce picked up the paper but did not read it. Mike turned away and returned to his room. She looked up from the note when he came out, his running shorts replaced by a pair of faded jeans. He sat back down at the table, and she read the note while he laced up on a new pair of running shoes with no socks.

"Gotta break these in," he said. "And I got no clean socks."

She stared at him and held up the note. He shrugged, and she shook the note at him.

"'Have a good life'? What does that mean?"

"Means have a good life, I guess."

"Mike, it means he's not coming back. You can't live here by yourself."

"Why not? I've been by myself most of the time since I was twelve. Who gives a rat's ass? Come on. I'll take you home."

"I can walk." Joyce got up to leave. She still had the crumpled note in her hand.

Mike followed, and before she reached the front door, he grabbed her arm. As soon as he touched her, Joyce spun around. Mike pulled his hand away and stepped back.

"I'm sorry, Joyce. I didn't mean to—"

"Stop it, Mike. Just stop it... You can touch me." She stepped toward him.

He started to step back again, but she grabbed both of his arms and pulled herself closer.

"I won't break," she said softly, "and I don't mind."

She touched his face with her fingertips and then turned and opened the front door. Mike did not move.

"I thought you said you would give me a ride home."

Joyce went out the front door and around to the side of the house where Mike's truck was parked.

A few moments passed before Mike managed to dislodge himself from the spot in the front room where Joyce had left him and join her in the truck.

While he fiddled with the key, Joyce finally spoke again.

"You can't stay here by yourself all summer. Pastor Kevin will come back when he finds out, and my mom will have the church ladies bringing food every day."

"That's okay." Mike nodded. "Church-lady food is great."

"You cannot stay alone all summer!"

"I've been mostly on my own since sixth grade."

Mike didn't shout, but his angry tone seemed to catch Joyce by surprise.

"I can cook a little. And I know how to use the washing machine. I've got new running shoes and plenty of socks. I've got a bank account that the old man puts money in every month."

"That is not what I meant."

"I manage to get myself out of bed every day. I run. I run a lot."

"You think because you run, you should be able to stay by yourself?"

"I don't have any other plans."

"Jesus, Mike. Jesus H. Christ on a cracker." Joyce was still not an expert with profanity. "Who else knows?"

Mike didn't answer. Joyce never sounded petulant or pouty. She could come across as very grownup when she encountered something she knew was wrong. She hated the "poor, little me" games some girls played when a teacher called them out. Worse was the phony, male, "what, me care?" posturing that came so naturally to boys.

"Who else knows?" she repeated.

Mike didn't know how to answer. The only other people who talked to him this way were teachers and cops.

"Tyler knows. I showed him the note after we finished our run this morning."

"I think teachers have to report stuff like this, or they get in trouble, so don't tell anyone else."

Mike and Joyce had been sitting in his truck with the engine running long enough that a leak in the exhaust system had begun to fill the cab with a toxic blue haze.

"We better get moving," Mike said.

He put the truck in gear, and soon, they were sputtering toward town with the blue cloud trailing behind. Mike turned left onto Scout Lake Road. He turned into Joyce's driveway and stopped.

"I think they're both in Abel," he said. "It was so long ago. Maybe she's changed."

25

JOYCE WRESTLED the door open and climbed down from the cab of the truck, and her father startled Mike when he appeared at the driver's side window.

"Turn the engine off, son. If I let you get away without bringing you inside to say hello to Joyce's mother, I'll be in the doghouse for sure and forever."

Mike followed Joyce into the house and stood inside the door. Even though he had his semi-clean jeans on, he wasn't sure what to do with his hands. Joyce's father sat in a huge, worn-in easy chair in a front corner framed by two large windows. He appeared to be concentrating on untying his boots when Joyce's mother came into the room from the kitchen.

"Joyce, are you going to make Mike stand there in the door all day long? We haven't seen you for a long time, Mike. Come in and sit." Molly sat on the couch.

Joyce nudged Mike toward a stiff-backed chair and then sat on the couch next to her mother. Don, Molly, and Joyce all watched him long enough to increase his discomfort. Mike was uncertain about what he should say or do. He started to rub his thighs, but then thought that might be impolite. Then he felt his feet begin to tap the floor, so he pressed down on his knees.

"Relax, boy. This isn't the principal's office." Joyce's father had finished untying his boots but hadn't taken them off.

"Sorry." Mike thought he might start to stammer. "I don't... I, um, haven't... Uh, I haven't been to visit anyone for a long time."

Don looked at Joyce and shook his head. He didn't say anything, but Mike could read the puzzled look on his face.

He started to get up. "Maybe I better—"

"I hear from a teacher friend that you still get in trouble a lot," Molly said.

Mike's jaw dropped. Molly smiled, but there was an edge to her voice that made him still more uncomfortable.

"Fights and truancy. And you called Joyce out to that party the other night?"

"Mother! It's none of your business."

"I'm going to try to do better." Mike was on the edge of panic.

"Mike," Molly continued, "I do not like fighting and carrying on. But I'm sure Joyce's father here could tell us a thing or two about young boys and parties in the woods and skipping school and whatnot." She paused and looked at her husband. "I think he even knows even adults carrying on and whatnot."

Mike let his eyes shift to Joyce's father. The older man had reclined all the way back in his enormous chair and closed his eyes.

"Long time ago, Molly," he muttered.

"Not so long," Molly said, glancing at Joyce.

Mike had never thought the name Molly fit Joyce's mom.

He tried to remember if he'd ever known anyone else named Molly. She looked like a...Joyce. It was Joyce who looked like a Molly. Mike's eyes shifted to Joyce's mother. She had dark, straight hair pulled into a girlish ponytail, and she sat prim and erect on the edge of the couch. Her long-sleeved dress stopped just short of the floor. She watched Mike with her hands folded in her lap and a slight tilt to her head. Joyce had told Mike her parents had gone to high school together, but Molly looked much younger than her husband, who was beginning to go gray on top and saggy in the middle.

"I don't recall you partying at all in high school," Don said, his eyes still closed. "So, I don't guess you'd know what went on back in the day, way out there in the woods."

"Or what goes on these days, either," Molly said. She turned and smiled at Joyce and then turned back to Mike. "It seems things haven't changed much. Have they, Joyce?"

Mike felt paralyzed. He could not speak. He could not think. He grasped his thighs because his hands were shaking.

"Jeez, Mom..."

"Oh, now you're cursing, as well."

"Mike, she's teasing," Joyce said. "Mother, *please*."

Mike looked to Don for support. He was still reclining in his chair, but now his eyes were open, and he was shaking his head.

Mike relaxed a little.

"Instead of terrorizing the boy, Molly, why don't you give him something to eat? I didn't see anyone home at his place last night, so I'm sure he could use a decent meal. Especially with all the running and...whatnot."

Mike exhaled and sat back against the hardback of the chair. When running came up, he was back on familiar ground.

"You're still running?" Molly wanted to know more.

"Yep," Don said with a nod. "Could be a champion is what his coach says."

"Could be? Then why isn't he?"

When Mike was in a room with adults who weren't Tyler, they talked at him. He could not remember ever being in a room with adults talking about him as if they were interested.

Molly turned to Mike. "Why aren't you a champion, Mike?"

Mike didn't know what Joyce's mother wanted to hear, and, thankfully, Joyce answered for him.

"Because he hasn't been able to stay out of trouble for a whole season. But last night, Coach Tyler made him promise that next year will be different. He's going to win state in cross-country this fall."

Molly seemed impressed. "Is that right, Mike?"

"I'm going to try to do better."

Molly stood and faced Mike, but he was watching Joyce's dad. "Well, we forgive in this house."

Don rolled his eyes, and she continued.

"And something good to eat will surely help Mike make a good start."

26

"I CAN'T THINK of a single reason why you shouldn't run every day," Tyler told Mike. "Twice a day. You don't have a job or a girlfriend. Dahlia doesn't count, and Joyce knows better. You don't have any guy friends, nobody likes you—"

"Yeah, I know," Mike said. "A complete loser."

"Some people would say so, but I don't think they're applying the appropriate criteria. You don't care about college. You don't have anything to do but run."

So, Mike ran. Every day. All summer.

He ran in the hills and on the rocky trails along the Silver River. He ran on the narrow, undulating country roads that took him away from town and then looped back onto Main Street. He ran around the grass track and up and down the rutted football field.

He ran so often that the locals began to move aside on the sidewalk or drift toward the center line when they saw Mike. The sight of Mike running along the Mountain Loop Highway or on the secondary roads around town became as common as the log trucks lumbering back and forth between the mountains and the mills. Only on Sundays, when Tyler drove Mike deep into the hills so they could run for two hours through barren clear-cut or lush old growth, did Mike run once a day. And with every run, Tyler seemed to become more convinced of Mike's unique capacity.

As June ended and the summer progressed through a hotter and drier-than-normal July and August, Tyler expected the miles to take a toll. He planned for Mike to take a break before school started so he'd be fresh for the cross-country season. But by the beginning of August, Tyler noticed Mike was slowing down on their Sunday runs, but only so Tyler could keep up.

As the summer days got shorter and the start of school approached, Tyler worried Mike might forget his promise to stay out of trouble. Settling the score with James might be too great a temptation. While they rested on the tailgate of Mike's truck after their long run on the last Sunday in August, Tyler decided to remind Mike of his promise. Tyler was shirtless and dripping sweat.

"School's about to start." Tyler stood and leaned with both hands on the tailgate. "Remember your promise to stay out of trouble. No fights. No backtalk. I know you have an issue with James, but you need to let that go."

Mike leaned back into the bed of the truck, his feet dangling off the end of the tailgate, and stared into the endless deep of the blue sky. After a few seconds, he sucked in a long breath, held it, and let it rush out through his nose. "I haven't seen James since that night at Junior's."

"That's good. Leave it be, okay?"

Mike sat up and turned toward Tyler. "James has got a beat-down coming."

"And it would be good for him. But he's got nothing to lose. You do."

. . .

Mike hopped down from the tailgate and walked toward the front of the truck, thinking over Tyler's words. Mike stopped at the driver's side door and stared at the low mountain he and Tyler had just run up and back down. The visible hillside was lush and green, thick with fir near the road and with cedar higher up. But the beginnings of a new clear-cut started at the crest of the hill, bare and ugly and invisible to anyone driving by on the highway.

He put both hands on top of his head and shrugged to stretch out his back. Then, without turning around, he said, "I won't do nothing to James."

"Good."

Mike had planned to settle his issue with James before the school year started. But Tyler had become one of two adults Mike did not want to disappoint. Joyce's mother was the other, though Mike was not sure why. Besides, Tyler was right. James wasn't worth it. Mike would let it go.

27

INTROSPECTION WAS NOT a quality encouraged among Silver-ton's young males, but after his confrontation with Joyce in front of the church, James began to wonder about things, but just a little. As the summer progressed, he became more and more ambivalent about Mike. Still, Tall Paul and Pork, who were not given to either self-aware contemplation or ambivalence, reminded James frequently of his promise to get back at Mike.

As is the case with most runners, there was a predictable pattern to Mike's training routine. Each Monday, James had seen Mike running the rolling, eight-mile Scout Lake loop in the morning and the Jordan Road out and back in the evening. He would run past the Sportsman's Club and onto the trail behind Morton Shingle on Saturdays when the mill was closed, and the log trucks would not be stirring up dust on the gravel access road.

On the last Saturday before school started, James and the boys were drinking beer on the rocks at the bottom of Silver Falls, less than a mile from Morton Shingle. James stared at the white water churning at the base of the falls and thought about what Joyce had said back in June. *Just stop. That's all. Stop.* The two other boys were debating whether Pork could fart louder than Tall Paul could burp.

"Hey, James." Tall Paul threw an empty bottle toward the river and missed. "You gonna get that faggot for cuttin' you short with Joyce at Junior's?"

"I ain't thought about it. My old man's had me sweepin' out his shop all summer."

Pork was composed of soft fat, which made him think he was bigger and tougher than he was. "No one's got the right to stop you from gettin' some."

"Whatever." James could not get the conversation with Joyce out of his mind, but, apparently, the germ of an idea had begun to form in Pork's alcohol-clouded brain.

"You know what?" Pork turned to James. "He runs by the shingle mill every Saturday. We could wait there by the Sportsman's Club and get him when he runs by."

"Right on," Tall Paul said. He threw another beer bottle toward the river. He missed again. "Let's go get 'im."

James shrugged. "Whatever you guys want to do."

As the summer had progressed, things that used to matter to James had become less important. He'd begun leaving more and more decisions up to Tall Paul and Pork, though neither was quite sure what to do with the responsibility.

"Let's go get 'im, then," Pork said.

Tall Paul nodded, then both boys looked toward James. "Yeah. Let's go get 'im?"

"Whatever," James said.

James and the boys stumbled up the footpath to the parking lot at the top of the falls and piled into James's truck. James backed the truck into the highway, forcing a minivan full of church-camp kids to swerve, and then burned rubber back toward town. He took a left onto the access road leading to the shingle mill and parked in front of the Sportsman's Club.

"I guess we could wait here. See if he comes by," James said, tapping the steering wheel with one hand.

Pork looked down the road. "What if he don't?"

"Then we'll drink more beer."

James reached into the cooler in the front seat and grabbed another beer, but Pork slapped him on the shoulder and pointed down the road toward where Mike had just emerged from the woods. James dropped the beer back into the cooler.

"Let's get 'im," Tall Paul said.

The three shuffled out of the car and formed a less than straight line across the road. James was in the center but a step or two behind the other two. When Mike saw James and the boys, he stopped running and walked toward them.

Pork called out, "You best turn around and run on back the other way. You ain't good for nothin' but runnin', anyway."

James stayed a step or two behind Tall Paul and Pork and watched Mike, who had stopped about ten feet away.

"You shouldn't have messed with James and Joyce," Pork said. "They was about to have fun."

"Shut up, Pork," James said. Guilt was still a new feeling, and he did not like it.

The other two boys giggled, but when Mike stepped forward, they both moved back behind James. Pork held a beer bottle in one hand and tapped a tire iron against his thigh with the other. Tall Paul held an unopened beer bottle by the neck.

"You was with Dahlia, anyway," Tall Paul said, poking his

boney head forward. "You wanted the same thing, and I bet you got some."

Mike opened his mouth, took in a deep breath, and closed it again.

Pork swung the tire iron at Mike, but it slipped out of his hand and clanged at Mike's feet. James stepped back, and Tall Paul threw the beer bottle at Mike's head and missed.

James came forward again and bent down to pick up the tire iron, but Mike already had it in his hand. James sighed, straightened up, and threw a slow-looping, uninspired, right-hand punch at Mike. Mike swung the tire iron at James, and a cracking sound filled the air when the steel bar hit James's wrist.

James screamed and dropped to his knees, holding his bruised wrist against his chest, his mind scrambled by shame, guilt, and regret.

28

WHEN MIKE GOT HOME, a strange man was sitting in a kitchen chair on the front porch. Mike stopped running when he reached the driveway and walked toward the house, on edge, feeling a little like he should not be there. The man stood and moved to the top of the steps. Mike stayed on the ground, looked up at the man, and waited.

"Good run?"

"Yeah. I guess. Who are you?"

"It's a small town. I thought everyone knew everyone."

That's what the youth pastor said.

"I guess not," Mike said, trying to be clever. "You must be from the church."

"Well, I'm sort of in charge of the church. I'm Pastor Clem. Can I sit back down? I've got a bum leg."

Joyce had never talked to Mike about church except to explain something Pastor Clem had said about her decision to stop going. Mike knew everyone else connected with the church was unhappy about Joyce's defiance and refusal to attend. The exceptions were Pastor Clem and maybe Joyce's mom, which seemed odd to Mike.

"Yeah," Mike said, "Sure." Pastor Clem was someone Joyce admired, so Mike was less uncomfortable, but still wary.

When Pastor Clem turned back toward the kitchen chair by the door, he skipped a little to protect an old leg injury, but once he got turned around, he managed to get back to the chair with a minimal limp.

Mike stepped up onto the porch and said, "Be right back." He went into the house and returned with another kitchen chair, which he placed on the other side of the porch and a little to Pastor Clem's left, closer to the steps. Mike had learned a little about how to treat a visitor from paying attention to how Joyce's parents treated him, so he did not sit right away.

"You want a glass of water?" And then, before he could catch himself, "Or a beer?" Mike cringed as soon as he said *beer*. "Sorry. I didn't mean to offer you a beer."

Pastor Clem laughed. He stretched his long legs and linked the fingers of both hands behind his head.

"I've been in my hot, stuffy study all day. I'm trying to write another sermon about forgiveness and loving your enemies so the members of my congregation will either nod knowingly or nod off, and then go out into the world Monday morning and forget every damn word. So, yeah, I'd love a beer."

"Um. Actually, I don't have any beer—I promised Coach Tyler. I offered 'cause I figured you'd say no."

Pastor Clem laughed again. "Well, I wouldn't want it to become common knowledge, but I don't mind a cold one now and then. I'm a preacher, Mike, not a monk."

Mike was not sure of the difference, but he was sure Pastor Clem was not what Mike had expected. He had concluded Pastor Kevin was a judgmental jerk who didn't want Mike seeing Joyce because he had designs on her himself. And he had some vague recollection of his mother talking about a Reverend Park in Abel, but he had been too young to tell whether Janine had been afraid of the man or in awe.

"I guess you'd like to know why I'm here."

Mike shrugged, not sure he wanted to know. He thought of Pastor Kevin. Pastor Clem nodded for Mike to sit, and Mike felt like an interloper again.

"I didn't come before because Joyce asked me not to."

Mike started to shrug and say, "*Whatever*," but he stopped himself.

"I want to apologize. No...that's not quite it. I want to *explain* Pastor Kevin's visit."

Here it comes, Mike thought. *I'm not the right kind of boy*. "Me and Joyce are friends. I don't...I won't...I wouldn't..."

Pastor Clem waited, but Mike didn't finish his thought. He just shook his head.

"Mike, I'm not here about Joyce. I've come because of Joyce. But look, I'm not worried the way Pastor Kevin is."

Then what? Mike knew from tedious experience that when he wasn't certain what an adult wanted to hear, it was best to shut up. So, he waited.

When Pastor Clem remained silent, Mike said, "Then what are you worried about?"

"Good. Now we can have a conversation. Joyce said I might have to talk at you instead of to you because you've never learned how to talk to an adult."

"She said that?"

"Mike, Joyce is the most intelligent, most thoughtful young person I've ever come across."

"Joyce doesn't go to church. She comes over here on Sunday, or I go to her house. Her mom makes me eat."

"Mike, I try not to preach unless it's Sunday morning, so I'm not going to preach at you. But you don't have to go to church to be in *The Church*. Most people who show up on Sunday are good people to start with, and they try to do good most of the time. The best I can hope for is they get a little better over time and try to do good a little more often. If I were honest, I'd like to see more serious sinners in church. But I'm realistic, which isn't always the same as being honest."

Pastor Clem shifted in his chair. "Joyce listens. She studies. I don't tell her what to do. She will think about what I say, compare it to what the Bible says, and come to her own conclusions. Church is like school. It has something to offer if you don't stray, but maybe even more if you do. Joyce has strayed, but onto a narrower, steeper path, I think. Maybe you have, too."

"So...what do you want from me?" Mike stood and crossed his arms, then put his hands in his back pockets. "What do you want me to do?"

Pastor Clem held up both hands and then dropped his hands to his knees and leaned forward.

"I don't want anything." He struggled to his feet. "But keep what I've said in mind. It will help you understand what Joyce says and what she does."

"Okay."

"And maybe it will help you understand James."

"James?"

"Yes. James. Joyce mentioned that you and James have an...uh, an issue. I don't know the details. She wasn't specific."

Mike waited for Pastor Clem to tell him it would be best

not to worry about James. To let it go. To be the bigger man and to forgive James.

"I won't tell you what to do, but I know James. I know the family. If you want my help, I'll do what I can."

Mike was used to being told what to do by teachers and cops, and he was familiar with indifference from his father. But an offer of adult help with, as far as he could tell, no strings attached, that was something new.

"There might be trouble." Mike thought Pastor Clem should know about James and the boys.

"What kind of trouble?"

"James and his two mouth-breather buddies, Pork and Tall Paul, were waiting for me by the Sportsman's Club. Pork tried to hit me with a tire iron, but he dropped it, so I picked it up. I think I broke James's wrist with it, and I may have hit Tall Paul on the side of the head."

"May have?"

"I'm not sure. I threw the tire iron at him and took off into the woods and ran back here."

"That could be a problem, but I'm sure James and the boys had it coming. School hasn't started, so those folks can't do anything. And James won't want anyone to know the three of them couldn't take you."

"I was lucky, I guess."

Pastor Clem stepped toward Mike and put a hand on his shoulder, the same way Joyce's father had. Mike shuddered, and after a few seconds, Pastor Clem took his hand away and walked down the steps into the front yard.

Mike remained at the top of the steps, and Pastor Clem looked up at him.

"Mike, I know you've been living alone since June."

"Joyce told you?"

"Yes. She's worried. Or rather, she's concerned."

"What did you tell her?"

"I told her not to worry, Mike. I think you'll be fine."

For the first time, Mike noticed that Pastor Clem had not come in a car or truck. He walked down the driveway, turned left when he reached the highway, and limped back toward town, facing the traffic.

29

ON A DARK LATE afternoon at the end of the first week of school, James swaggered into his father's auto and truck repair shop and pretended to sulk about how his injured wrist had kept him from starting football practice with the rest of the team. In truth, James's injury was not that bad. And what he did not tell his father was he'd decided not to show up for football practice at all.

James's father, Ollie, had been the star of the Silverton High football team twenty-five years earlier. He would have played football at Western Washington State College up in Bellingham, but in the last game of his senior year, a fat tackle rolled onto his left leg and bent his knee ninety degrees sideways. The resulting ruptured medial collateral ligament and ripped-clean-off-the-bone meniscus caused the college coaches to reconsider Ollie's football value and withdraw their scholarship offer.

"How long you gonna be out, boy?" Ollie never referred to James by name.

James did not answer.

"I sure don't know why you didn't kick that Beck kid's

ass. His old man was a pussy. Can't imagine a skinny turd like that being too awful tough."

"He ain't that skinny no more."

"There was three of you, and you still had one good hand. The other two coulda held him for you."

Ollie had tools and a clean rag on the fender of someone's newish pickup. He was meticulous about his work. Ollie's workshop was spotless, with dozens of tools and pieces of equipment organized, so it was easy to move around. If Ollie needed a tool, he knew where to get it, and he put it back in the same spot when he was done.

His family life was less well organized. James was the last of three children. But the two girls, born a year apart, realized early their father had little use for daughters. Both married young and left Silverton, mostly to get away from Ollie. Their father would have been hard-pressed to say where either of the girls lived, and people who knew him were smart enough not to ask.

The first was born six months after Ollie and James's mother graduated from Silverton High. At first, Ollie refused to admit the child was his. JoAnn had a reputation, well earned as it turned out, but she insisted only Ollie could have been the father. And in the socially ambivalent and morally ambiguous sixties, a hasty marriage had to be arranged. The immediate shame of unwed motherhood outweighed the potential pain of a long life in a loveless marriage. Even though Ollie and JoAnn could barely stand the sight of each other, a second girl came along less than a year later.

"She-it," he'd said when the doctor in Everett called Ollie to tell him he was a father again. "Another useless girl."

Then Ollie moved out. He would stop by a couple of

times a month for what he called a *conjugal* when he'd failed at trolling for drunken coitus at the Cavern Tavern or the Tree Top Inn. JoAnn granted Ollie conjugal privileges so he wouldn't smack her around as much when he came by for other reasons. JoAnn had resumed the activities that had resulted in her questionable reputation and uncertain popularity in high school, but Ollie pretended not to know. And JoAnn was better at trolling than Ollie, hence the inevitable rumors about James's parentage.

Ollie had lined up three wrenches on the rag. He picked up the largest wrench and shook it at James.

"You better not screw up this football season."

James knew his father was still bitter about the exploded knee that had derailed his own football fantasy, so again he remained silent.

Ollie reached far down into the guts of the truck. Out of habit, James bent forward to see what his father man was doing. Ollie stood up, and James leaned back, out of his father's reach.

"I didn't get nothin' playing football for that damn school except a good excuse not to get drafted. But I got plans for you, boy. You already been all-state. I was never more'n all-county. Three straight years, though."

Ollie bent down into the truck's innards again. He pushed down hard on the wrench and grunted.

"You are going to get back at Mike Beck. I don't want it to get around that a pussy that don't even play football beat your ass and got away with it."

"I'm thinkin' I'll let it go." James was thinking of both football and Mike. "No one knows but Tall Paul and Pork, and they won't say nothin'."

"You afraid, boy?"

James was certain he could take Mike, and Tall Paul and

Pork would help. He took half a step back, wary, and then he lied.

"I ain't scared."

"Boy?"

"I ain't."

Without warning, Ollie came up from the truck's entrails and hit James with the back of his right hand hard enough to rock James's head back. James knew better than to wince or cry out.

Ollie pointed at James with the wrench. "You get that sumbitch. No way you don't get that sumbitch."

"Yeah." James clenched his teeth so his father would not see his jaw tremble. "Okay. Okay. I...we got plans for Mike Beck."

"And you get on the football field. Don't want the coach to find out you're gettin' to be a pussy...*boy*."

For the third time, James said nothing.

James left the shop and drove to his mother's house, which he had never quite thought of as home. He sat in his truck and leaned against the driver's side door, wondering if his mother was alone. He winced when he touched the tender spot under his left eye.

He massaged his cheekbone and watched his mother's open window. There was no sign of activity other than the occasional fluttering of the curtain. He got out of the truck and leaned on the fender nearest the house and listened. No sound came from his mother's window, so maybe she was alone. He rubbed his cheekbone again. He thought about checking the mirror but decided it didn't matter if he was bruised or not because his mother would not say anything about it anyway. They'd both been bruised before.

He walked to the porch and sat on the middle step. It was late afternoon, so the east-facing porch was now in the shade. He massaged the slight swelling below his eye. Then, by habit, he began to organize a familiar hostility in his mind.

He knew what Tall Paul and Pork would expect him to do. If the three of them cornered Mike and beat the crap out of him, no one would think much about it. Plenty of people had seen what Mike had done at Junior's party, and Tall Paul and Pork wouldn't be able to keep the "fight" to themselves. And as long as he didn't get Mike at school, the principal couldn't do anything to him.

Ollie's voice began to echo in James's brain... *Don't want the coach to find out you're gettin' to be a pussy...boy.* Then a pause and a different voice... *This is not the way you have to be.*

James walked around to the back of the house and went into the shop. He took the cedar box down from its place on the high shelf and set it on the workbench. He opened the box and removed the gun. He jammed the gun into his hip pocket, and the weight of it tugged at the waistband of his jeans.

He picked up the box and ran his hand over each corner, making a mental note when his fingers passed over a rough spot. Then, with fine sandpaper and a delicate touch, he smoothed out the rough spots. He planned to apply several coats of clear stain to preserve the wood's natural character, perfecting every flaw. His shop teacher, Mr. Short, had told James that a well-finished project would outlast the workman.

"The wood is perfect to start with. Our job is to make

perfection last." Mr. Short was six-foot-six, rail thin, and awkward when he moved, but he had graceful hands and a shop filled with small boxes and large chests. There was even a grandfather clock made from the same dark cedar as James's box.

The cedar box was the first project James had devoted any serious time to. He had turned it in unfinished back in May. Mr. Short had examined James's work, told him it was "a wonderful start," and to take the summer to finish it.

"It will take all summer if you don't rush it. Art takes time, James. Do not take shortcuts. Show it to me again when school starts."

"Art? It's a box."

"What do you think art is, James?"

James had shrugged and had taken the box home for the summer.

James heard the shop teacher's voice in his head as he worked the wood with the sandpaper. After four or five strokes with the sandpaper, James would stop and test the wood with his fingertips. Each pause revealed another rough spot, so James would shift his attention and continue. As the rough edges of the perfectly joined corners of the box became smooth, James noticed the stiffness in his wrist begin to dissipate.

While he worked, the loud memory of his father's harsh grumbling began to drown out Mr. Short's encouragement, and James's attention shifted from the surface of the wood to the purpose of the box. He stopped working and replaced the lid, pleased by how well it fit, and then put the box back in its place on the high shelf.

Dusk had settled by the time James stopped working. He went into the house through the back door. His mother was sitting at the kitchen table smoking a cigarette, her left foot resting on her right knee. She was wearing a thin housecoat, and her hair did not appear to have been brushed that day. She looked up at James when he came into the house, her gaze settling on the bruise on his face.

"Been to see your dad." It was not a question.

James paused and nodded, then continued through the house and out the front door. If his mother noticed the gun in his hip pocket, she didn't say anything.

James didn't think about where he was going when he left the house, but when he got to the corner at the end of the block, the truck made a left. The sky in the east was dark, and the streetlights had begun to come on. As James passed the last streetlight before he reached Scout Lake Road, he saw Joyce walking toward him and waving her arm.

JAMES ALMOST DIDN'T STOP. But when his truck reached Joyce, he hit the brakes hard, and the tires squealed as the truck lurched to a stop. She pulled the passenger-side door open, climbed up into the seat, and stared straight ahead. James looked over at her and waited.

"Drive," Joyce told him. She pointed with her chin, indicating James should drive on out Scout Lake Road.

"Can I take you somewhere? What?"

Joyce didn't answer, but James knew that the road would loop back into Silverton at the west end of town after eight miles. He figured Joyce would have something to say before they got that far.

James's introduction to male-female interaction came from watching his father knock his mother around as a prelude to knocking James around. As a result, his attitude toward girls had been that he was the stud duck in town. And any female who wanted to ride in the stud duck's truck or even be seen with the stud duck had to come across for the stud duck.

Despite his intimidating demeanor, James was attractive

to a certain type of female. That is any girl whose introduction to male-female interaction was watching her father knock her mother around, usually as a prelude to knocking her around. A mutual familiarity with domestic abuse not being the best foundation for a long-term relationship, James and the girls in his life spent only enough time together to either consummate a brief and awkward intimacy or a quick brush-off if the girl were the least bit discerning.

Joyce was discerning, and James disgusted her. So, what was she doing in the front seat of his truck with her hands folded in her lap, staring straight ahead without saying or doing anything to give James even the slightest hint of why she had flagged him down?

He knew how to deal with the sort of desperate girl he was normally in search of. At Junior's party, James had known he had no chance with Joyce. Even if Mike hadn't meddled, James hadn't intended to force the issue. In fact, he had never forced the issue. If a girl said no, James would back off, although he might smack her once or twice because that was what he'd learned to do when he didn't get what he wanted from a girl.

He stole a glance at Joyce. She was still staring straight ahead with her hands folded in her lap. James could see how different she was from his mother, sitting at the kitchen table in her thin housecoat sucking on her cigarette, but he could not account for the difference.

As he approached the dirt road that led to the Scout Lake trailhead, by habit, he let the truck slow down and started to turn into the dark lane. After one hundred yards, the dirt road came to a dead-end, where the trail began. The end of the road, invisible under a thick canopy of vine maple, was the perfect parking spot.

As soon as the truck started to slow, Joyce looked over at James and said, "Keep going."

But James had already sped up. At last, Joyce turned a little in the seat. She bent her leg and sat on her left foot but made sure her longish skirt was pulled down below her knee. Her hands were still folded in her lap.

"I guess you're wondering why I stopped you," she said.

James nodded and kept his eyes on the road.

"I was frightened when I found you waiting outside the church. I thought if I said something to you, I wouldn't be frightened. It worked, and I'm not scared of you anymore."

James slowed down to about twenty-five miles per hour so he could concentrate on what he wanted to say. "There's a turnout up here. Can we stop? We'll still be on the main road, and anyone who drives by can see us, so I can't *try* anything."

31

JOYCE THOUGHT about James's question. What if someone saw her parked out here with James?

"Yes," she agreed. "You can stop."

James pulled off the road onto a wide turnout but left the engine running and the lights on. He turned toward her.

"But stay over there behind the wheel," Joyce added.

His shoulders dropped, and the corners of his mouth fell. "You don't have to say nothin' like that," he said. "I ain't going to try anything. I was drunk that night at Junior's. I haven't had much to drink since then. I don't like myself after...when I drink."

That revelation surprised Joyce. "So, you know you shouldn't drink. That's good, James."

"I didn't say I *shouldn't* drink. You scared me a little, too, that day outside the church."

"What could I do to you?"

"Nothin'. But you said I didn't have to be this way—that being an assho—being a jerk isn't who I am. It's who everyone expects me to be, though."

"That's true. But you don't have to be what anyone else expects."

"Yeah, well, I'm still a jerk."

"Not if you don't want to be."

"My old man is the king of the jerks, and my old lady is the town pump."

Joyce knew about James's father, but she blushed at the crude reference to his mother and remembered what Georgie had said about her.

Joyce took a deep breath and held it. Then she told James his own life story, based on a couple of things she knew, a lot of things she had heard, and a few good guesses.

"Ollie and JoAnn never got along, right?"

James sat still for a moment and then nodded.

"Your dad moved out and came back just long enough to get your mom pregnant, first with your sisters and then with you, and then he left again."

"That's what everyone says," James said.

"JoAnn did enough to keep you alive, and your father showed up a few times every year to take you hunting and fishing so you wouldn't embarrass him by not knowing how to do that stuff."

"I work in his shop sometimes, too."

Joyce was becoming agitated, but she wasn't exactly sure what annoyed her. "I'll bet Ollie could not stand the thought of a boy of his not knowing how to hunt or fish or shoot or fight or screw or fix a motor. What would people think?"

"I don't know," James's words were barely audible. "What do people think?"

She lowered her voice. "Not all women are weak, James. And being a man and being mean isn't the same thing." Joyce stopped talking, but the dispositional math was inescapable. James was a purebred and certifiable jerk.

James got out and walked around to the front of the truck. Joyce watched through the windshield as he put both hands on the hood and dropped his head between his shoulders. After a few seconds, he raised his head, and his damp eyes glistened in the glare of the headlights. Joyce got out and stood next to the right front fender, out of the light. With his arms still on the hood of the truck, he turned toward her.

"How do you know all that?"

She remained in the dark behind the headlights. "I don't know. It's what I've heard."

"Well...maybe what you have *heard* about Ollie and JoAnn isn't true of me?"

Joyce did not respond right away, then she sighed. "It doesn't have to be this way."

She stepped to the front of the truck and put her hand on his shoulder. James stood up and stepped back, and Joyce retreated to the darkness behind the headlights.

"I'm sorry about that night at Junior's," he said.

"Okay."

"But I don't know any other way!"

"Pastor Clem says there's always another way."

James was about to slam his fists on the hood of the truck. Instead, he squeezed his fingernails into his palms and tapped the hood gently.

"Pastor Clem is wrong," he said, just loud enough for Joyce to hear.

He climbed into the truck. The engine roared, and the tires squealed as he hit the gas, leaving Joyce standing alone on the side of the road in the dark.

32

SCHOOL STARTED, and Mike kept his promise to Tyler. He went to class and did his schoolwork, though without enthusiasm. Every morning he ran for an hour, and every day after school, he went to Tyler's semi-organized practices with Silverton High School's new cross-country team.

Mike was impatient with the ritual of practice, but most of the other runners seemed to need repeated encouragement from the coach. Mike would sit on the old bleachers and rest his elbows on his knees with the heels of his hands pressed against his eyes and wait. Tyler preached about the need for consistency in training or the virtues of various running shoes or stretching or eating right or getting enough sleep or working together as a team. On and on for up to twenty minutes every day before the actual running began. Tyler never mentioned these things when he and Mike ran together. Maybe it was the job. The role. The profession. Mike wasn't sure, but he was impatient for Tyler to get done talking so he could run.

Then there was the warm-up, jogging three or four laps around the grass track. Mike would play the martyr during this daily ritual by jogging along with little Georgie at the back of the small pack. After the warm-up, the team would sit in a neat circle while Tyler directed the stretching routine. Mike sat outside the circle, so his deliberate inattention to the stretching exercises would not distract the other runners. Stretching made his legs hurt.

Joyce had become a sort of unofficial manager and was always nearby.

The other runners were as conscientious about the jogging and the stretching as Mike was apathetic. He approached Tyler's pre-training liturgy the same way he approached his classes. Silent and indifferent. At least once a day, Tyler would cast a critical glance in his direction, as if to make sure Mike was not setting a careless example for the rest of the team.

When at last the running started, Mike separated himself from the rest. Most of the team's training would take place on an assigned loop on the trails and roads around Silverton. But as soon as he was out of sight, Mike would go off on his own. Except for his Sunday run with Tyler, he had never gotten used to running with anyone else. The other boys ran in the hills or on the narrow roads, chatting about the same inconsequential issues they chatted about in the cafeteria or in the crowded hallways. But Mike ran in a different direction and with a different purpose.

There were few locations as lush and green as the foothills of the Cascade Mountains of western Washington in the early fall. Though the western slope of the Cascades was not exactly rainforest, first-time visitors, whether driving or hiking, were often surprised by the impenetrable ground cover. Dark-green thickets of salal often grew as high as a man's head. Yellow and orange salmonberries that began life as brilliant pink flowers in the spring grew in low spots of clear-cut, where the ground was open to the sun. Vine maple wrapped around larger trees or twisted around itself to form a vegetative barrier that had to be either bypassed or chopped through. Well-named devil's club and bear grass covered the ground between decorative and unpalatable Oregon grape, with its deep-green, holly-like leaves and globular fruit. And then there were the trees— ancient cedars, some as tall as twenty-story buildings and fifteen feet in diameter. And the smaller but more numerous Douglas Fir.

But Mike neither sought nor found solace in trees or mountains, in the extraordinary natural beauty surrounding his hometown. He did not notice or care to identify local flora. His mind did not wander. Running was neither an aesthetic experience nor a psychological release. Every step had a single purpose, to be as quick and as powerful as possible. Every run up every hill had a single objective: to engage every muscle in the long drive to the top. And then at the top to push harder until the terrain relented, and he could coast down the other side.

Mike never considered time or pace, nothing except exertion. Tyler lectured him about the need to slow down, moderate his effort, and leave something for the races. But even if Mike began at a jog, he'd be running hard again after a mile or two.

Mile after mile after mile.

Day after day after day.

By the time he returned to the grass track, the other boys were either finished and gone or in the last stages of gathering their gear and their schoolbooks and heading home. But Joyce always waited. Mike didn't know why she waited, but he allowed himself to be glad she had.

33

SINCE VERY FEW small schools had cross-country teams, Tyler had to talk his team into races against the area's larger schools.

Among a few kids at the larger schools, there was a subtle disdain for the "backwoods" kids from Silverton. One group of runners from Puget Sound High School in Everett even laughed when they saw Mike and the rest of the team get off the bus in their mismatched sweat clothes.

"What are they doing here?" a muscular runner from Puget Sound—a guy who'd had some modest success—asked.

"Don't worry about it," a young assistant coach said. "They're probably going to run in the JV race, and they'll be so far back, they won't get in the way."

But only Little Georgie ran in the JV race, and he was thrilled to finish with two runners, both from Puget Sound High, behind him. The other five kids from Silverton were entered in the much tougher varsity race.

"We're going to crush 'em," the stocky boy from Puget Sound bragged.

Mike liked to be left alone before he raced, so Tyler had talked about strategy during the thirty-minute bus ride to Marysville. Tyler had Mike sit across the aisle from him in the first row of seats. Mike had faced the front, and Tyler had sat with his feet in the aisle.

"There's no point in telling you to be patient at the start. But keep in mind that the best Snohomish kid was third in the state last year, and they have two other kids in the top twenty. If you run the first mile and a half too fast, they could—"

"They won't." Mike leaned back with his legs stretched out and closed his eyes.

Tyler wasn't sure whether Mike meant he wouldn't start out too fast or they wouldn't beat him.

At the starting line, the Silverton team was stacked into a narrow space on the far left. The race would begin with a sweeping left turn before the course rose gently for about 500 yards. The single significant hill was a steep incline the length of a football field that flattened out near the end of the first lap and then again on the second lap, three hundred yards from the finish.

The other runners milled around near the starting line, jogging and striding back and forth while Mike waited. He yawned and twisted his neck from right to left to stretch out a tight spot.

The Puget Sound High School team was lined up next to Mike and the other boys from Silverton. The stocky runner took his place at the front of the Puget Sound line. He looked over at Mike, smirked, shook his head, then stared down the course toward the first turn.

At the same time, one of the Snohomish runners, another stocky kid with a crooked smile and hard eyes, walked up to Mike and said, "Hey, good luck."

Surprised, Mike shook his hand weakly and watched him jog back to his team.

"The Snohomish guys suck," the Puget Sound kid said.

Mike huffed but didn't respond because he knew the Puget Sound kid would be far behind by the end of the first mile. A stooped man in baggy sweatpants was describing the course through a bullhorn. Mike had jogged the course with Tyler and the rest of the team, so he wondered why another detailed explanation was necessary.

"Any questions?"

There were none.

"Good luck, gentlemen."

A second man, shorter and soft around the middle, appeared in front of the runners. He held a pistol pointed toward the ground.

"On your marks!" the man shouted.

The pistol shot was not as loud as Mike expected, but he was distracted by the fleeting memory of real gunshots and of Junior falling on top of him. The rush of runners away from the starting line brought Mike back to the present, and he found himself pulled along in the middle of the pack. He looked toward the front. Two runners in red Snohomish singlets and the stocky kid from Puget Sound High in yellow were pulling away from the field.

After two hundred yards, Mike heard Tyler yell.

"You're fine! Long way to go!"

Mike relaxed. The runners completed the first long turn, and the field thinned out as they climbed the first hill. Mike stepped between two slowing runners to get to the outside, where he had a clear path to the front. As soon as he was free of the pack, he sped up and caught the leaders before they reached the top of the hill. He caught the Puget Sound runner first, taking a measure of wicked satisfaction from the surprised look on the kid's face as Mike ran past.

"Go with him!" a coach yelled from the top of the hill. "He won't be able—"

The rest of the Puget Sound coach's admonition was lost as Mike raced past.

At the crest of the hill, he caught the two Snohomish runners. He charged over the top and went by both as the course began to drop. The first Snohomish runner, the same kid who had shaken Mike's hand before the race, stayed close behind him.

Now that he had the lead, Mike began to run the way he did in the mountains around Silverton. The long downhill allowed him to lengthen his stride until he was almost sprinting. He could still hear the Snohomish runner's breathing close behind, so Mike ran even faster. The next hill was short but very steep, with a sharp turn to the left at the top. By the time Mike made the turn, he could no longer hear the Snohomish runner.

He was alone.

He completed the first lap ten seconds ahead of the Snohomish runner.

Mike raced past the small gathering of friends and family at the end of the first lap and around the big, sweeping turn again. At the top of the first hill, he began to feel tired, and by the time he got to the short, steep hill, he was suffering. He remembered what Tyler had told him in the final miles of one of their harder Sunday runs. *Relax. Run quicker, not harder.*

Mike's attention was focused on each step and on each yard of green grass as it disappeared behind him. By the time he reached the top of the last hill, he allowed himself a quick glance over his shoulder, out of curiosity, not fear or uncertainty. When he turned back, he could see the finish line. He was beginning to hear scattered cheering, and he saw Georgie running back toward him. When Mike ran by, Georgie jumped up and down and clapped his hands. Mike crossed the finish line before the kid from Snohomish even reached the top of the last hill. Mike slowed to a walk, strolled through the chute, then jogged back toward the finish line.

34

TYLER STARED at the watch on his wrist, his most ambitious suspicions confirmed. He looked around for Mike and found him watching the other kids finish. Mike seemed pleased when the second Silverton runner, a gaunt sophomore named Toby, sprinted past the stocky kid from Puget Sound to finish fourth. A look of distressed confusion had replaced the Puget Sound runner's arrogant smirk. And Tyler was a little surprised when Mike gave his teammate a fraternal hug when he emerged from the chute.

Tyler waited until the last Silverton runner had crossed the finish line then found the Marysville coach near the end of the chute.

"What's the course record?" Tyler asked the coach.

"It *was* 15:05 by Reed Meagher. He *was* one of the best I'd ever seen," the coach said. "But your kid just ran 14:45."

Tyler smiled. *Fourteen forty-five and a hug for a teammate,* he thought.

* * *

Mike didn't race anyone as fast as the kid from Snohomish for the rest of the fall season. And Tyler began to see a gradual change. After two or three more races, Mike began to realize the Puget Sound High kid's disdain had been the exception.

As Mike continued to win, word got around. Cross country had never been a sport that attracted large crowds to weekday meets, but others were beginning to see what Tyler had seen that first day in PE class. The kid from the mountains could run.

"The boy's special," the Snohomish coach, a stout, non-runnerish-looking, older man, told Tyler. "I didn't think anyone in this state was going to beat our best kid, except maybe Jonah Hart over in Richland, but your boy destroyed our kid."

Tyler smiled and shook his head. "I've never seen anything like it either, Coach."

"He's a freak of nature," the Snohomish coach said. He slapped Tyler on the back and laughed. "No other explanation. Can't be the coaching."

Tyler worried that Mike might be getting bored and began to think about putting him in a longer race against older runners. But at the same time, Tyler understood that Mike was challenged by the simple act of seeing how hard he could push himself. Who he beat or how fast he ran didn't matter. And Mike seemed to delight in mastering the unique challenge presented by each new course.

"Every course seems to have something meant to slow you down," Mike told Tyler after the next-to-last meet of the season. "Big hills. Sand. Tall grass. Mud." But he never slowed down. And he continued to win and to win by wider and wider margins.

After a half-dozen local races, there was the formality of

the district qualifying meet. One of the better kids in the small-school district meet tried to stay with Mike, but he disappeared after less than a mile, and two of Mike's improving teammates passed the kid near the finish.

Mike was going to run in the state meet and win a state championship. Tyler could see no obstacles remaining. But some obstacles are unseen.

35

By the last week of October, the air on the western slope of the Cascade Mountains had begun to drip. While waiting for Mike to finish his run, Tyler and Deputy Dodge huddled under a leaky awning that provided minimal protection for the high school's back doors. The other boys on the team had already run and gone home. Joyce leaned against the railing behind Dodge and Tyler. She pretended to be reading a book but listened hard to what they had to say about Mike.

"I wonder how good he'd be if he came from a better family," Tyler said.

"I think an intact family might have acted as both a security blanket and a governor for a boy like Mike," Dodge said. "From what I've seen of some of these kids, *normal* isn't always best."

Tyler nodded.

Dodge continued. "If he'd come from a better family, Mike would be just like all the other *good* boys in town. Baseball when he was little. Good grades. Then football and basketball. A runner? In Silverton? Could only happen by accident."

Mike emerged from the woods and continued across the track and the football field. He enjoyed the squishing sound his shoes made when the grass was soaked. Little splashes exploded up from the ground with each step, and Mike could feel the cold water against the back of his legs. He saw the truck with the brown sheriff's department star on the door before he noticed the two men standing under the awning. He slowed to a jog and then walked the last few yards to the bottom of the steps. Joyce pushed herself away from the railing and stood next to Tyler and Dodge.

"Mike, do you remember me?" Dodge asked. "We talked at Junior's cabin back in June."

Mike started to answer, but he stopped when Mr. Thompson came through the double doors.

This can't be good.

"Coy, it's good to see you." Thompson slapped Dodge on the shoulder and then put his hands in his pockets and rocked back on his heels. "What can we do for you?"

"I'm just checking up on some of the kids who were at Junior's last summer. A couple kids are still a bit trauma-tized. Nightmares and such."

The principal stared at Mike.

"I'm fine." Mike was still standing at the bottom of the stairs in the rain.

Thompson started to speak, but Deputy Dodge raised his hand to indicate that he shouldn't.

"Do you want to come up here out of the rain?" Dodge asked. He turned the fur collar up on his leather coat and raised the zipper a few inches.

"I'm not gonna get any wetter." Mike looked at Tyler. "Am I in trouble?"

"No one said anything about being in trouble," Joyce said. "No one is in trouble, right, Deputy Dodge?"

Dodge looked at Joyce and smiled. "I thought you were reading."

"Why do you want to talk about what happened at Junior's after all this time?" Mike suspected this might be Dodge's excuse to talk about something else. "I didn't shoot him."

"We know who shot Junior," Dodge said. "But he did bleed on you."

"Deputy Dodge is just checking in," Tyler interjected, "to see how you're doing."

Mike waited. Rainwater dripped off his nose, and his hair was plastered to his forehead. He had discarded the hooded sweatshirt he'd been wearing when he started his run because it had become waterlogged. It was hanging on a tree branch somewhere along the trail about three miles out.

"So, how are you doing, Mike?" Dodge said.

"I'd like Mike to get out of the rain," Tyler told Dodge. "The state meet is a week from tomorrow, and it would be good if he didn't get pneumonia."

Dodge stepped down and motioned for Mike to follow. Then Dodge turned around to Joyce. "Come on, young lady. You might as well join us. We can talk in my car. It's warm, and I've got a dry sweatshirt."

"We can use my office," Thompson offered.

Dodge ignored him as he ushered Mike and Joyce away from the building. Dodge's Sheriff's Department SUV was parked next to Mike's truck. Joyce climbed into the front seat, but Mike waited for Dodge to unlock the back door.

"Force of habit?" Dodge said. "You can both sit up front."

Joyce scrunched into the middle of the front seat, and Mike slid in next to her.

"I'm dripping all over your upholstery."

Dodge handed Mike a dry sweatshirt emblazoned with the same star on the truck's door. "Put that on. A lot worse than rainwater has dripped onto that seat."

Joyce cringed, and Mike laughed.

The front seat was crowded, and Mike had to twist awkwardly to strip off his wet T-shirt and pull the dry sweatshirt on.

"Cross-country, huh?" Dodge said, lowering the zipper on his coat. "They didn't have that when I went here. All the guys played football. I was pretty skinny back then, and I didn't like football that much. My specialty was catching the ball and running out of bounds. I didn't really like to get hit, so I don't think the coach thought much of me. Might have been better at cross-country."

Joyce glanced at the deputy, then at Mike.

Dodge looked at Joyce and said, "Girls had tennis."

"Am I in trouble?" Mike asked again.

"Not that I know of. But then, there must be stuff goes on around here I don't know about."

"Like what?" Joyce said.

"This will just take a minute, young lady," Dodge said. "You know, it says a lot about Mike that a good girl like you would wait out in the rain for him. It's admirable."

Joyce turned away, and her cheeks grew a little red.

"The thing is, Mike, I'm curious. By the time we arrived at Junior's that night, most of the local kids had vanished, and the out-of-towners still there were pretty shook-up, but you seemed more nervous than upset. Almost as if what happened to Junior didn't faze you, that it didn't matter Junior had been shot."

"It mattered," Mike countered. "I don't mind that Junior's not dead."

"Is he all right?" Joyce said.

"He's fine. The wound looked worse than it was. He spent a day in the hospital. Then we cited him for providing liquor to minors, but a judge took pity on him because he'd been shot. No jail time. He's back to selling liquor and drugs to any underage kid willing to pay. We've got an eye on him, though."

"So, it would be good to avoid Junior's place?" Mike started to smile.

"Yeah. If I were a big-shot runner trying to stay out of trouble, I'd stay away from Junior."

"That's the plan," Mike said. He turned and looked out the window at Tyler and Thompson still waiting under the awning. "I don't want to be in trouble anymore."

"That's good, Mike. Good."

Mike started to push the door open to leave when Dodge interrupted him.

"One more thing about that night," he said. "Why didn't you wait for your ride like I told you?"

"I didn't want to be there anymore, so I ran. That's what I do."

"That's what Joyce and Coach Tyler said. I don't think I believed it at the time."

"There are trails and logging roads."

"You just ran?"

Mike nodded.

"That's right," Joyce said.

She put her hand on Mike's knee. The gesture surprised him.

"Well, Mike, that's also admirable, but there's something else."

There is always something else.

"I said I'm fine," Mike insisted. "I washed Junior's blood off and went running with Coach Tyler the next day."

"I get that. But I also hear you've been living by yourself."

"So?"

"So...you're a minor. The law says you need adult supervision. You can't live alone. I could take you in and get you into foster care until we figure out what's up with your dad. And I could arrest your dad for neglect...and maybe your mother...for desertion or something."

Joyce turned toward Dodge but scooted closer to Mike.

"I don't feel neglected. My mother left when I was twelve, and *Bobby* left back in June."

"My parents have been sort of keeping track of Mike," Joyce said. "Isn't that good enough?"

"For the law? No."

"To Hell with the law. I can leave, too, you know. Take off any time I want. Runs in the family."

Joyce leaned back harder against Mike.

Dodge cocked his head slightly. "You think the law doesn't apply to you." It was not a question.

Mike put his hand back on the door handle.

"Look, Mike, I know where your parents are. And I suspect you do, too."

Mike nodded and took his hand away.

"I'm going to look the other way on your living situation for a while."

"Thanks, I guess."

"But it needs to be resolved. Mr. Thompson suspects something. And he can pressure Coach Tyler."

Mike did not like the sound of that. "Coach hasn't done anything wrong."

"There's right and wrong, Mike. And then there's legal and illegal. They're not always the same."

"What are you saying I should do?"

"I'm not saying you should do anything, but when you do, take Joyce with you."

Mike nodded and nudged the door open. The rain had stopped, but a frigid wind blew the residual dampness through the narrow space that separated Mike's truck from the sheriff's vehicle. Dodge left, and Mike pulled the passenger-side door of his truck open for Joyce and then dashed around and climbed into the driver's seat.

The sodden wind outside was seeping in through the old truck's assortment of imperfections. Joyce hugged herself and shivered, so Mike pulled a wadded-up T-shirt from behind the seat. He pulled off the sweatshirt and handed it to Joyce and then put on the T-shirt.

"Thank you," Joyce said. "You've never done anything like that before."

"What?"

"You opened the door for me. And you gave me your sweatshirt because I'm cold."

"It's Dodge's sweatshirt."

"I still think it was nice of you."

Mike's face felt hot. He left the truck running when he pulled up in front of Joyce's house, but she did not get out.

"So, what are you...what are *we*...going to do now?" she asked him.

Mike shrugged and shook his head. He was confused about what Dodge had said, and he did wonder what a future in Silverton would hold for him. And for Joyce.

"I'm going to Abel," he said, looking at Joyce. "Tomorrow. First thing."

"*We're* going to Abel. There was a man who had two sons..."

"What is that supposed to mean?".

"For this my son...was lost and is found."

"I don't understand.

"I'm sure you don't. Prodigals, Mike. It's all about prodigals."

36

WHAT DEPUTY DODGE had said kept Joyce awake most of the night, but she was still up at sunrise, just like every other Saturday. She could never quite understand her classmates' need to sleep away the only two days of the week they were not held hostage by the ritualistic clanging of bells and the obedient shuffling from room to room. Her parents made few demands, so she guarded the free and unoccupied hours on the weekend with the ferocity of a soldier on furlough.

Joyce was waiting on the porch when Mike's truck rattled into the circular driveway a little after seven. She hoisted a book bag over her shoulder and climbed into the truck. Mike drove away from the house around the circular driveway and took a left.

"Dodge is cool," he said.

Joyce could not remember Mike ever using the word *cool* before.

He turned right when they reached the edge of town and rumbled past the high school. "Seems as if everyone in town went to school together. My dad. Your mom and dad. James's parents. Thompson. Even Sorenson."

"And Pastor Clem. Silverton is a little inbred. My mom said everyone was surprised when Dodge became a deputy sheriff because he was the kid who never followed the rules." All at once, Joyce realized why Dodge had taken an interest in Mike. "Oh. Oh! I think I see why Deputy Dodge is so interested. Mike, don't you get it?"

Mike shrugged. "Get what?"

Joyce sighed. "Deputy Dodge? You? Rules? Getting into trouble at school?"

Mike shrugged.

"Clueless." Joyce shook her head and stared at Mike.

"What?"

"Never mind." She held her breath for a second and then exhaled loudly. "How do you expect to get to Abel? I thought some guy sent you and Tyler away last time."

"We're not going to drive. A trail at the end of Snow Lake goes over the ridge and down into Abel. Remember?"

"We're hiking?"

"No. You'll wait in the truck while I run to Abel and see if there's anything to see."

"I'm going to sit and wait?"

"Mike patted the book bag. "Looks like you've got plenty to do."

"Then why did I need to come along?"

"I thought you'd want to be there when I got back."

"No, Mike. I want to be there when you get there."

Joyce was annoyed, but Mike seemed excited about the prospect of sneaking up on Abel, so she bit her lower lip and didn't say anything. Joyce watched the forest slide by and realized the vegetation did not change much from season to season, only the colors. The underbrush was nearly as thick in October as it had been during the summer but was brown or gray instead of green.

"The only difference is that it's wetter," she said.

"What's wetter?"

"Things don't change much, do they?"

"Yeah, they do. Everything's different." Mike glanced over at Joyce. "I'm a little different."

"Not just people. The woods. The town. School. The church. The sameness feels as if it's closing in. Like there's no way out. When I left the church, it was summertime, and I felt like I might suffocate if I didn't get out. Now, I feel like I might drown if I don't go back."

"Well, that's change, isn't it?"

Joyce reached into the book bag and pulled out her Bible and set it unopened on her lap. "Yes, Mike. That is change."

They passed the road to Abel, and Mike pointed across the seat. "There it is."

A mile farther on, he pulled off the highway and parked the truck in a wide turnout. Joyce started to get out, but the door was blocked by the pile of dirt and rock left behind when the turnout was last graded. She pulled the door shut and sat back.

"This won't take long," Mike assured her. "Two miles to Snow Lake. Less than a mile to the other end. Maybe two or three over the ridge and down into the town."

"Mike, they may not even—"

"I want to take a look."

Joyce reached out and touched his arm. "Mike, maybe it's not the town that has kept her away."

"What else could it be?"

Rain had been predicted for later in the day. Mike pulled on a heavy black windbreaker with orange sleeves over his long-sleeve shirt. Neat orange print on the left breast encircled a cartoon tiger and read *Silverton High Coaching Staff*.

Joyce reached across the seat and touched the tiger.

"Coaching staff? Really?"

"Tyler doesn't want me to catch a cold. I'm sure he has another raincoat."

Without another word, Mike was out of the truck and bounding up the dozen crude, wood-and-stone steps that led to the trail. He leaned into the hill and settled in for the two-mile climb to Snow Lake.

Joyce opened her Bible and thumbed through the pages, waiting for a passage to catch her eye. She looked up through the windshield at the gathering clouds in the narrow ribbon of sky between the trees that lined both sides of the highway. She stopped leafing through the Bible, and when she looked down, her index finger had come to rest on John 19:26.

When Jesus saw his mother there, and the disciple whom he loved standing nearby, he said to her, "Woman, here is your son."

"Woman, here is your son," Joyce said aloud. "Mike, here is your mother. Now, what are you going to do about it?"

A little more than an hour later, Mike appeared at the top of the stone stairs. He paused before walking down carefully, step by step. He climbed into the truck and started the engine without speaking. He began to put the truck into gear, but Joyce put her hand on his arm and pulled it back.

"Mike?"

Mike stared straight ahead. Joyce put her hand on his chin and turned his face toward her.

"Mike, what did you see?"

"Rooftops. There was smoke coming from all the chimneys, and I could smell wood burning."

"And?"

"I didn't see anyone except—" Mike pushed Joyce's hand away from his chin, but then he grabbed her wrist and started to squeeze before he let his hand relax. "A woman and a kid walking up the trail, maybe a quarter-mile below me. The kid had a backpack. I didn't want anyone to see me, so I ran back up the trail."

Mike and Joyce drove back to Silverton in silence, but when they passed the turnoff to Abel, Joyce moved away from the door and put her Bible on the seat between her and Mike. Mike looked down at the Bible and then tapped it with his index finger. Neither spoke until they reached Joyce's house. He stopped the truck at the end of the driveway.

"Do you want me to get out here?" Joyce asked.

Mike looked at her without expression and then drove up the driveway and stopped in front of the porch.

"Mike, do you want me to get out here?"

Mike looked down at the Bible again. Joyce moved it across her body and set it down next to the passenger door. Then she turned toward Mike, scooted a little closer, and put her arm on the back of the seat behind his shoulders. Mike glanced at her arm and then put his hand in the small space on the seat that still separated them.

"Well, you wanted a look at Abel. You got a look."

Mike opened his mouth, but instead of speaking, he sucked in a quick breath and closed his eyes.

"So, what do you know now that you didn't know before?"

"I don't...know. I can't...tell... I didn't see much."

Joyce waited, but when Mike said nothing, she asked, "What did you expect to see?"

Mike stared out the driver's side window. "To see where

she's been." He shuddered as he took in a shallow breath. "And to find out why she doesn't come home."

Joyce's heart swelled. She moved her arm off the back of the seat and onto Mike's shoulders. Tears trickled out of the corners of his eyes, and little rivulets began to form in the trail dust on his face.

She remembered reading somewhere that tears of grief had a different chemical composition than tears of pain and did not taste the same. She wiped a new tear from Mike's face with her knuckle and put the knuckle into her mouth. The taste revealed no hint of the content of Mike's tears, but she was beginning to understand the heft of the lonely cross he had to bear and wondered what she might do to counter-balance the weight.

Joyce leaned forward and whispered in Mike's ear. "You didn't go down into Abel. You could have, but instead, you came back here."

She pulled her head back for a moment and then turned Mike's face toward her. She looked into his eyes and kissed him on the mouth.

37

JOYCE SPENT most of the next day, Sunday, alone in her room, thinking about Mike and Abel and the kiss. And she read her Bible, certain she could find a passage that would explain precisely how the kiss had made her feel. But nothing she could find about love satisfied her curiosity about what she thought she might be feeling about Mike. Only *Love God, love your neighbor, love one another, and love your enemies.*

Matthew 5:44 imprinted itself in some prominent place in her brain. *But I say to you, love your enemies, bless those who curse you, do good to those who hate you, and pray for those who spitefully use you and persecute you.* This was James. That wasn't hard to figure out. And the implication was clear, easy to understand. After one brief kiss, Joyce's feelings about Mike required no effort. In fact, it was something of an effort to keep those feelings under some semblance of good-girl control.

But she had also had a feeling about James, and Matthew 5:44 seemed to condemn her for those feelings. So she spent most of what was left of that Sunday wrestling with that most difficult scriptural obligation.

Then on Monday morning, despite a misty drizzle, Joyce left the house earlier than usual so she could walk for an hour before school and think.

There was no traffic on the road in front of her house, but as she approached the church, thinking of maybe going inside, Pork's ugly yellow Bug screeched to halt with both front tires on the sidewalk. She had to jump back to keep from being hit. She collected herself and then tried to continue around the back of the car, but Pork had jammed the pudgy vehicle into reverse and backed up into the street to stop her. She tried to go around the front, but Pork shoved the gear lever into first and blocked her way again. Joyce moved toward the back of the car once more, but James's pickup pulled off the street and stopped close behind Joyce.

When Joyce turned to see what James would do, Tall Paul unfolded himself out of the VW, grabbed Joyce by the arm, and squeezed. James was out of his truck by then. He strode quickly toward Joyce. She thought about screaming but didn't because Matthew 5:44 was still on her mind. James yanked Tall Paul's arm away from Joyce and then shoved his friend back toward the VW. Joyce started to walk on toward school, but now James had her by the arm. He did not squeeze, but he did not let go, either.

"Would you get in the truck, please?"

Joyce pulled her arm away, and James let go. She looked up the street and then back the way she had come to make sure no one was watching and then climbed into the front seat of James's truck. James just stood there for a long moment. He raised his hands and shrugged at the boys in the VW as if to say, *Well, are you coming?*

Pork pulled the VW the rest of the way off the road, and

he and Tall Paul bundled themselves into the back seat. James had remained standing in the road, but he rolled his eye and shook his head before climbing into the truck and pulling out.

Once he was settled, Joyce said, "James, what do you want?"

"I don't know exactly." He was rubbing his wrist. "I guess I just want to talk for a minute."

Tall Paul and Pork snickered in the back seat.

"Hey," Pork said. "I'll bet Mike-effing-Beck is out running somewhere. Whyn't we go see if we can find him. Show 'im we got his girlfriend."

Joyce waited for James to answer, but he just watched Pork in the rearview mirror for a few seconds and then said, "That's kinda what I had in mind."

"Really, James," Joyce said. "Is that really what you had in mind? Is it?"

James stared straight ahead and shook his head slightly.

"And I'm not Mike's girlfriend," Joyce said, turning to face the boys in the back. "Were just..."

"*Friends.*" James completed the sentence for her. "Yeah, right. Why can't you tell the truth about Mike, Joyce? It is a sin to lie."

Joyce was confused.

"James, I thought you were going to try to... I thought you'd decided not to..."

He turned to see what the boys in the back were doing. They were still snickering, waiting for James to proclaim their next move. Pork reached over from the passenger side and slapped James on the shoulder with a meaty left hand.

But James's attention was back on Joyce.

"I thought so," he said. "But maybe I can't."

"I think finding Mike might be kind of fun," Tall Paul said.

"Especially with Jesus-freaking-Joyce with us," Pork chortled. "We'll get 'im good this time, right, James?"

James didn't answer.

"James," Joyce said. "What is this about?"

James reached under the seat and showed Joyce the gun from Junior's party.

"Jesus," Joyce said. "Sweet Jesus. What are you going to do with that?"

"I don't know. I guess we'll find out."

38

MONDAY MORNING, Mike left the house to run for an hour. He cruised through the drizzle out toward the countryside west of town. Just past the city limits, he turned left onto Crooked Mile Road toward Harden Lake. The road was lined on both sides with damp cedar and dense underbrush and began to roll gently as it neared the lake. He was tempted to push the pace through the rolling hills, but Tyler had told him to save his legs.

"You can run as much as an hour Monday and Tuesday," Tyler advised, "but slow down. Take it easy—don't push anything this week."

Mike thought about the almost visit to Abel and about Joyce's kiss. He was having a hard time working out the connection between Almost Abel and The Kiss, so he welcomed the opportunity to do his Sunday long run by himself. Something else to wonder about.

Mike had just turned onto the two-mile loop that would take him around the lake when he saw James's truck coming from the opposite direction. The truck veered across the road, and the tires screeched when James hit the brakes.

The engine roared, and the tires squealed as the truck accelerated backward in his direction. Mike jumped across the shallow barrow pit to keep from being hit, but as the truck skidded to a stop in the middle of the road, he stepped back onto the shoulder with the barrow pit behind him.

The back doors on both sides of the truck flew open, and Tall Paul and Pork appeared. James hesitated with both hands on the wheel and his eyes down. He climbed out of the truck and leaned against the fender with the gun dangling from his right hand.

After a few seconds, the front passenger-side door opened, and Joyce stepped out of the truck. Mike stepped toward Joyce but stopped when James moved in front of the truck, the gun dangling at his side.

Mike knew a narrow footpath ran along the lakeshore down a short incline through the underbrush about twenty feet from the road. Gun or no gun, James and the boys weren't going to pursue Mike into the woods, but he stood his ground anyway.

"Big-shot runner, huh?" Pork said.

Tall Paul and Pork had remained on opposite sides of the truck. They seemed to be watching for traffic from each direction. There was none, so they turned their attention back to James and Mike.

"You need a gun, James?" Mike said. "You really are a—"

"Shut up," Tall Paul said. "We'll see how fast you run with a bullet in your leg."

Joyce moved forward, a step outside the ten-foot space separating James and Mike.

"Let it be. And we'll leave. Okay?" Joyce eased herself a little closer to James. "He doesn't mean anything."

Mike looked back and forth between James and Joyce. Who was she speaking to?

Mike glanced over his shoulder to be sure of his escape route, but he didn't run. Then he turned his attention toward Tall Paul and Pork. Tall Paul was leaning against one side of the truck with his arms extended. Pork was on the other side, leaning on his forearms.

"Do what you're going to do," Tall Paul said to James, "so we can get out of here. I'm gonna need some coffee 'fore school."

"I'm going to finish my run," Mike said.

When he started to step back across the barrow pit, James raised the gun in Mike's general direction. Joyce reached out and slapped James's arm. A shot exploded, and a bullet buried itself in the ground a few inches from Mike's left foot. He bolted across the ditch and heard the sharp explosion when James pulled the trigger a second time.

Mike stumbled down the slope to the lakeshore. He turned right when he reached the narrow path, but as he was about to sprint up the trail away from James and the boys, his right foot crashed down onto a tree root protruding from the trail. Mike's ankle rolled ninety degrees to the side. Searing pain enveloped his ankle and lower leg all the way to the knee., and a flash of white light blinded him. The ankle bone touched the ground and then snapped back. Mike crashed to the ground and lay there, writhing in agony.

Had he broken his ankle? He had no idea, but it hurt. A lot. He rolled onto his back and remained still with his head in the dirt and his forearm covering his eyes.

39

JAMES JUMPED into his truck and slammed it into gear. Tall Paul and Pork were barely able to scramble into the front seat before James sped away. He raced back toward town with the gun in his lap and turned right when they reached the main road.

"Jesus!" Tall Paul cried. He was leaning forward with his hands on the dashboard, rocking back and forth. "I never thought you'd shoot him, man. We're in big trouble. We're *all* going to jail."

Pork was wedged in between James and Tall Paul with his round back turned halfway toward the driver's side. James slowed down at the city limits sign and pulled over on the shoulder just short of where the concrete sidewalk began and tossed the gun into Tall Paul's lap.

"Jesus! I don't want it," Tall Paul said, tossing the gun around Pork back to James. While he was fumbling to hide the gun under the front seat, a green and brown Sheriff's Department SUV slowed down and stopped on the other side of the road opposite James's truck.

"That's Dodge," Pork said. "He's going to find out what you did, and then *you* are so busted. You are going to jail."

Dodge stepped out of the SUV and sauntered toward the truck, indicating that James should roll his window down with his finger.

When he reached James's truck, he was silent for several seconds. "Everything okay here, boys?" He looked past James, who glanced over to see Tall Paul and Pork sitting up straight, silently staring straight ahead. James waited several seconds before responding to Dodge. He knew the other boys would say nothing until he did, and even then they'd make sure not to contradict whatever James would tell the deputy. It crossed his mind to tell Dodge about Mike and Joyce, but he did not after thinking about it for a second or two.

"Yes, sir," James said. "We're just going to school."

"If I remember correctly, all three of you boys live in town."

"That's right," James said. "We do."

"Then what are you doing out this way?" Dodge leaned forward and craned his neck so he could see into the front seat. All three boys leaned back and held up their hands to offer Dodge an unobstructed view and confirm their innocence. Dodge took a step back and looked carefully into the back seat. Then while James watched in the rearview mirror, he continued around the truck and examined the empty bed. By the time he got back to the driver's side window, Pork had begun to sweat.

"Are you sure you're okay, Peter?" Dodge said, using Pork's given name.

Pork nodded vigorously but did not speak.

Dodge made another quick scan of the interior of the truck. "Well, you boys get on to school." He stepped back.

"Thank you, sir." James put the truck in gear and, without checking for traffic, drove away. In the mirror, he could see Dodge on the shoulder, looking back in the other direction.

"He's suspicious," Tall Paul said.

"Dodge's going to find Mike, and he's going say what happened." Pork sounded as if he might cry.

"No, *Peter*," James said. "Mike ain't going to say nothing. Or Joyce, neither."

"What? You got a thing with Joyce now?" Pork said.

James glared at Pork, but he had become curious about the sudden sadness that was welling up from somewhere down deep. Pork let out a loud fart, and James shook off the strange emotion and drove back through town toward the high school.

40

JOYCE STEPPED over the barrow ditch and peered down the slope. Mike lay writhing on the ground a few feet away. A cold fear raced through her. Had he been shot?

"Mike, what happened? Did James shoot you?"

He didn't answer.

"Oh, Jesus, please."

She started down the slope, but her feet slipped, and she slid the rest of the way on her butt, her feet barely missing Mike's head when she reached the trail. She raised herself onto her knees with her hands clutched beneath her chin.

"Oh, Jesus, please," she repeated. "Can you talk, Mike?"

"I don't even think I can walk."

"Oh, Jesus. What now?"

"It's my ankle. Help me up."

"Oh, God. He shot you in your ankle."

"No, I twisted my ankle. Running away."

Joyce helped Mike to his feet, and they hobbled together back up the slope to the road. Mike slid down onto his butt with his feet in the shallow ditch when they reached the barrow pit. Joyce stepped across the ditch and stood help-lessly in front of Mike.

"What can I do, Mike?"

He grimaced as he pulled his ankle up onto his opposite knee so he could examine the damage. Joyce was horrified at the sight of Mike's grotesquely swollen ankle.

"Mike, can I help?"

Mike shook his head. "What were you doing in James's truck?"

"That doesn't matter," Joyce said.

Mike waited.

"Alright, then. I was walking to school. Tall Paul and Pork almost hit me with their car, and then James showed up. I think he kind of rescued me."

"Rescued you? Right. They had this planned."

"I don't think so. Not until James met up with the other two."

"No. Tall Paul and Pork aren't that smart. They do exactly what James says."

"You don't know *what* I know." Joyce was angry at Mike's presumption, but she was even more annoyed at James. But Matthew 5:44 was still emphatically on her mind. *Love your enemies. How to do that now?*

"Mike, you can't walk on that ankle. So how are we going to get back to town?"

"Maybe I can." But Mike's voice was shaky, and his hands were trembling. "If you help, maybe I can limp to the main road. We could get a ride."

Joyce thought about it and then shook her head. "No. You can't, but I can walk back toward town and get help."

"I really think I can make it to the highway, Joyce. Help me up."

But before Joyce could get Mike to his feet, Deputy Dodge's SUV approached from the direction of the highway.

"Thank God," she said. "One of us must be living right."

The narrow road to the lake had only a thin shoulder, so the deputy stopped in the middle of the road when he reached Mike and flipped a switch to turn on his light bar.

Dodge called out from inside the truck. "You two okay? What happened?"

Mike lowered his foot to the ground. "I twisted my ankle. Pretty bad."

Joyce tried to help him stand one more time, but he plopped back down before he was halfway up.

Dodge was already out of the truck with a first aid kit in his hand.

"Stay down, Mike. Let me take a look. What happened here?

Mike inhaled through his teeth and shuddered. "I was running on the path by the lake and stepped on a root. My ankle is hurt pretty bad, I think."

When Dodge attempted to lift his ankle, Mike gasped loudly through clenched teeth.

The deputy took his hand away. "Take your shoe and sock off."

He broke open a chemical ice pack from the first aid kit and placed it on the outside of Mike's ankle. While he wrapped Mike's ankle with an elastic bandage, Dodge asked Joyce, "And what were you doing out here, young lady?"

Joyce hesitated, and Dodge held his hand up to prevent her from having to say anything. "I saw James and his boys heading toward town from this direction. Do either of you know anything about that? Did James have anything to do with this?"

Mike looked away, silent.

Joyce looked Dodge full in the face and lied. "We haven't seen James."

* * *

Dodge watched the nurse push Mike into the clinic in a wheelchair, then he and Joyce followed Mike and the nurse into the building. Dodge pointed to an old couch in the waiting room, and Joyce sat in the center with her back straight and her hands folded in her lap.

Dodge called the school and explained to Mr. Thompson what was going on. He also told the principal that Mike's father was out of town working, and Mike was not sure how to get in touch with him. He did not tell Mr. Thompson Mike had been living alone. Dodge hung up the phone and leaned over the counter and tapped a frumpy, gray-haired woman on the shoulder.

"They take the kid in back, Wilma?"

"You see 'im out here?" She shook her head in mock exasperation and then looked up at Dodge and smiled. "Yes, Deputy. He's in the back being x-rayed. Is the county going to pay for this?"

"Kid's not destitute. I imagine someone will be in to settle up, one way or the other. I need to talk to the doc about the boy's situation. He may need to bend a few consent rules." Dodge rapped the countertop twice with his knuckles then headed down the hall. He found Mike in the first examination room.

"What's the verdict, Doc? Kid gonna live?"

Dr. Magnuson was past eighty. He'd been an orthopedic surgeon at one of the big Seattle hospitals. Then he retired to a four-thousand-square-foot "cabin" near the Verlot Ranger Station ten miles up the Mountain Loop Highway.

When he discovered he needed more to do than stare at trees and catch fish, he reopened the Silverton Clinic, which had been closed since the last doctor left town almost ten years before. He seemed to enjoy suturing nasty gashes caused by every imaginable type of cutting tool, setting broken bones, and treating accidental gunshot wounds.

"It's a severe sprain. Hurts like the dickens but looks worse than it is. He'll be off his feet for a while. Four to six weeks."

"I'm a runner," Mike explained.

"I know you are," Dr. Magnuson said with a nod and a sad frown.

"The state meet is—"

"Saturday. Yes, I know." The doctor put his hand on Mike's shoulder. "I'm sorry, son."

Mike lowered himself all the way back onto the treatment table and covered his eyes with his forearm.

Deputy Dodge approached the table. "Mike, I've got to ask you a couple of questions."

Mike didn't move. "So, ask."

"When you were running this morning, did you see James with Tall Paul and Pork?"

Mike hesitated and looked away before answering.

"No."

"Are you sure, Mike?"

Mike watched Dr. Magnuson gently probe his swollen ankle. After a few seconds, he turned and looked Deputy Dodge in the eye.

"Yes. I'm sure."

41

MIKE DIDN'T ARGUE when Dr. Magnuson insisted he'd have to convalesce on crutches and in a clumsy walking boot. Nor did Mike complain when the doctor ordered him to submerge his foot and ankle in ice three times a day. Mike shook his head when the doctor told him "no running" for four to six weeks.

"I'll be able to run in a couple of days."

Mike had run every day since he was twelve years old, and running every day had become more than a habit. The ritual of running, the daily ablution in sweat, pumped the emotional and spiritual lifeblood into each day. Running with such single-minded devotion, with no apparent purpose beyond the primal act of putting one foot in front of the other, was essential because it was particular to Mike. And because nothing else in his world made sense. Except now and then and more and more often, Joyce made sense.

So, the day after he hurt his ankle, Mike sat at the kitchen table and brooded over the formlessness that would define the weeks ahead as his ankle healed. He removed the walking cast, placed it on the tabletop, and then tried to put on his running shoes. He put a shoe and sock on his left foot first, but he could not get it past the greenish-purple bulge behind his toes when he tried to put a sock on his swollen right foot.

I'll run without socks, he decided.

He got up, hopped to the back door, threw the offending sock outside, and tried to put his shoe on again. Of course, the absence of the sock made no difference. Since he could not get his right shoe on, he pulled off his left shoe and flung it over his shoulder down the hall. The shoe bounced off the wall, and a faded photo of Robert and Janine standing in front of the courthouse in Everett on their wedding day crashed to the floor. The sound of glass breaking did not divert Mike's attention from his pulverized right ankle.

Maybe I can jog barefoot.

He left the walking cast on the table and stood up. Balancing on his left foot, he took a tenuous step toward the hall. Using his left leg for support, Mike stepped down on the ball of his right foot and tried to push off. The result was a replay of the searing pain and white light of the day before when his foot had hit the exposed root, and his ankle bone had hit the ground.

"Ahhhh. Ow. Ow. Ow."

Mike stumbled onto his left leg and hopped three awkward steps down the hall. He tried to regain his balance by grasping at the knob on the door to his room, but the momentum of the inward swinging door spun him around. He lost his balance, fell backward, and landed on the shattered glass from the picture frame.

42

JOYCE HAD STEPPED up onto the porch when she heard Mike's first pain-filled howl. She burst through the front door in time to see him land on the broken glass. Mike rolled onto his stomach. Tiny splotches of blood where the glass from the picture frame had lacerated his left butt cheek had already begun to seep through his running shorts.

"Mike, what are you doing?" Joyce rushed forward and bent over Mike with her hand on his shoulder.

Mike started to get up but instead dropped his forehead onto his folded arms, and with his mouth an inch or two from the floor, said, "I was trying to run down the hall."

Joyce pulled her hand away and sat down on her heels.

"You were what?"

"I couldn't get my shoe on, so I thought I'd run up and down the hall barefoot."

"How did that work out for you?"

"Shut up." Mike dropped his forehead to the floor and closed his eyes.

Joyce turned around and sat on the floor. She scooted

back a little and hugged her knees so her feet were next to Mike's head.

"Do you know you're bleeding?"

"I cut my butt." He lifted his head and tried to twist around to see his injured backside.

"That seems appropriate. Probably serves you right."

Mike dropped his forehead back to the floor. "Oh, God."

Joyce reached down and tried to put her fingers under the waistband of Mike's running shorts. "I better take a look."

"Look at what?"

Mike reached back and gripped his shorts, pulling up as Joyce pulled down.

"Your bloody butt cheek. What do you think?" She pulled her hand away from his waistband and slapped him on his unscathed right butt cheek. "Don't be such a baby. You may need stitches."

Mike winced but would not relinquish the grip on his shorts.

"There's no one here, Mike."

"You're here."

Careful to avoid the shards of glass, Joyce scooted onto her side next to Mike so she could speak into his ear.

"Yes, I am. And what does that suggest to you?" Joyce stood up and looked down at Mike. She shook her head and added, "It means you need to get a clue. I'll be on the phone in the front room. I'm going to call Tyler. Maybe you'll let him look at your butt."

43

MIKE PUSHED HIMSELF INTO AN AWKWARD, one-legged, push-up position and maneuvered onto his side, away from the broken glass, but when he tried to sit up, he discovered only his right butt cheek would bear any weight because the cuts were all on the left cheek.

Joyce returned and placed the walking boot on the floor next to him. "Tyler is on his way. At least he will be when he stops laughing."

"I don't see anything funny."

Joyce stepped over Mike and the broken glass and went into his room. She returned after a few seconds with Mike's crutches and a pillow. She dropped the crutches onto the floor and then headed toward the front room with the pillow.

"We'll wait for Tyler out here. You may need to sit on the pillow."

Mike crawled to the table, hefted himself onto a chair, and snapped the walking boot back on. He retrieved his crutches from the floor where Joyce had dropped them and hobbled into the front room. He sat in the center of the couch, where Joyce had placed the pillow. Joyce sat in the old chair in the corner. She picked at the duct tape repairs on the arm of the chair and then folded her hands in her lap and watched him.

"I think you're supposed to elevate your ankle."

Mike scowled. He tried to lift his ankle onto the armrest but was too close, so he used his good foot to push himself back. He slid off the pillow and winced when the rough surface of the old couch aggravated the shallow lacerations on his butt. He got his right foot situated on the armrest and tried to twist his body to take the pressure off his left butt cheek. The pillow was in his way, so he tossed it onto the floor. He was working hard to get comfortable when he noticed Tyler standing in the open front door with a red-and-white plastic box in his hands.

"That looks uncomfortable." Tyler shook his head and chuckled. "But you need to turn over onto your stomach so I can take a look," Joyce said. "You cut your butt."

"Turn over?" Mike did not move. "Really?"

"Tell him what you were doing when you fell on your butt, Mike."

Mike flushed and did not say anything.

"The genius here was going to run up and down the hall."

"I'm not surprised. On your stomach, genius."

Tyler knelt by the couch and waited while Mike struggled to maneuver himself onto his stomach without banging his ankle or scraping his butt. Tyler started to pull Mike's running shorts down to inspect the cuts, but Mike grabbed the waistband and gestured toward Joyce with his head.

"What?" Tyler said, pulling his hands back. "Oh, I figured you and Joyce had..." He glanced over his shoulder at Joyce. "Never mind."

"Had already what, *Coach*?" Joyce was standing up with her fists on her hips.

"Um…" Tyler stuttered. "Um. Nothing… Maybe you had better wait in the kitchen."

Joyce spun around and slammed the front door as she left. A framed picture of a much younger Mike crashed to the floor behind the couch, but Mike didn't hear any glass break this time.

44

Confused by Mike's lack of perception and disappointed by Tyler's crass assumption, Joyce hurried toward home with her head down and her arms crossed. As she approached the high school, James honked his horn as he sped past her toward town. He made a U-turn and parked in front of the building with the passenger-side tires on the sidewalk. Joyce was about to turn back toward Mike's, but when James made no move to get out of the truck, she approached the passenger side and stopped two steps back from the open window.

"What are you doing here, James?"

"I parked up the road from Mike's house and waited until you left."

"Do you want me to get into your truck, James?"

He was quiet for a long moment and then said, "Yes. Please."

"I need to ask you something first."

"Okay."

"Are you going to leave me on the side of the road again?"

"No."

When Joyce climbed into the truck's cab, the first thing she saw was the cedar box on the seat next to James.

"That's a nice box, James. Did you make it?"

"It doesn't matter who made it." James did not take his eyes off the road.

"It does matter. James, things like that matter." Joyce was not sure what to say next. So, she remained silent for a long moment. "So, what's in the box?"

"The gun used to shoot Junior."

"Really, James? Is it the same gun you...?"

"Yeah. The one I used to shoot at Mike."

He put the truck in gear and drove up the highway past Mike's house toward the mountains.

James drove Joyce out of town and stopped the truck in the middle of the bridge above Silver Falls. In the gathering darkness, he could hear the water rushing over the granite boulders far below. The falls and the river downstream were shrouded in the greenish shadow cast by the steep cliffs that rose on either side, even though the sky still held some light. He got out of the truck and held the cedar box in both hands. Joyce slid out of the passenger side and joined him at the railing. As he was about to fling the box off the bridge, Joyce grabbed his arm.

"Don't, James." She jerked the box out of his hands, and the gun rattled around inside. Then she gently opened the lid and removed the gun. It felt cold and unfamiliar in her hand. She gripped the gun by the barrel and pointed it at James. "This is not who you are." Then she lowered the gun and held the box up. "This is."

He stared at the box for several seconds, then reached out, took the gun from her, and shoved it into his back pocket. Then she handed him the cedar box. He walked around the front of the truck and climbed up into the driver's seat.

* * *

Joyce put both hands on the railing and carefully peered over into the damp abyss. She pulled herself forward until her waist rested against the railing and leaned as far out as she dared. The frigid mist roiling up from Silver Falls felt good against her face, but she was surprised by a vague, rotten-fish smell that came with it.

She bent at the waist and gripped the railing with both hands as her feet lifted off the concrete walkway. She released her grip and spread her arms, weightless, as she balanced above the falls. Joyce closed her eyes. *And to the woman were given two wings of a great eagle, that she might fly, into the wilderness, into her place... Revelations, 12:14.*

She pushed herself back, walked to James's truck, and climbed into the passenger seat.

"Okay," she said. "*Maybe* it's a start."

"Maybe. Maybe I don't know how to be anyone else."

James drove back through town, took the familiar left onto Scout Lake Road, and stopped at the head of Joyce's driveway. When she moved to get out of the truck, he touched her on the shoulder. When she turned around, he attempted to hand her the cedar box.

She put her hand on the box and said, "I can't... It doesn't seem right. It's too...you should keep it."

James looked down at the box and then pulled it back. He looked hurt.

"I'm sorry, James."

"Can we talk again?"

"Of course… Whenever you like."

James turned his head and stared out through the windshield. The light was fading, and Joyce's house was dark except for a bright light on the porch and a duller glow through a small window in the front door.

She climbed out of the truck and closed the door. But before he could back out of the driveway, she turned back and stepped up to the open passenger-side window. The box was on the seat next to James. She reached into her cloth book bag and pulled out her Bible. She reached through the window and placed it on the seat where she had been sitting. "This might help, James. You can give it back the next time I see you."

James picked up Joyce's Bible, stared at it, and then put it inside the cedar box. The Bible fit perfectly. She turned and walked up the driveway with the empty cloth bag dangling from her shoulder.

45

JOYCE HAD BEEN THINKING LONG and hard about what she should tell Mike about her ride onto the bridge with James, but she had decided to wait. She knew James was not likely to say anything about their nascent, if awkward, friendship since she was so far outside his normal delinquent circle of acquaintances.

Joyce was not ashamed, and she did not concern herself with what Mike or anyone else thought or might say. She also knew any attempt to convince James to have a change of heart and not worry about what people expected of him would disintegrate at the first whisper of disapproval or uncertainty.

She talked to Pastor Clem about James but never mentioned the situation to anyone else.

"He left me on the side of the road and drove away the first time."

Pastor Clem frowned. He was tolerant of the hormonal influences teenagers often succumbed to but disdainful of behavior that put other kids at risk.

"What happened this last time?"

Joyce and Pastor Clem often talked in his study on the first floor of the parsonage, an ancient house next to the church with cramped rooms and a narrow staircase. The overhead light in Pastor Clem's study was seldom lit, and the single shaded lamp on his desk emitted an eerie glow that diminished as it radiated into the narrow room.

Floor-to-ceiling bookshelves covered two walls, each shelf crammed with scholarly tracts, religious histories, and eschatology. Spiritual biographies intermingled with trashy westerns and lurid detective novels. Against a third wall, old magazines stacked to the ceiling parted like the Red Sea around an unframed portrait of Christ.

Joyce's first impression upon entering the room was of deep shadow with an acute brilliance at the center and the smell of old paper and ink. She was aware of the portrait of Christ but had a hard time making out the details of the mysterious face. She sat in a comfortable straight-backed chair. Pastor Clem leaned back in his squeaky office chair on the other side of the desk, his face obscured by the shadow cast by the desk lamp.

Pastor Clem's study was Joyce's favorite place.

"Nothing happened," Joyce told Pastor Clem. "We drove out toward the mountains, but he parked in the middle of the bridge above the falls."

"*Parked*, Joyce?"

"Not *parked*. He stopped the truck and left the engine running."

"After what happened the first time, it may not have been wise to ride in James's truck a second time. The boy does have a rather unsavory reputation."

Sometimes, Pastor Clem used words that made Joyce smile. She had always thought of *savory* having to do with food. She tried to come up with her own tasty metaphor, but nothing came to mind.

"It would have been a long walk back to town," he said. "You're a brave girl, but sometimes, it's better to be smart."

"When he first stopped in front of the high school, I almost turned around and went back to Mike's house. I could have gotten a ride home with Coach Tyler. Or I could have apologized to Mike."

"Why didn't you?"

That was the question, wasn't it? Joyce did not trust adolescent impulses. The problems her school and church friends struggled with—the drama of relationships, the pressure of adult expectations, the guilt, uncertainty, and anxiety, the wasted emotional energy spent worrying about the past, present, and future—were the inevitable result of ceding authority to impulse. Joyce believed in both the blessings of desire and in the danger of instinct.

Still...

"It felt like... I knew it was the right thing to do."

"And you trust what you know rather than your feelings?"

"Should I not?" Joyce asked, a wee bit defiant.

Pastor Clem smiled. "What did you talk about? Did you give him your *testimony*?"

There was the edge of a sneer in Pastor Clem's voice, and Joyce wasn't sure if he was mocking her or issuing a challenge. She decided to respond to the challenge.

"That night at Junior's, James tried to force me into the back seat of his truck."

Pastor Clem shifted in his chair and looked Joyce in the face. His hands were tented against his lips, and he nodded for her to continue.

"The next day, when I was coming out of the church, he

tried to apologize. He said he wouldn't have done anything. I told him he didn't have to be the way he is. That he's not the kind of person everyone thinks he is."

"What did he say to that?"

"Nothing that time. He just drove off."

"What did he say this last time?"

"Not much. He just listened. I told him the same thing. That it doesn't matter what anyone else thinks about him."

Joyce waited for Pastor Clem to say something. He remained silent and attentive, so Joyce continued.

"He got back in the truck and said he didn't know how to be anyone else. I thought that was a strange thing to say, that he didn't know how."

Pastor Clem smiled. "What did you tell him?"

"That anyone can learn, anyone can change. But I think he'll need help. Will you talk to him?"

Pastor Clem leaned forward and stared into the circle formed by his arms and clasped hands. Then, without looking up, he said, "I'm very proud of you, Joyce."

"Proud?"

"You may have been foolish to get into James's truck a second time, but you wisely told the boy the truth. And I think he does need to talk to someone, but I'm not the right person."

"Then who is the right person?"

"Salvation doesn't always take place in church, Joyce. Sometimes, salvation and the church are at odds. Often, a believer must leave the sanctuary, the safety of the congregation, to do God's work."

Pastor Clem stood up, and Joyce decided not to tell him about the gun or her Bible.

46

OVER THE NEXT SEVERAL WEEKS, Mike spent every lunch period with his foot and ankle submerged in an icy tub in Tyler's tiny office. A thick, rubber sleeve protected his toes from frostbite. Mike had told Tyler he had sprained his ankle while running, but he'd said nothing about Joyce or James or the gun or how he got home. He did not have much to say about anything. But he did listen when Tyler talked about rehabbing the ankle. Joyce was there most days, and Mike had asked her not to say anything about James or the gun.

The lacerations on Mike's butt turned out to be minor, and they healed at about the same rate as his ankle, but he was still careful about how he sat and where he stepped.

After two weeks, Dr. Magnuson told Mike, "You can walk on your ankle as much as the pain allows—but walking on it is going to hurt."

"I don't mind." Mike shrugged.

Mike discarded his crutches but limping around school was still painful and awkward. Most teachers were sympathetic and would let Mike leave class early to avoid the crush of students racing to get to their next class. And even though he managed to get around a little better each day, his ankle throbbed if he could not elevate it.

Joyce continued to show up and stand against the wall with her arms folded while Mike iced his ankle in Tyler's office. She would watch while Mike removed his shoe and sock and plunged his foot and ankle into a tub of ice. Each time, he'd grimace and cringe, and Joyce would smile.

"You love this, don't you?" Mike said.

"I won't lie. Maybe the ice is penance for the way you acted when I tried to help after you cut your butt."

Mike frowned and stared into the tub as his foot and ankle went numb, and Tyler tried to talk to him about running. After twenty minutes, he would pull his foot out of the ice, put his sock and shoe back on, and limp out of the office. Joyce would follow a few seconds later.

After another couple of weeks, Mike was walking with less of a limp, and the cuts on his butt had healed enough that he could sit in class without having to squirm onto his right butt cheek. But for some reason, Mike became more sullen and more distant as the time when he'd be able to run again got closer.

One day, as Mike iced his ankle, Tyler said, "You'll be able to run in a week or two."

"Whatever. It don't matter."

Joyce pushed herself off the wall and took a tentative step in Mike's direction. "Mike, it does—"

"It. Don't. Matter."

Mike pulled his foot out of the tub and limped out of Tyler's office, carrying his shoe and sock. Joyce followed his single damp footprint and found him sitting on the top step of a steep stairway at the back of the building staring at a heavy steel door at the bottom of the steps. The door was much wider and heavier than normal and had a fading yellow-and-black sign that read *Fall-out Shelter*. Joyce sat down next to Mike, careful not to get too close.

"What do you think is down there?" Mike said, nodding toward the sign.

"My mom said there's a bomb shelter. They used to have drills. Everyone had to go down to the basement. In case the Russians dropped a bomb."

"On Silverton?"

"Mom said it might be an improvement." Joyce smiled. "And my dad said there are big green boxes and barrels that were supposed to have food and water, just in case. But later, someone found out the boxes had always been empty."

"Hmm. Empty." Mike stared down at the heavy door and shook his head.

"The boxes and barrels were supposed to make the kids feel safe."

"But they were empty. Typical."

Joyce scooted a little closer to Mike. He did not move away.

"I guess people will believe just about anything," she said, "if it makes them feel safe."

47

THE BELL SIGNALING the end of lunch rang, and Joyce stood. Mike slipped his shoe on and left it untied. He stumbled when he tried to stand on his sore ankle, so Joyce offered her hand. He hesitated and then took it. Mike shuffled down the hallway and out the double doors at the back of the building. He leaned against the railing with his shoe in one hand and his sock in the other while the frantic hoard of kids returning from lunch attacked the building. When the crowd cleared, he sat on the steps and put his shoe and sock back on.

"Mike, you need to get to class. Do you need help?" Mr. Thompson asked, coming to stand behind Mike.

Eyes stinging, he looked up at Mr. Thompson and then stood and stared across the parking lot.

Thompson spoke again. "It looks like you're getting around better. But you need to get to class."

From behind him and just inside the open double doors, Mike heard Joyce say, "No, Mr. Thompson. He doesn't need to get to class."

Thompson swung around and said, "Young lady, you need to—"

But Joyce was already headed down the stairs to join Mike.

She said nothing and did not touch him. Instead, she stood next to him and looked out toward the green-clad mountains beyond the parking lot. Thompson stepped back, just inside the double doors.

Mike turned toward Joyce. "They thought they were safe, but it was a lie."

"Typical," Joyce said.

"I need to go home and then..."

Joyce nodded once, put her hand on Mike's shoulder, and turned away. She walked up the stairs past Thompson and turned down the hall toward her next class.

"Go on home, Mike," the principal said.

Mike stood and walked carefully down the stairs and then jogged toward his truck in the parking lot, listing only a little to the left.

* * *

The next day at the beginning of lunch, Joyce was nearby as Mike hobbled toward Tyler's office, moving slowly but barely limping. She caught up with Mike and was at his side when the sea of adolescent humanity parted, and Pork lumbered down the center of the crowded hallway with Tall Paul in his wake. Mike shuffled sideways to let them pass, and his still tender ankle tipped to the outside. Joyce took his arm as he hopped backward and leaned against the wall to let the pain subside.

Pork stopped and smirked. Mike flipped him off, but

Joyce stepped in front of Pork when he took a menacing step in Mike's direction.

"Go away, Pork." She crossed her arms and stared up at him. "Leave him alone."

Behind her, Mike pushed himself off the wall and stood up straight on both legs.

Joyce became aware that a small crowd had formed a semicircle to watch the confrontation, but the expectant gathering began to disperse when Mr. Sorenson came down the hall. She was not surprised when Sorenson slipped into his empty classroom and watched from the safety of the open door. Pork raised his hands to shove Joyce out of the way, but Tall Paul grabbed the back of his shirt and pulled him back.

"Sorenson's watching," Tall Paul said. "We should go."

Pork backed away with Tall Paul still tugging on his shirt. Pork pointed at Mike over the top of Joyce's head and backed away down the hall.

Joyce put her hand on Mike's arm and said, "Are you okay?"

Mike shook his head. "James is not in school anymore, so I didn't think I'd have to fight."

"You don't have to fight them. You don't *have* to fight."

Mike looked at her for a few seconds and shook his head again. He shrugged her hand away and headed down the hall toward Tyler's office. As she followed, Joyce noticed he was limping a little more than before.

Joyce followed Mike into Tyler's office and stood in the corner.

Mike plunged his foot into the ice, but after a few seconds, he said, "Screw it all...just screw it," and stormed out of Tyler's office with his shoe and sock in his hand and no trace of a limp.

"Someone needs to talk to him," Tyler said. "He's not listening to me, Joyce. Can you talk to him?"

"We talked a little at lunch yesterday."

"That's good. About what?"

"The bomb shelter."

"There's a bomb shelter?"

"Yeah. There's a bomb shelter. My mom and dad say there used to be empty food boxes and empty water barrels in the basement. I thought that was strange, but Mike just shook his head and said it was *typical*."

* * *

Mike grabbed two blankets off his bed, jerked a hooded sweatshirt off a hanger in his closet, and crammed everything into an old canvas backpack. He had running shorts on under his jeans, and his extra pair of running shoes dangled off the bottom of the pack. He found two semi-dry T-shirts in a pile of laundry in the hall and added them to the collection stuffed into the backpack. He grabbed a bag of cookies in the kitchen, a jar of instant coffee, an unopened pound of bacon, and a box of matches. He shoved everything into the backpack.

He found a metal cup and a warped frying pan in a dented mess kit his father had probably brought home from the Army from a shelf in the cluttered garage. Both went into the backpack.

He strode from the garage, tossed the backpack into the front seat of his truck, and climbed up into the driver's seat. He paused at the end of the short driveway and stared for a long time in both directions before turning right onto the Mountain Loop Highway.

When he reached the turnoff to Abel, he stopped the

truck and peered down the gravel road. He didn't think he could get past the guard at the general store, so he decided to take a more indirect approach...the trail from Snow Lake over the ridge and down into Abel.

When he arrived at the Snow Lake trailhead, he parked his truck well off the road. He shouldered the backpack and hefted it a couple of times, trying to find a comfortable position, but the haphazard nature of its contents made comfort an unreasonable goal.

As soon as school ended for the day, Joyce went to Mike's house. His truck was gone, so she sat on the porch until the temperature began to drop and then went inside to wait. She sat on the couch for almost an hour before going into Mike's room. Mike kept an extra pair of running shoes in his closet because winters in western Washington were so wet, it was impossible to keep a single pair dry.

Mike's extra shoes were gone.

She sat on his bed and stroked his uncovered pillow. The tenderness she felt for him was stronger than ever. She could see he'd left, and she knew where he'd gone. She needed help, so she walked back into town.

Joyce stopped on the sidewalk outside James's house. She did a quick double-take to make sure she was in the right place because the peeling picket fence had been repaired and painted, and the gate rehung. The front of the house had also been painted. The ancient dingy orange was now covered by a sedate gray, with the windows trimmed in white. On the front porch, carpenter tools lay neatly arranged next to a sawhorse, which straddled a pile of sawdust swept into a neat pyramid.

What had James been up to?

Joyce lifted the new latch on the gate and walked toward the house. She paused at the steps to see if she could figure out what the tools had been used for. Just as her foot hit the first step, James emerged from the house. Joyce had not seen him since the night she'd given him her Bible, but he seemed different. He was barefoot, and his pants sagged. James normally wore his hair in a tight buzz, but now it reached his ears, curling away from his head on the left side.

He had Joyce's Bible in his hand as he walked to the edge of the porch. Joyce stepped back onto the sidewalk.

She wanted to ask him what he'd been reading in her Bible because the first thing she noticed when he stepped out of the hose was that he had marked his place with his index finger. James hadn't returned to school for the remainder of his senior year. Joyce had heard all the ridiculous rumors: He was on drugs or in jail, gotten a girl in another town pregnant, and even that he might be dead. But she'd also seen the work that had been done on James's house and was certain Ollie had done none of it.

Joyce had overheard adults at school say all sorts of things about James, now that he was not at school.

"Always knew he was a loser," Mr. Sorenson had said.

"What does he think life will be like without an education?" Mr. Thompson had muttered.

Joyce ignored what the gossipy kids said. Gossips of whatever age never knew what they were talking about, but she didn't like what she heard from the grownups.

So, she'd asked Pastor Clem about it.

.   .   .

Pastor Kevin had been in Pastor Clem's office when Joyce came by. She'd wanted him to leave, but Pastor Clem had motioned for her to sit. Kevin had stood directly behind Pastor Clem, looking down at Joyce. Joyce had looked up at Kevin and then across the desk at Pastor Clem, who motioned for her to proceed.

"I haven't seen James for a long time, but he has my Bible," she'd told the pastor.

Pastor Clem had started to say something, but Kevin jumped in first.

"Joyce, I think you have a thing for bad boys."

Pastor Clem had rolled his eyes and then looked straight at Joyce. "Bad boys, Kevin?"

"I think Joyce knows what I mean. But, Joyce, you need to be careful who you associate with. You will become like the five people you spend the most time with."

Then I'll make it a point to spend less time with you, she'd thought.

Pastor Clem had continued to look across his desk at Joyce. "Who do you think she should spend time with, Pastor Kevin?"

"Matthew, Mark, Luke, and John," Kevin replied.

Pastor Clem had rubbed the bridge of his nose with his thumb. "That's only four, Kevin."

"And Paul," Kevin had added. "Can't forget Paul."

Pastor Clem had folded his hands and stared hard at Joyce.

"What about Jesus?" she'd said.

Kevin had started to respond, but Pastor Clem held up his hand.

"Most kids like James figure things out, but they need help. If I were you, Joyce, I'd pay attention because I don't suspect anyone else is."

. . .

Still on the sidewalk in front of James's house, Joyce started to speak. "I need—"

But she stopped talking when James reached out to hand her the Bible.

"No, James," she said. "I need your help. I need you to take me somewhere. I need a ride."

James held up his hand, a signal for her to wait. "Just a minute." He went back into the house and closed the door.

Joyce did not move. When James returned after about five minutes, he had changed into clean jeans, and his dingy T-shirt had been replaced by a new-looking red flannel shirt. His newly shaggy hair was covered by an old baseball cap with a Scott Paper logo above the brim.

He walked past Joyce and then stopped and turned back. "Let's go."

"Don't you want to know where?" she said. "This might take a while."

"I got time. Let's go."

James climbed into the driver's seat of his truck. Joyce hesitated, wondering whether she was pushing her luck. She shoved her misgivings aside and climbed into the passenger seat.

"Have you got a flashlight? We might have to do some hiking in the dark."

James reached under the seat and pulled out a three-foot-long Maglite. He flipped the flashlight on and shined the bright light into Joyce's eyes.

"Jeez, James..." Joyce squeezed her eyes shut and turned her head away.

"That bright enough?" James flipped the light off. He set the flashlight on the seat and started the truck. "Where to?"

Joyce was still wary of James. "You might not like it."

James turned toward Joyce and lowered his voice. "Don't matter." Then he repeated, "Where to?"

"You don't have to help me."

Joyce pushed the passenger-side door open and started to get out of the truck, but James reached across the seat and gently grabbed her arm.

"Then why'd you ask me to help? Where to, Joyce?"

Joyce pulled the door closed and leaned back against the seat.

"Mike has disappeared. Well, not disappeared, but he left school at lunch, and he's not at home."

THE SUN WAS SETTING, but Mike had just enough daylight left when he reached Snow Lake to set up his minimal camp. The lake was deep and clear, fed by snowmelt and half a dozen small streams that trickled down and filled the hollow formed when a glacier had receded. The remnant of the glacier, thinning and softening as it inched its way down the steep moraine separating the lake from the valley where Abel was located, was still visible at the far end of the egg-shaped lake.

A little-used trail forked off to the left, and even though the underbrush at this elevation was sparse, Mike knew that trail petered out after about half a mile, replaced by an impassable animal track.

Mike took the trail to the right. The Forest Service maintained the trail and carved out several crude camp-sites along the western shore. During the summer, campers needed a reservation from the ranger station at Verlot to reserve a campsite, but by November and December, the temperature might plunge to below freezing overnight, and rain or snow was a near certainty.

So, Mike did not expect to see any other campers at Snow Lake.

The sun had dropped below the ridge to the southwest and took the temperature down with it. Mike set his backpack on the ground and pulled on his hooded sweatshirt. He shouldered the pack again and walked another quarter mile. The first campsite he came to was little more than a wide patch of dirt covered with fir needles and cedar fronds surrounding a rock circle placed by the Forest Service to form a crude fire pit.

Mike set his pack down against a large log facing the lake about ten feet from the fire pit and began the crucial task of finding firewood. He began by gathering several handfuls of twigs covered with moss. There had been no rain for two days, so the dry moss would make adequate tinder, and the twigs were excellent kindling. He laid the moss and twigs at the bottom of the fire pit. Next, he scoured the area beyond the campsite for larger wood, blown-down branches or logs other campers might have thought were too long to use for firewood.

He crisscrossed several small fir boughs on top of the kindling. It took several more trips, each farther into the lengthening shadows, to find enough wood to build a fire that would last the night.

By the time he returned to camp for the last time and struck a match to the moss, it was dark. Mike nursed the tentative sparks in the tinder into an earnest flame and breathed on it until the kindling crackled and the small sticks at the top ignited.

While he waited for the fire to build itself up enough to add proper fuel, Mike removed one of the blankets from the pack, folded it, and placed it across the log. He sat on the ground and leaned back against the blanket and rubbed the ache out of his thighs, satisfied with the steep hike. He looked up at the sky and was gratified and relieved to see stars. To the east, the rising full moon cast eerie shadows among the trees.

Mike rested for several minutes and then got up to add more fuel to the growing fire. He placed a seven-foot-long log across the rock circle of the fire pit. When the log burned all the way through at the center, he would be able to shove both ends of the log into the fire and replace it with another long log, then another, to keep the fire going all night.

Sitting with his back against the log, he was close enough to the fire to stay warm, even as the temperature continued to drop. After an hour, the moon rose above the trees, and the shadows were replaced by the pale reflection of moonlight off the lake.

Mike's campsite was bathed in the reflected moonlight, and when a breeze rippled the surface of the lake, the light fluttered into the camp like evanescent butterflies. Mike preferred the moonlight reflecting off the lake to the clear light of day. The light filtering through the trees or dancing off the surface of the lake revealed just enough.

Sometimes it's better not to see everything.

Mike did not care for introspection. Yes, he often wondered about things when he ran, but generally he kept his mind occupied with more immediate concerns. How far did he have to go? How steep was the next hill? Should he run hard or take it easy? During the weeks he'd been unable to run, when he'd been unshielded by the familiar fatigue, questions had begun to haunt him in the long minutes before he fell asleep each night.

What happened between my mother and father? No answer. *What will happen between James and me? James has disap-*

peared from school, and Joyce seems to know something about that. But what? No answer.

What about Joyce? No answer.

Before his injury—when he could still run—each day had organized itself around that certainty, the one thing he understood and could rely on, even if the purpose of his daily pilgrimage onto the roads and into the hills was a mystery to everyone else.

Everyone except Joyce.

Mike thought about how he'd treated Joyce and about how she had probably prevented him from getting into more trouble when she'd stood up to Pork. *She even talked back to Thompson.* And he wondered if Joyce had anything to do with the fact his James problem seemed to have been, if not resolved, at least postponed.

No, Mike did not care for introspection because private emotion seemed pointless. But as he sat on the cedar stump, he realized he was capable of private guilt as far as Joyce was concerned. And he recognized he should do nothing to cause more damage to Joyce's opinion of him.

The fire had settled. Mike munched on a cookie and watched the reflection of the moon make its way across the lake. He thought about how long it would take the fire to settle enough to cook the bacon in his backpack when a glimmer of light from the trail startled him. He stood up, stepped gingerly over the log, skulked about thirty feet into the dark of the forest, and hid behind a tree.

50

JOYCE, uncharacteristically impulsive, had brought along nothing to keep her warm on a cold night in the mountains. She had only the raincoat that had been in her locker and the hooded sweatshirt she'd been wearing when she left school.

"I got a blanket in the back seat," James said. "Better than nothin', I guess."

Joyce wanted to ask James why he kept a blanket in his truck but decided she didn't really want to know.

It had been nearly dark when they left Silverton, but James did not turn on his headlights until they were about a mile from the trailhead. Joyce was struck by how the tunnel of light enhanced the gloom beyond the headlights. She hadn't thought about what they were going to do until the dark had settled completely. As the daylight dissipated, the forest and the dense underbrush along the road seemed to become impenetrable.

. . .

James pulled into the turnout at the trailhead and parked behind Mike's truck. He started to get out, but Joyce grabbed his sleeve.

"Will we be able to see well enough to get to the lake? How will we find Mike? What if there's someone else up there?"

Like most boys who grew up in Silverton, James knew his way around the woods and was disgusted how little some kids, like Joyce, knew about the woods. She had lived on the verge of the mountains her entire life but apparently had never left the safety of the paved roads.

"I got this." He flashed the Maglite in Joyce's face again. "It's a good trail, and there's a full moon. If Mike's got a brain at all, he'll have a fire going. It's almost fu—freakin' winter, so no one else is going to be up there."

Joyce followed James up the trail. The powerful Maglite provided ample illumination for James, but if Joyce got more than eight or ten feet behind him, she lost sight of the ground. Although she walked to and from school every day and preferred to walk to get from place to place in town, she was not prepared for the strenuous first mile.

By the time they reached an old cedar stump next to the trail, she had to beg James to stop. She sat on the stump, and James leaned on a tree on the other side of the trail. Joyce had felt a little better when James mentioned the full moon. She had visions of summer nights when the moon was bright enough to read by in the backyard. But here in the deep woods, moon shadow obscured the trail, and the trees morphed into eerie, ever-changing shapes that combined with the nighttime forest's covert sounds to create in Joyce a shallow sense of dread.

She was scared. But... *Faith is easy in daylight*, Pastor Clem had told her once. *In the light of day, we can see a threat coming. The world does not change in the dark, but we no longer see it for what it is. We think we need protection, but what we really need is faith. Faith that the world is as it should be. Dark or not.*

Joyce stood up. "How much longer?"

"About thirty minutes if we don't stop. It's not so steep from here."

James led the way up the trail, but Joyce stayed back a little this time, watching his back and feeling the ground with her feet. When clouds covered the moon, she was disconcerted by the woods' total blackness, and she was still afraid. Yet, despite her fear, she followed James until they reached the boggy, northern end of the lake.

James pointed to the orange glow of a campfire visible roughly a quarter-mile away.

That's gotta be him," James said.

Joyce took the flashlight from James and led the way up the trail toward Mike's camp.

"He's not here." Joyce scanned the entire campsite with the Maglite. She stopped when the light reached the log. Mike's backpack leaned against the log, and the orange and black blanket had been folded across the top. Joyce picked up the blanket. "This is the blanket from Mike's bed."

"Really?"

Joyce turned the Maglite on James, illuminating his smug smile, and her cheeks grew hot. She turned the light back on the log and then raised it to scan the woods.

"Mike?" Joyce did not shout.

She continued to scan the woods with the Maglite until Mike stepped out from behind a tree, shielding his eyes.

When she lowered the light, James stepped up close behind her and little to her side.

Mike strode into the campsite, but when he stepped over the log, his injured foot turned over, and he had to bounce on one leg to regain his balance. Joyce started toward Mike, but James grabbed her arm and pulled her back. She jerked herself free and stepped forward to help Mike.

He sat on the log and reached down to massage the outside of his left ankle. James retreated a couple of steps.

"Jesus, Joyce," Mike said, shaking his head. "What are you doing up here? And what is he doing here?"

James stepped forward and stood looking down at Mike. "Look, motherfu—" Whatever he'd intended to say trailed off in the dark, and he stretched the fingers on both hands to keep them from closing into fists.

Mike stood and started to step toward James, but Joyce, for the second time, stepped between Mike and a potential adversary. This time, she was facing Mike.

"I was worried when you left school," she said. "You didn't come back to school, so I came to find you. And I needed help. You looked...hurt." She had started to say *lost*.

She realized she was standing close enough to James to feel his hips against her butt, so she shuffled a half step toward Mike and James took a step back. "I had an idea where you might go. If your truck hadn't been down at the turnout, we'd have gone back and taken the road to Abel. I needed a ride either way."

Mike stared past Joyce at James. "Maybe I'm not going to Abel at all. Maybe I just wanted to be by myself."

James met Mike's eyes, then moved back to the other side of the fire pit, squatted on his haunches, and stared into the fire with the blanket from his truck clutched to his chest. After a few seconds, he set the blanket on the ground, moved to the far side of the campsite, and leaned against a tree just inside the limit of the orange light cast by the fire.

Mike continued to watch James until Joyce nudged him a step or two backward so he had to either sit on the log or trip over it.

51

MIKE REMAINED ON THE LOG, staring at the ground, and Joyce stood over him. She turned slightly to watch James.

"So? What *are* you doing up here?" Mike said again. "It's dark. You don't do dark. Nice, Christian girls don't do dark. But whatever, I see *James* has a flashlight."

"What is that supposed to mean?" Tears welled up in Joyce's eyes and spilled out onto her cheeks. When she looked down at Mike sitting on the log, tears dripped onto his jeans and formed damp, dime-sized circles. "When are you going to get a clue? Jesus Christ, Mike, can't you see? You're the one in the dark."

Joyce instinctively searched her mind for a dependable Bible verse. *Sight*? *Vision*? *Revelation*? *Light*? Nothing came, so she squeezed her hands into fists and placed them on Mike's shoulders. "It's not that dark."

James stood and stepped away from the tree, but Joyce held Mike down with her hands on his shoulders. James took another step toward the fire, and when Mike tried to sweep Joyce's hands away, she pushed him hard enough that he tumbled backward off the log with his butt on the ground on one side and his feet on the other.

"Stay there." She pointed at him and then wiped her cheek with her sleeve. "This is not why I followed you up here."

Mike pushed himself back up onto the log.

James started to step around the fire, but Joyce turned on him. "You're not helping, James." Joyce stepped back to keep Mike from standing up. "You said you'd help."

James picked up the blanket and backed away from the fire. Scattered raindrops began to bounce off the hard dirt of the campsite, making the fire hiss.

"If you're done with me, I can head back down the hill," James said. He held up the Maglite. "Remember? I got a flashlight." He lowered the Maglite and looked off into the dark woods.

"No." Joyce stepped away from Mike.

He stood up but stayed behind her. The light rain caused the ashen scent of an old forest fire to drift out of the woods, and the campfire continued to hiss.

James retreated to a spindly fir tree about ten feet from the fire. "You think to bring a tent, Mike?"

From behind Joyce, Mike put his hands on her shoulders, but she still felt defeated. She shivered and hugged her raincoat around herself. Mike bent down and pulled the other blanket out of his backpack and handed it to her. She wrapped it around her shoulders and felt warmer at once.

"I guess I don't need a tent," Mike said. "Pretty dry under here."

Joyce pulled the blanket tighter and sat on the ground. She leaned against the log and pulled her knees up inside the blanket.

Joyce could see that James was getting wet under the

inadequate fir tree. She looked up at Mike. He put his hand on her cheek and nodded.

"Give me a hand," Mike said to James.

Mike picked up one end of a fifteen-foot-long log. James hesitated and then took the other end. Together, they placed the log on the fire so it would burn into two shorter lengths.

Joyce looked up at James and patted the ground. James wrapped the wool blanket around his shoulders and sat about three feet to one side of Joyce in the shelter of the grown-together cedars. Mike sat down closer to Joyce on her other side. He pulled a bag of cookies out of his pack, took two for himself, and then passed the bag across Joyce's body to James. James grabbed two cookies and set the bag on the ground next to Joyce.

Even though it rained most of the night, the ground beneath the entwined cedar trees remained dry. James got up twice to keep the fire going, and during a lull in the rain, Mike rearranged his blanket to cover himself and Joyce, and she slid over until she was close enough to put her head on his shoulder and feel the warmth of his body.

52

DESPITE THE LIGHT rainfall most of the night, by sunrise, Mike, Joyce, and James were still dry, if not very well-rested. They were mostly silent as each, in turn, drifted off into the woods to pee. Mike went first and then James. Joyce hesitated when it was her turn, confiding to Mike while James was out of earshot that she had never peed outdoors.

"It's easy for guys," she said.

"I don't think I can help you there." Mike was shocked and a little disappointed that Joyce could live her entire life in Silverton without having learned to pee in the woods. "You'll figure it out, or you'll have to wait 'til we get to Abel, but maybe everyone there pees outdoors."

Joyce was not sure he was joking.

When James returned, Joyce trudged into the woods farther than was necessary. She agonized a little over the delicate task ahead of her. But, at the same time, she was awkwardly charmed by a nascent intimacy with Mike. Not so long ago, he had refused to let her examine the cuts on his butt, and now they were talking about outdoor peeing. She considered that progress of sorts.

When she returned from the woods, she went immediately to the lakeshore to rinse off her hands. James and Mike were eating the last of the cookies out of the bag. James took the last cookie, but instead of eating it, he offered it to Joyce. She shook her head, and he popped the cookie into his mouth before pouring the last of the crumbs into his mouth directly from the bag.

"It's really cold," Joyce said. "Can we get the fire going again?"

"We?" Mike smirked.

James began to stir the fire and stack small bits of leftover wood onto the embers.

"No time for that," Mike said. "You'll warm up when we get moving, Joyce."

"Moving?" James said. "Going back down?"

Joyce picked up the blanket from where she'd left it on the log and wrapped it around her shoulders again.

"Not down," Mike said. "Up. And over. We're going to Abel."

"We can go back down the way we came and then drive to Abel," James said.

"There's a guard on the road. We're going in the back way."

Before James could respond, a crashing noise followed by, "Crap on a cracker. I hate the woods," sounded from behind them. All three turned to look toward the trail.

"Jesus," James said. "It's Pork."

Mike finished stuffing his blanket into his backpack and then hefted it onto his shoulders. Tall Paul stumbled into the campsite with Pork huffing and puffing a few feet behind. Tall Paul stopped, and Pork shouldered past him to stand directly in front of James.

"James has got 'em both," Pork said to Tall Paul. "Let's get 'em. We'll take care of Beck, and James can finish up with her while we make Mike-effing-Beck watch."

Tall Paul pulled a tire iron out of his belt, the same one he'd thrown at Mike earlier, and tapped it against his leg, just as he had back in August. Pork started past James, but James put his hand in the middle of Pork's chest and stopped him.

"I don't know why anyone would want to go to Abel," he said without turning away from Pork, "but you'd better get moving. And these boys are going back down the trail."

"Bull crap!" Tall Paul threw the tire iron at Mike. He missed badly, and the makeshift weapon ricocheted off a tree and splashed into the lake. "Damn it!"

Mike started to laugh and took a step toward Tall Paul. Joyce grabbed Mike's arm and pulled him away from the campsite, and they hurried up the trail away from James and the boys.

Pork tried to slap James's hand off his chest, but James brought his other hand up and pushed Pork hard. Pork stumbled back a few steps. James followed and pushed him again, and this time, Pork tumbled backward and plunged into the lake.

James was soaked by the enormous splash, but he turned on Tall Paul, who was already backing away. James continued in his direction, but Tall Paul turned and began running away from the camp.

"Help, James! Help me! I can't swim!"

James turned back to the lake and watched Pork thrashing about in the shallow water.

"Stand up, peckerwood. It ain't that deep."

Pork stopped thrashing and sat still in about three feet of

water near the shore. "Oh... I ain't gonna drown. So...are we going after 'em?"

James watched as Pork rolled over onto his hands and knees and crawled out of the lake. He shook his head in disbelief and followed Tall Paul down the trail. Pork struggled to his feet, shivered once, and then waddled along behind James.

"Wait up, James. I got beer in the car."

53

MIKE AND JOYCE had heard the splash.

"What was that?" Joyce asked.

She started back toward the campsite, but this time, Mike grabbed her arm.

"Sounded like someone's big butt hitting the water."

"James?" She looked back in the direction they had just come.

"I doubt it. Probably Pork."

Mike started back up the trail, and after a few seconds, Joyce turned and followed. "Does it seem like James is..."

"Less of a jerk?" Mike said. "Maybe, yeah."

The trail remained flat along the lakeshore. Then it twisted and climbed for a half-mile past the diminishing glacier to the top of the ridge. From the top, they could see the lake and the highway, which snaked east along the bottom of the narrow Silver River Valley with Sauk Mountain on the far side.

Mike had taken a step or two down the other side, but Joyce stopped at the top of the ridge.

"Oh, my. Look how far you can see from here." This

time, her memory of the Bible did not fail her. "The fool hath said in his heart, 'There is no God'."

"What?" Mike stepped back up to where Joyce was standing.

"Psalms 14:1. The rest is something about corruption and abominable deeds. But I like the first part best."

"A fool, huh?"

Joyce touched Mike on the arm. The clouds were breaking up, and rain seemed at once a distant memory and a nearby possibility. A shaft of sunlight shining through a low break in the clouds flashed off the lake's mirrored surface, and Mike and Joyce had to avert their eyes.

Mike turned and started down the trail on the other side of the ridge. The switchbacks ended, and the trail reentered the woods. After half a mile, Mike stopped at an opening in the trees and pointed to the narrow valley less than half a mile below. Joyce could see perhaps two dozen houses with smoke rising from blackened, stovepipe chimneys protruding from green metal roofs.

"Do you think they're still there? Your mom and dad?"

"I don't know."

Mike started down the trail, but Joyce did not move. After a few steps, he stopped and turned back toward her.

"Joyce," he said. "I'm no fool."

The trail emptied into the town between what appeared to be the last two houses on a wide gravel street. As they headed down the street, Joyce noticed all the houses were nearly identical. The old-growth forest loomed ominously above the tiny town. Each house appeared to be one story with a little lawn, a neat porch, and two windows in front, one on each side of a red door. That every door should be red seemed odd to Joyce.

After they had passed half a dozen houses on each side

of the street, a green pickup truck appeared from the right and sped straight toward them fast enough to make Joyce nervous. She pulled Mike to the side of the street in front of one of the houses. Joyce noticed a curtain flutter in the window to the left of the door.

The truck stopped, and the same security man who had confronted Mike and Tyler back in June stepped down from the truck and crossed the street to where Mike and Joyce were standing.

"May I ask who you are and what you are doing here? This is a private community." The security man looked at Mike and nodded. "I know you. You were here last summer." He took a notebook from his pocket and thumbed the pages until he apparently found the entry he'd been searching for —no doubt the one for Mike and Tyler from back in June. "You were here with a man not much older than you are," he said, looking at the notebook. "You said you wanted to see where the road went. I told you that you needed to leave, and you did so without incident."

"Do you write everything down in that little book?" Mike said.

Joyce had retreated a half step.

"When I am on duty, yes."

"Well, then you probably have it written down that another man showed up on the same day or the day before."

The security man flipped back one page.

"That is true. How did you know that?"

Mike didn't answer.

"That man is his father," Joyce said. "We think he came here to meet up with Mike's mother, his wife."

The security man remained impassive. "Wait here." He returned to the truck and spoke through the window to a man in the passenger seat. When he finished speaking, the security man turned and leaned against the door.

The other man got out of the passenger side and slowly came around the front of the truck and stopped. He was old, taller than Mike, and very thin. The man put his hand on the fender and motioned with a walking stick for Mike and Joyce to approach. Mike did not move at first, but when Joyce started across the street, he followed.

"You must be Mike," the old man said. He did not appear ill, but he leaned heavily on the walking stick in his left hand, and his right hand fluttered slightly. "I suspect you're here to see Janine. She is your mother, after all."

Mike swallowed hard. "I haven't seen her for—"

"More than five years," the man said, knowingly. "Yes. It's time, I suppose. And I don't know who you are, young lady, but I've seen those green eyes before, so I think I can guess."

The old man told Mike and Joyce to climb into the back of the pickup and directed the security man to take them to see Janine. The old man did not get into the truck but headed toward the house across the street. He stopped in the middle of the street. "By the way," he said, "I'm Reverend Park. I used to be in charge around here. Say hello to Pastor Clem for me, won't you?"

By the time Joyce had thought to ask how he knew Pastor Clem, the old man had disappeared into the house.

54

THE SECURITY GUARD motioned for Mike and Joyce to get into the truck. He made a tight U-turn and headed back in the direction he had come and then stopped in front of a much larger house on an oversized lot with a neat lawn in front. The security man waited silently for them to get out of the truck and then drove away.

Mike and Joyce stood on the edge of the lawn and stared at the house. It was similar to the others, but the porch was wider, and there were two windows on each side of the red door. Mike waited and did not move until Joyce started up the gravel walkway that dissected the lawn. By the time Mike caught up and stood beside her, Joyce was knocking on the door. The door opened at once, and Robert stood in the doorway. Mike could see Janine sitting on a couch and a small girl playing on the floor. Even from the doorway and behind Joyce, when the child looked up, Mike could see she had green eyes.

"Mike? I...we didn't expect to see you." Robert remained in the doorway.

Mike looked past him and stared at his mother. At least,

he thought she was his mother. The woman stood up. She did not seem as tall as he remembered, and her hair was much longer. The girl remained on the floor, gathering several wooden toys and putting them into a tiny backpack. *The woman and the child from the trail.*

He turned sideways to get past his father. Robert moved out of the way, and Joyce followed Mike into the house. Mike stood just inside the door, and it was Joyce who approached Janine.

"Mrs. Beck? Janine?"

Janine said, "I was—um, I am. Yes."

Mike did not move. Janine looked up at him. Her lip trembled, but she did not cry.

"Janine?" Mike spit the word, and Janine took a step toward him. He stiffened and did not move.

"Who's the kid?" Mike's voice dripped with disdain. "You taking care of someone's kid? Better than you took care of your own, I hope."

Joyce turned toward him. "Mike. Stop. That's not why we came." She looked back to Janine and then motioned to the child still playing on the floor. "She's a cutie, for sure. Who is she?"

Janine sat back on the couch and folded her hands in her lap. "You're Joyce, yes?"

"Yes. I am."

"Joyce, this girl is Grace. She is…Mike's sister."

Mike's knees buckled, and he nearly fell over.

"And yours."

"Mine?" Joyce's draw dropped, and her mind raced.

She turned and looked at Mike, who had stepped back just outside the open door with his hand on the outside of the doorjamb. They stared at each other for a long moment before Mike began to turn away.

"Mike, wait," Joyce said.

He took his hand away from the jamb and took half a step back inside. Joyce dropped to her knees, placed her hand under the girl's chin, and raised the child's face.

"You have green eyes like me," she noted softly. Joyce looked closer, then withdrew her hand and brought it to her mouth. "And, Sweet Jesus, just like my dad."

Dodge's truck pulled up outside the big house in Abel. The door was still open, but Robert had retreated to the couch to sit next to Janine. Mike took another step into the house and leaned on the wall next to the door.

Dodge came up the walk, reached through the doorway, and knocked twice on the open door. Everyone in the room, except Grace, looked toward the open door and remained silent. Dodge stepped inside.

"Everything good here? No need for the law?" He smiled without warmth. "Mike, you good?"

Mike opened his mouth, but nothing came out.

Joyce stood.

Dodge told her, "Your dad's in my truck outside. He didn't want to come in."

Joyce left the house, marched to the truck, and stared at her father through the open driver's side window. "Does Mom know?"

Donald looked away. Joyce gripped the door with both hands.

"Does she?"

"Of course, she knows."

"And she didn't leave...she didn't—"

"No. She forgave me."

"She would forgive. Wouldn't she?"

Mike came out of the house and stood next to Joyce. "They're going to stay here, but Dodge told Robert to be home a couple of days a week so he doesn't have to haul me off to some foster family."

"And what about Grace?"

"She's *our* sister. Is that weird?" Mike jammed his hands into his pockets and shook his head.

Joyce turned and gazed through the still open door at the child playing on the floor. "Yeah. I think that qualifies as weird."

Joyce opened the back door of Dodge's truck and climbed into the back seat. She stayed on the driver's side and stared at her father through the screen. "What are you going to do, Mike?" She said, still staring at her father.

"I'm going to go get my truck and drive home."

Mike took off his shoes and jeans and tossed his jeans through the front window of Dodge's truck. He adjusted the waistband on the running shorts he always wore under his jeans and stuffed his feet back into his shoes. Without another word, Mike ran to the corner and turned left onto the same gravel street he and Joyce had walked down when they came into town. He ran into the woods and sped up as the trail rose in front of him. He reached the switchbacks and slowed a little when the trail narrowed, but then he sprinted over the top of the ridge, and with the endless vista of the lake and the distant mountains in front of him, he ran as hard as could down the other side.

His ankle held up, and by the time he reached his truck, he knew he was ready to run again in earnest.

55

Robert was true to his word. He showed up at the house outside Silverton at least two days a week, although he never spent the night, preferring to spend most of his time in Abel with Janine and Grace. Mike and Joyce spent at least one day a week, usually Sunday, in Abel. She was determined to get to know Grace, and Janine began trying to rebuild a tenuous relationship with her son. Mike's antipathy toward his parents had not cooled, but every time he saw Grace's green eyes, he felt an unfamiliar thrill of affection and thought of Joyce.

Ironically, while Mike was resistant to getting reacquainted with his mother, Joyce was trying to find some basis for maintaining a relationship with her father. Don apologized daily, but Joyce didn't want to hear it. Finally, Molly stepped in.

"Your father has done nothing he needs to apologize to you for. I've forgiven him, and he's done nothing, ever, to betray you."

Joyce understood what her mother saying in the abstract. But the up-close-and-personal reality of sin and disappointment was hard to meet face-to-face. Forgiveness was much easier from a distance.

Pastor Clem was even more blunt, and his admonition surprised her.

"Get over it, Joyce. If you need to forgive your father, forgive him before his sin eats *you* alive."

Joyce didn't like the metaphor, but she got the point.

* * *

Tyler did not ask Mike about his night in the woods or his visit to Abel. The only thing Mike told him was he was ready to run again. But Tyler insisted Mike see Dr. Magnuson before he resumed full-out training.

"I've never seen anyone recover this fast," Dr. Magnuson told Tyler as they watched Mike run around the track with no trace of a limp. "Remarkable. You take good care of that boy."

Dr. Magnuson and Tyler had decided it would be safer to run around the track than on the trails, where there was more danger of re-injuring his ankle. Mike did not mind. Without the distraction of traffic or unstable ground, he could get into a zone. On the track, he was conscious of nothing except the effort and the grass disappearing beneath his feet. He was even able to calculate his speed based on the number of steps he took each lap. And he discovered there was an optimal rhythm, the perfect combination of stride length and stride rate.

Grace had been a disruption. He felt something for her, something just on the affectionate side of ambivalence. But getting to know the child left him feeling unbalanced and off-center, as if every time he thought about how he should feel about Grace, he'd misstep and stumble and have to get up again and rethink the whole situation.

On the day after Christmas, Mike added a morning run at the track. By the first of the year, Dr. Magnuson told Tyler there was no need to restrict Mike's running to the track.

"But tell him to be careful," the doctor added.

The winter months on the western slopes of the Cascades were notorious for being dark and gloomy, but then after the months of cold rain and damp snow, the forest undergrowth would explode with green every spring. The new growth spilled onto the older trails, and Mike had to be extra cautious when he ran in the woods. He did stumble once or twice, but the ankle held up each time.

That year, the sun didn't shine in Silverton for the entire month of January, and the community fell into its annual damp funk, a sodden depression made worse by seasonal unemployment in the woods. And without James's enormous presence under the basket, the basketball team at the high school did not win a single game.

But Mike continued to run. Every day. Sometimes with Tyler, sometimes with a rangy sophomore who would run with Mike for as long as he could and then walk or jog back to school. The younger boy managed to keep up a little longer each time, and he didn't seem to mind when Mike increased the pace. Mike liked to test the younger runner and was pleased when he saw him running with Tyler or by himself on the days he didn't run with Mike.

James hadn't attended Silverton High since September, and in January, as Deputy Dodge had predicted, he dropped out of school officially. He avoided contact with Tall Paul and Pork and worked at his father's shop or on his mother's house while he waited for summer and a promised job setting chokers for his uncle.

Tall Paul and Pork were still at school and never missed an opportunity to let Mike know they were watching. The boys shared one class with Mike and would spend the entire period glaring at him. When they'd pass him in the hallway, Pork would drop his shoulder as if to hit Mike in the chest. Once, Tall Paul faked throwing a punch. Mike would have responded with a punch of his own, but Joyce had both hands on his right arm.

Mike continued his habit of eating his lunch in Tyler's tiny office in the gym basement. He never said so, but he was glad Joyce was there every day, too. Since that first kiss in Mike's truck, there had not been another. Mike became aware of a quiet equilibrium, a sort of emotional holding pattern that settled between him and Joyce during the dark days following his ankle injury and the tension over his lacerated butt. Most boys would have found such an arrangement with a girl intolerable.

But Mike was not most boys.

What was Joyce to him?

Sister? Not really. But what about Grace?
Girlfriend? What does that even mean?
Something else? But what?

* * *

On a Friday during the first week of February, Mike came into Tyler's office, and Tyler handed him a copy of the *Washington Track and Field News*. On the front was a grainy photo of a tall, hard-boned runner crossing a finish line. The headline above the photo read *Jonah Hart Sets HS Indoor Record: 4:10.3!*

"What do you think?" Tyler said.

"How does anyone run a mile inside?"

Tyler laughed. He'd forgotten Mike had never completed a track or cross-country season and had never raced anywhere more than twenty miles from Silverton, so he knew next to nothing about the sport.

"I think you can beat this Hart kid," Tyler told him.

I've only run 4:22," Mike said.

"Jonah Hart won the state cross-country meet in 14:43," Tyler said. "You ran 14:45 last fall, and you were never pushed after the first mile."

"When can I race this guy?" Mike looked at Jonah's photo.

"He's from Richland in eastern Washington. The biggest high school meet in that part of the state is the Pasco Invitational, the second Saturday in April. They have a special invitational mile. Jonah will be entered, and maybe Micah Madrigal from Spokane and Matt Jarvis from Boise. They've all run about 4:12."

"Can I get invited?"

"I know the meet director. I've already talked to him."

Mike said nothing. He glanced at Joyce, standing against the wall behind Tyler with her hands folded and her eyes down.

"If you run 4:17, he'll let you in."

"Four seventeen? I can do that."

"Right on!" Tyler said. "Piece of cake."

So, Tyler and Mike met at the grass track every Tuesday for a session of quarter-mile repeats. Ten the first week, then twelve, then fourteen, and so on, until Mike was running twenty by the middle of March, each under sixty-five seconds.

56

ON THE FIRST day of March, a drizzly Tuesday, Tyler had Mike run a time trial on the grass track. He was to run at a modest pace for three-quarters of a mile and then run the final lap as fast as he could.

The track was wet, and the inside lane was slick, worn down to the dirt by the hundreds of laps Mike had run during the winter. He stood bare-legged at the starting line, wearing an oversized, hooded sweatshirt and rolling his right ankle gently to the outside. Dr. Magnuson had pronounced the injury healed, but Mike constantly manipulated the joint anyway. Flexing, twisting, and rotating his ankle, not so much for reassurance but testing its limits, exploring how far he could push before the pain stopped him. For the first time, he could not feel any residual pain, no matter how far he bent his ankle to the outside.

"You ready?" Tyler said.

Mike shrugged and tested the ankle joint once more. "Sure."

Mike was never nervous before a workout or a race, although he knew his racing had been limited by his inability to stay out of trouble and by Tyler's habitual caution. Mike approached training sessions with indifference and races with a sense of curiosity. He was not curious about whether he would win—he'd never lost—or what his time would be because until then, time hadn't mattered. He wondered about one thing: *How hard could he run?*

"Remember," Tyler said, "today, we want to see how fast you can run the last lap. Not how fast you can run a mile. Run each of the first three laps between sixty-seven and seventy seconds, then go."

Mike nodded. His lack of familiarity with the idiosyncrasies of the sport that consumed other runners made him a perfect coaching subject. He didn't know enough to question anything he was told. Everything Tyler said made sense, so he nodded, pulled off his damp sweatshirt, stepped to the starting line, and waited.

"Tyler held up a stopwatch and said, "Go!"

Mike left the starting line at a little more than a jog.

After the first turn, he heard Tyler yell across the infield, "That's too slow!"

Mike increased his speed on the backstretch, concentrating on his tempo, and completed the first lap in seventy seconds.

"That's good! Don't break rhythm!" Tyler called out.

Mike glided into the second lap, feeling as if he could run at that pace all day, so he increased the tempo. He began to feel loose and free. It had begun to rain harder, but Mike barely noticed. The track was sodden and heavy in spots and slick in others, but he managed to stay light on his feet. He completed the second lap in sixty-seven seconds.

"Two seventeen—be patient now!" Tyler shouted.

Mike was in no hurry. He didn't mind the long runs in the woods, but there was nothing like the sensation of control he felt running on the track, the subtle awareness of how far he had already run and how far he had left to run, and the certainty of knowing he could match his speed with the remaining distance, each measured lap completed in a prescribed time.

The third lap was an afterthought. And Mike was not aware he'd increased his speed again.

"Three twenty-two!" Tyler yelled. "Hit it, Mike! Go hard from here."

Tyler's voice set him off like a sprinter leaving the blocks when he crossed the starting line with a lap left. His loose, relaxed movements became frantic. He began by pumping his arms harder. His knees came up, and his spiked shoes began to tear at the grass track. He slipped when he came out of the first turn but regained his balance in a single stride and tore up the backstretch as fast as the heavy track and thick air would allow. With half a lap left, he felt the effort for the first time. But he did not hesitate. He pounded around the turn.

He felt himself letting up with a hundred meters left, but he resisted the temptation to relax and slow down. The familiar discomfort deepened and spread as he neared the finish line. He flew by Tyler and slowed to a jog.

Tyler stared at his watch. *4:20.2.* Mike had run the last lap in fifty-eight seconds. He needed to drop three seconds to qualify for the Pasco Invitational.

Tyler watched Mike jog around the first turn and onto the backstretch. By the time he completed one more gentle lap and returned to where Tyler was standing, the rain had stopped, and Mike was moving easily again. Tyler handed

him his sweatshirt and showed him the stopwatch. Mike
nodded.

"You need to cool down," Tyler said. "We'll get that 4:17
at Lake Stevens in a couple of weeks."

Mike pulled on his sweatshirt and jogged off toward the
trail into the woods behind the track. An hour later, he
returned to the track and ran five more laps, sprinting the
straights and jogging the turns. Then he jogged home in the
dark.

57

THE TRACK TEAM left Silverton for their first meet in a steady drizzle. The meet was to be held at Lake Stevens, a larger school south of Silverton.

Mike had continued to run twice a day. He had seen Pork's VW parked in the shadows or on a side street once or twice but was determined to leave his plans for James and the boys on hold until school ended in June. He didn't think about James at all until he saw his truck parked across the road from Joyce's driveway as he finished a run late on a Wednesday afternoon. The engine was running, and the driver's side window was down. James appeared to be watching the house. Mike noticed the lights in Joyce's second-floor bedroom were off, and Joyce was entering the house through the front door.

Mike stopped at Joyce's driveway. James nodded at Mike and then drove off toward town. Mike looked back at the house, and the light in Joyce's room came on. *What is James doing here? Where has Joyce been?* He thought about running after James but remembered his promise to Tyler. He watched James's truck disappear and then ran on back to the track.

Tyler had told Mike to skip his morning run the day before the meet at Lake Stevens, but Mike woke at his usual time and couldn't relax. He got up and dressed and did his usual one-hour run. His ankle felt strong, but he was still careful about where he put his feet. He ran through town onto a flat loop to the northwest, slow and easy. That afternoon, as they stretched, Tyler talked to the team about the meet the next day, and Joyce handed out copies of the meet schedule. Mike was entered in both the mile and the half-mile.

Tyler explained the race plan to Mike. "You'll run like you did in the time trial. But this time, you'll run the last two laps hard. There'll be a pretty good kid from Arlington. I figure he'll run the first two laps in about 2:15. Then you take off. Run the third lap hard and see what you have left. The half-mile is for fun, and it's good speed work."

Mike had never considered the half-mile fun. No one ever had.

As the other kids milled around after practice, Mike started off across the track to run on the trail around the cranberry bog.

"Mike," Tyler called out. "You're done. You've got plenty to do tomorrow. Give it a rest."

Mike turned back, raised his hands in a gesture of mock disgust, and then nodded.

* * *

The track at Lake Stevens was hard-packed red clay. Even though it was still raining, the track drained well, so the damp surface was firm. Four shorter races were scheduled before the mile, so the first lane was not used for the earlier races to preserve decent footing.

There were nine runners in the boys' mile. Mike was assigned a starting position on the far outside of the track with the Arlington runner one position to his left.

"Do not take the lead the first two laps," Tyler told him before the race. "I don't care if you have to walk. Do not lead."

The rain stopped while the starter was giving final instructions to the competitors. When the starter's gun exploded, the Arlington runner bolted into the lead, and Mike found himself in last place around the first turn. He moved past the field and was on the shoulder of the Arlington runner by the time they'd completed half a lap.

The leader settled into an even pace, and Mike followed along effortlessly. He glanced at Tyler, who was leaning against the low fence that surrounded the track as Mike and the leader came out of the second turn. Tyler made a *relax* gesture with his hands, as if to say, "Perfect. Stay right there."

Mike did not want the pace to slacken, so he moved up next to the Arlington runner as they crossed the start-finish line at the end of the first lap. Mike heard a man with a stop-watch on the infield call out, "Sixty-five, sixty-six, sixty-seven."

Faster than the time trial, Mike thought. *But easier.*

"Too slow!" someone yelled.

They'd just reached the top of the first turn.

"You've got to get away from him," the same voice called out.

Mike realized it must be the Arlington kid's coach, and he remembered something Tyler had said once. *Anyone who thinks he can beat you will have a plan, but your plan is to be*

*alert, pay attention to what's going on around you, and cover
every move the leader makes.*

So, Mike watched the Arlington runner. He could tell
the boy was trying to speed up because he was breathing
louder and working harder with his arms. When they
reached the backstretch of the second lap, Mike made a
move as if he intended to pass. When the Arlington runner
increased his effort, Mike backed off, but the other boy did
not slow down.

As they came off the second turn, Mike moved up next
to the Arlington runner again. He noticed that Tyler had
moved down the track closer to the finish line.

"Wait!" Tyler yelled.

Mike and the other boy raced past the finish line side by
side with two laps to go. A thin man in a floppy, wide-
brimmed hat shouted out their time.

"Two fourteen, two fifteen."

As soon as they entered the turn, Mike took the lead.
The speed of Mike's move must have stunned the Arlington
runner because he did not respond. He glided down the
backstretch and all the way through the second turn before
he noticed the first signs of fatigue, a slight heaviness in the
thighs and a hot feeling behind his sternum. As he crossed
the finish line with one lap to go, Mike was tiring but not in
any real distress.

"Three thirteen, three fourteen," the man in the floppy
hat shouted.

Mike could do the math. He needed to run the last lap in
sixty-three seconds to qualify for Pasco. He completed the
first turn for the last time, and he could see Tyler on the
infield halfway up the backstretch.

"Stay quick!" Tyler yelled. "Pick up your feet!"

Mike was starting to hurt now. But with half a lap

remaining, he realized he could run even harder. Around the last turn and into the homestretch, the hurt morphed into real suffering, but he didn't falter. Every muscle, every sinew cried out for him to back off. Every oxygen-starved cell begged for relief.

As he entered the final straightaway. Mike was aware of nothing but the track during. He flashed through the finish line, slowed to a walk, and bent at the waist with his hands on his knees. He straightened after a few seconds and looked back up the track. The Arlington kid had just come out of the second turn. Mike waited, and when the Arlington runner crossed the finish line, Mike extended his right hand. The other boy took it and squeezed.

"Great run," he said. "

+Just great."

Mike nodded and turned away. Tyler was standing on the infield grass halfway between the finish line and the backstretch. On the track, eight girls were lining up for their own mile race. Mike walked past a group of men comparing times on their stopwatches.

"Is this right?" one of the men asked the others. "Did he run the last two laps in 1:58?"

"That's what I got," another man said, "4:12.7."

Mike continued on to where Tyler was standing. Tyler held up his own watch for Mike to see.

"You're in," he said, smiling.

The rain started up again and continued all night.

58

LATE THE SAME AFTERNOON, when James pulled up in front of his mother's house, he spotted the taillights of a new-looking pickup partially hidden behind the house. His mom had a visitor. Without thinking, he reached down and pulled the gun from under the driver's seat, where it had remained untouched since the day he shot at Mike. James waited. It wasn't quite dark, but the heavy clouds and drizzle, along with James's mood, made it seem as if full daylight had been in hiding since sunrise. When a violent gust slapped the rain against the windshield, James decided he'd better get inside before the weather got worse. He gathered up the cedar box with Joyce's Bible inside and stuck the gun into his back pocket. He slid across the seat and got out of the truck through the passenger-side door. He held the box under his sweatshirt as he lumbered across the sodden yard and onto the porch.

James pulled the box with the Bible from under his shirt and paused with his hand on the doorknob, listening. He took a deep breath and opened the door, hoping his mother and her friend were not at the kitchen table, which would be visible as soon as he stepped inside.

He pushed the door open. No one was at the table, and no sound came from the second floor where he knew his mother would be entertaining her *friend*. He started up the stairs, stepping carefully so he'd not alert his mother and the man she was with, and paused at the landing. Still no sound. He listened hard for a few more seconds and then continued up the stairs to his room.

James stretched out on the bed with the box in one hand and the gun in the other. He squeezed his eyes shut and clenched his fists when he heard the bedsprings in the next room squeak. He had taken Joyce's Bible out of the box several times but had only opened it once, the day Joyce had asked him to help find Mike. When the squeaking in the next room stopped, he sat up, set the gun on the table beside the bed, and removed the Bible from the box.

"Oh, what the hell," he said to himself. "Lightning didn't strike last time." He opened the book and read the first page he came to, Psalms 27:1.

The LORD is my light and my salvation—whom shall I fear? The LORD is the stronghold of my life— of whom shall I be afraid?

James realized he'd been afraid every day, but he had never spoken of fear or of uncertainty because the consequences for a young man in Silverton off appearing fearful or uncertain would have been far more severe than any benefit to be gained by facing whatever had made him afraid.

So, Psalms 27:1 made him shudder. He read Psalms 27:1 over several times and then turned to a page closer to the back, Titus 2:11.

For the grace of God has appeared that offers salvation to all people.

"All people?" James thought about how he had bounced some unsuspecting kid off the wall at school or forced an intoxicated girl into the back seat of his truck. "Not *all* people."

He flipped back to another random page, Acts 2:21.

And everyone who calls on the name of the Lord will be saved.

"Everyone?" James remembered the part he'd played the last time Mike was suspended from school.

He flipped through a few more pages, to Acts 16:31.

They replied, "Believe in the Lord Jesus, and you will be saved."

The word *you* jumped off the page, and James shivered as he thought about Joyce and the night at Junior's party. He leaned over the edge of the bed and retrieved the cedar box from the floor. He sat up on the edge of the bed and put the Bible back into the box. He looked around for something to write on. He found a half sheet of notebook paper in the trash can and a dull pencil under his bed. Using the lid of the box as a makeshift desk, he wrote: *Joyce, can we talk some more?* He opened the box, slipped the note into the Bible at Acts 16:31, and placed it back inside the box. He returned to his bed, stretched out, cradled the box against his chest, and went to sleep without removing his shoes or his clothes.

* * *

Well after dark, James woke to the sound of his father's logger boots clomping up the stairs. A crash in the hall told James his father had banged open the door to his mother's room. A series of guttural howls and a thump told James his father had dragged his mother's companion out of the bed.

James grabbed the gun from the table, dashed into the hall, and stopped in the doorway to his mother's room. His father was on the floor, struggling with a man James did not recognize. His mother was trying to crawl over the two men to get away from the fight. James rushed into the room and helped his mother get away. He nudged her up against the wall opposite the bed and then grabbed his father by the back of his shirt to stop him from bludgeoning the man with his fists. Ollie turned on James and took a wild swing toward his head. James leaned away, but his father got his hands on James's chest and pushed him toward the door. He kept pushing until they were across the hall at the head of the stairs.

Teetering at the top of the stairs, James yelled, "Dad!"

Showing no recognition, Ollie looked into James's face and tried to push him away, but James stepped aside and spun his father around. Ollie stepped back to the edge of the top step, and James raised the gun and fired one shot that struck Ollie in the middle of the chest. Ollie slumped toward his knees and stared at the blood oozing through his shirt. James put his free hand in the middle of Ollie's chest above the bullet wound and pushed him down the stairs.

James's mother screamed. She pushed James aside and stumbled down the steps to the landing where Ollie lay motionless. James turned away. The man Ollie had been fighting stood in the doorway. He had a cut above his eye and was shirtless, his clean dungarees held up by a single suspender. A single logger boot dangled from his left hand.

James stared at the man for a long second.

"Shit," he said finally.

James raised the gun once again. But when he pulled the trigger, the only sound was the loud click of the hammer snapping down on an empty chamber.

59

THE HALF-EMPTY SCHOOL bus trudged back toward Silverton through a steady rain.

Mike sat sideways in the seat behind Tyler, feet planted in the aisle. He was ambivalent about the race because he still wasn't certain about the meaning of any particular time, but he was pleased so many people—adults and other runners—seemed impressed with how he ran, not to mention the time, 4:12.7.

Joyce sat across the aisle from Mike and read until it got too dark, the faint glow of the overhead lights in the bus insufficient for anything but eyestrain. She closed her chemistry book and turned a little toward Mike, who was leaning back with his eyes mostly closed. After several minutes, Joyce turned and sat with her feet in the aisle so her knees brushed against Mike's. He opened his eyes all the way when Joyce leaned forward and put her hands on his thighs. She glanced at Tyler, but the coach was facing the front of the bus.

"What?" Mike sat up.

"What? What?" Joyce answered. "What do you think?"

"Riddles. Always riddles with you. Why can't you say what you mean?"

"Okay. But what do you think I mean?"

She narrowed her eyes and smiled. The look made Mike uncomfortable.

She turned and scooted over near the window and patted the seat. Mike stared at the empty spot and then sighed and moved across the aisle to sit next to her, careful to leave as much respectful space as the narrow bus seat allowed. The movement must have alerted Tyler, and he turned to see what was going on. He glanced at Mike, smiled at Joyce, and then turned back toward the front of the bus.

"Okay," Mike said. "What is it? You've been staring at me for like ten miles."

"I've been thinking about purpose. Do you get it now? You made an impression on all those people who saw you race. You did something people will remember."

Mike blushed. He had liked the attention, but he didn't want anyone to know he liked the attention.

"The Arlington kid was cool," he said. "I think he expected to win."

"But he didn't mind losing. He understands."

Joyce was not a runner. In fact, Mike didn't know anyone less interested in sports. Everyone else in town seemed embarrassed when the Silverton High basketball team went winless or that the football team won only one game. Even Joyce's mother, who scrutinized the local teams, had commented on the recent athletic futility of Silverton's youth, but Joyce did not care at all, except when it came to Mike's running. Her interest had little to with Silverton High and even less to do with winning races.

"He's pretty good, so, yeah, I guess he'd have to understand," Mike agreed.

"It's not about winning—or losing, is it?"

Mike didn't answer. He dropped his eyes to the two books in Joyce's lap. American history and chemistry.

"Where's your Bible?" he asked.

Joyce turned to look out the window, but after a moment, she turned back toward Mike and said, "I gave it to James."

"James? Why James?"

"He didn't have a Bible."

Mike tried to look miffed because disdain seemed an appropriate reaction, but what he felt was new and difficult to identify.

"I don't have one, either."

Joyce flashed the same smile that had made Mike uncomfortable before.

"But you don't need a Bible, Mike. You have me."

* * *

The bus slogged through town, and the driver sped up over the potholed-gravel road that led to the parking lot to make sure the kids snoozing in the back of the bus would be awake by the time he stopped behind the high school. Mike was first off the bus. He warmed up his truck while the rest of the team dissolved one-by-one into waiting cars and trucks, dome lights winking off and headlights blinking on as parental vehicles left the lot and retraced the bus's route back into town or into the surrounding hills. Joyce took her time, helping Tyler make sure the bus was clean, so Mike's truck would be the last vehicle to leave. Tyler always walked to and from school, regardless of the weather or the time of day.

When Joyce climbed into the passenger side of Mike's

truck, Tyler tapped on the driver's side window to get Mike's attention, and Mike rolled the window down.

"You want a ride, Coach?" Joyce said.

Mike felt foolish because it hadn't occurred to him to offer Tyler a ride.

"No, thanks. I need to walk, and you, Mike, need to understand how fast 4:12 is."

Mike shrugged. "I only ran the last two laps hard. I can go faster."

"At Pasco, you'll have to."

"I don't mind," Mike said without expression.

"I know you don't mind, Mike. But most people do."

The rain had slackened. Mike rolled up his window, and Tyler strolled toward the walkway that led to the street between the high school and the library. Mike put the truck in gear, and Joyce moved a few inches in his direction. He looked at her, but she was staring straight ahead toward the invisible hills looming in the darkness behind the school.

"It's always green," she said in a whisper, "even in the dark. Ever. Green."

"Huh?"

"If you can go faster, then you must," she said. She leaned toward Mike and turned his face toward her with her hand. "Otherwise, there's no point, is there?"

She took her hand away, and Mike drove out of the parking lot.

60

MIKE HAD INTENDED to take Joyce straight home, but as they drove past James's street two blocks before the turn onto Scout Lake Road, the red and blue lights of several sheriff's vehicles flashing in front of James's house caught their attention.

"Mike, turn here!"

Mike turned down James's street and parked at the corner. Joyce jumped out of the truck, but Mike waited a few seconds before following her. The same tall, female deputy who had interviewed Joyce after the shooting back in June was leaning against one of the sheriff's trucks. When Joyce approached, the female deputy took a few steps in her direction and put her hand up. Joyce stopped, and Mike caught up.

"What's happening?" Joyce said.

"There's been an...an incident."

Mike glanced beyond the deputy. An ambulance idled in front of the house without its emergency lights on.

"I remember you," the female deputy said. "You were there the night Junior was shot. We had a talk."

"Yes, ma'am," Joyce said.

The deputy put her hand on Joyce's shoulder. "Wait here."

Mike stepped up next to Joyce, and when she leaned in next to him, he put his arm around her shoulders. After a few minutes, the female deputy returned with Deputy Dodge. Dodge whispered something to the female deputy. She nodded and returned to the house. Dodge stood in front of Mike and Joyce, chewing on his lower lip.

"How'd the race go, Mike?" he finally asked.

Joyce broke in. "What happened?"

"It was good, I guess," Mike said. "I won."

"What happened?" Joyce was insistent.

Dodge looked back toward the house, chewed on his lip some more, and moved half a step closer to Joyce and Mike when he turned back.

"There was a fight. We think James was trying to protect his mother. Nobody is saying much yet."

There was movement on the porch. The female deputy and a state patrolman were escorting James out of the house in handcuffs. They guided him down the stairs and put him into the back seat of one of the sheriff's trucks.

"What did he do?" Joyce said, motioning toward the truck with her chin.

"Like I said, there was a fight. James shot his father. We think he was trying to protect his mother."

Joyce remained calm. But she was trembling as she studied the ambulance. "Is Ollie okay?" She separated herself a little from Mike, but he kept his arm around her shoulders.

Not sure how much he should reveal, Dodge stared at the ground for a few seconds before meeting Joyce's eyes. "No, Joyce. He's not. Ollie was dead when we got here."

Joyce leaned a little farther away from Mike and clasped her hands beneath her chin. Dodge reached out to touch her shoulder, but Joyce shook her head.

"No...please...I'm fine. What about James?"

"We don't know exactly what happened yet. But we'll figure it out. There seems to have been someone else here."

"A witness?" Mike said.

Joyce shook her head. "One of JoAnn's *friends*, right?"

Mike removed his arm from Joyce's shoulders and stepped away. He was breathing hard and starting to shiver. Dodge moved toward Mike, but Joyce stepped between them. She put her arms around Mike, and when his shivering subsided, she stepped away. Mike started to speak but couldn't think of anything to say.

Dodge looked puzzled. "I know you and James didn't get along," he said to Mike. "No love lost, as it were. Plus, after the way you handled things back in June, I wouldn't think this would bother you much."

"Ollie's dead," Mike said. "And Junior wasn't killed. I don't know. I'm tired from the race, I guess. And I got wet, and it's cold."

"And you, young lady. I was under the impression you'd led a somewhat sheltered life. But a shooting. And now this? Are you going to need some help?"

Joyce shook her head. "I *have* resources," she replied. She stepped sideways and leaned toward Mike, and her shoulder touched his upper arm. She put her arm around his waist. "We'll be all right, Deputy."

Two paramedics and two deputy sheriffs carried Ollie out of the house on a gurney covered with a heavy gray sheet. They placed him in the back of the ambulance and closed the doors.

Joyce stepped around Deputy Dodge and approached the truck with James in the back seat.

"Joyce," Dodge said, "I don't think—"

Joyce turned back and said, "I'm fine."

Joyce approached James. She stood back but close enough to see James's blank face when he turned to look at her. The window was rolled up, but Joyce could tell what James said when he mouthed the words, "I told you."

Joyce shook her head and put her hand on the closed window. She said aloud, "No. You're wrong." She turned away and walked back to where Mike was waiting.

Mike and Joyce were headed back toward his truck when Deputy Dodge stopped them.

"Don't leave yet," he said. "Wait in Mike's truck."

Mike leaned against the front fender, and Joyce climbed up into the passenger seat and sat with her legs dangling out the door. Dodge returned to the house, and when he came back out, he had James's cedar box in his hand. Joyce climbed down and leaned against the fender next to Mike.

"We found this on the floor in James's room," Dodge said. He opened the box and took out Joyce's Bible. "Is this your Bible, Joyce?"

Joyce nodded and opened the Bible to the page marked by a piece of folded paper. Acts 16:31 had been underlined. She closed the Bible, opened the piece of paper, and read the note. *Joyce, can we talk some more?* Her cheeks grew warm, and her eyes filled. She turned toward Mike and handed him the note, unconcerned with how he would react.

Mike stared at the note for several seconds, waiting for the familiar rage and the habitual desire to run away into the darkness, but the urge and the desire both failed him. Instead, he folded the note in half and slipped it into the back pocket of his jeans.

Mike and Joyce climbed into the truck.

Dodge stepped up to the passenger side and spoke to them both through the open window. "I don't know how worried I should be about you two."

"Mike's got a big race in a couple of weeks," Joyce said. "The invitational meet in Pasco. We'll worry about that."

The ambulance eased away from the house, the emergency lights dark, and the siren silent. Dodge watched the ambulance disappear around the corner at the end of the street.

Joyce reached out the window and handed her Bible to Dodge.

"Please give this back to James when it's okay. Tell him to keep it as long as he needs it."

61

GEORGIE WAS NOT the smallest kid at Silverton High School, but he was shy and awkward and unathletic. He wore ill-fitting, hand-me-down clothes and carried a meager lunch to school in a rumpled paper bag. He had learned to hide in the social shadows, invisible to the inevitable tribe of marauding hulks in search of an easy victim. But with James gone, he thought he could relax. At least a little.

Georgie had one friend in school. Mike. He and Mike never hung out together. Mike didn't hang out. But Mike and Georgie were both on the school's track and cross-country teams. Georgie struggled to stay out of last place, but he was proud that Mike always returned to the finish line after he'd won to encourage Georgie and the other runners at the back of the pack. That, according to Georgie's limited expectations, made Mike his friend.

Then on Monday morning, the week of the Pasco Invitational, Georgie slinked toward his first-period class. He stayed close to the wall and maneuvered through the crowded hallway with practiced caution. But before he reached his classroom, he bumped into a girl hurrying in the opposite direction. She dropped her books, and Georgie bent down to help her pick them up. When they stood up, they bumped heads, and both stumbled backward. Georgie was sure there would be a scene, but when he started to back away, the girl grabbed him by the sleeve. Her arm was wrapped around her schoolbooks, and she released Georgie's sleeve to touch a small wooden cross swinging from a chain around her neck.

"I'm really sorry," he said.

"It's okay. Thanks." She reshuffled her books and headed toward the far end of the hall.

When Georgie turned to go, he crashed into the hulking form of Pork. In James's absence, Pork had taken it upon himself, with Tall Paul's inept assistance, to patrol the halls searching for threadbare, poor kids with sack lunches.

"What do you think you're doing?" Pork said. "You shouldn't be bothering a girl like that. You shouldn't be bothering any girl."

Pork was blocking Georgie's path to class, so Georgie took a tentative step sideways to go around and bumped into Tall Paul. Georgie knew the best way to remain unharmed was to make himself as small and as quiet as possible. So he backed away, hugging his backpack, and leaned against the wall with his eyes on the ground. Pork slapped Georgie's lunch sack from his hand and stepped on it, put a fat hand on the wall on each side of Georgie's head, and leaned down to squawk into Georgie's face.

Pork's breath reminded Georgie of the sour smell in the bathroom after his Uncle Joe had stayed out all night. He tried to turn away, but Pork's squishy forearms prevented Georgie from moving his head. He felt as if he might cry, which would have been a mistake. Then he heard Mike's voice from behind Pork's hulking mass.

"Leave him alone, fat boy."

Pork pushed himself away from the wall, and Tall Paul took one of Georgie's arms and squeezed. As Pork turned around, he pushed Mike hard with both hands toward the opposite side of the hallway. Mike was as tall as Pork but weighed at least a hundred pounds less. He stumbled backward, catching himself before he crashed into the wall. Pork moved toward Mike with his fists raised, but before he could swing, Mike slapped him on the left cheek. Mike's first-period teacher, Mr. Sorenson, came out of the nearest classroom and stepped in between the two boys. Pork backed away, but Mike stood his ground. Mr. Sorenson turned toward Mike and grabbed his arm.

"I knew you couldn't stay out of trouble."

Mike said nothing. Mr. Sorenson nudged him down the hall toward the principal's office, and Mike did not resist.

"I told Mr. Thompson it was only a matter of time. Let's see what he has to say about this."

Tall Paul had let go of Georgie when Mr. Sorenson showed up, but Pork gave Georgie a final push before walking across the hall toward the history teacher's classroom. Georgie picked up his backpack and tried to rearrange his ruined lunch as he headed down the hallway behind Mr. Sorenson and Mike.

62

MIKE SAT in the principal's office and stared at the ceiling.

"Mike, you need to answer me," Mr. Thompson said. He leaned back in his desk chair and sighed.

Mike lowered his eyes and stared at the wall behind the principal.

"Did you hit Pork or not? Was there a fight? And did you participate?"

Mike tapped his thighs with his closed fists and bit down on the inside of one cheek.

"Mike." The principal stood and leaned against his desk. "Answer me."

Mike looked up. "What did Sorenson say?"

The principal relaxed and sat back down. "*Mr.* Sorenson said he heard a scuffle, and when he came out of his room, he saw you hit Pork in the face. Is that what happened?"

"If that's what *Mr.* Sorenson said, it don't matter what really happened."

"Mike, you haven't been in here for a while, but you know if there's a fight, I have to suspend you. If you were provoked or protecting yourself or someone else, then the suspension doesn't have to be too long."

"How long?"

Mr. Thompson replied from memory, reciting some ritual admonition. "The minimum is five school days, and you cannot participate in any activities during that time."

Mike stared at the floor again, but he had opened his fists and was rubbing his thighs as he began to explain.

"Pork and Tall Paul had little Georgie pinned up against the wall. Pork was going through his backpack, throwing books on the floor. He stomped on Georgie's lunch."

The principal held up his hand. "Why would Pork do something like that?"

Mike was not surprised the principal would ask such a question. "Because—" Mike caught himself before he said *James*. "Pork is a... He's just like—" Mike caught himself again.

"Mike, there's no reason to use..." The principal rested his forearms on his desk. He straightened, folded his hands, and said, as if demanding an act of contrition, "I'm afraid I have no choice."

Mike slumped back in the chair and closed his eyes. He had not been in trouble all year, but it was the second week in April. And the biggest race of his life was Saturday.

The principal tapped a file folder on his desk with his index finger. "You've got quite a record here, Mike, but no trouble this year. Some of us thought you had turned a corner. What's going on?"

Mike thought about the thousands of miles he'd run on the roads and in the mountains and the endless laps on the track. He thought about training in the rain and about his injured ankle. He thought about Junior being shot. And he thought about James shooting at his foot. He thought about

4:12. He wondered about Jonah Hart and Micah Madrigal, and he wondered how much faster he could run. He thought about his absent mother and disinterested father. He remembered the last thing he saw before he turned and ran back to Joyce—his mother and Grace on the above Abel.

What would Joyce say? he asked himself. *Confess, Mike.*

So, Mike told Mr. Thompson everything. The principal listened. And when Mike was finished, Mr. Thompson nodded.

"I understand you've been through a lot, Mike. But my hands are tied."

Mike closed his eyes and thought about where he'd run when he left the principal's office. Out Scout Lake Road, past Joyce's house. He'd turn left onto the steep trail toward the old reservoir, but strangely, he could not imagine getting to the top of the hill without having stop.

"You'll have to go home now, Mike. You haven't been to class, so today will count. You can come back to school next Monday. You can resume the track season then. Any questions?"

Mike shook his head, stood, and headed for the door.

"Mike, wait. If I were you, I'd have questions about getting your schoolwork and about track practice."

Mike stopped in the open door and turned halfway around. He felt very tired. Like you said, Mr. Thompson, I've done this before."

As Mike left the principal's office, he saw Georgie seated in a stiff chair in the outer office with his backpack and crumpled lunch sack on his lap. Mike nodded to Georgie, then turned and took a step back into the principal's office. "What about Pork?"

"What about Pork?" The principal said. "Mr. Sorenson didn't bring Pork down here. He brought you."

"Right... Mr. Sorenson."

Mike turned to leave. Georgie stood and put his backpack and smashed lunch sack on the chair.

"I'm sorry, Mike."

"Sorry?"

"Sorry you got in trouble. Did you get suspended?"

"Yeah. Five days. Thompson said he had no choice."

"But that's all week. What about the race?"

Mike was flattered that Georgie knew about the race.

"I guess I'll miss it." Mike tried to sound unconcerned.

"Jonah Hart will be there. He's run 4:10. And Micah Madrigal has run 4:13. It's the one chance you'll have to run against guys like that."

"Never heard of 'em," Mike lied. He reached out and put a hand on Georgie's shoulder, as much to smother his own anger as to reassure the smaller boy.

"They can't do this, Mike."

"I guess they can. Maybe there will be other races."

63

ON WEDNESDAY MORNING, Tyler went to Mike's house before school. Mike yelled for him to come in without coming to the door himself. When Tyler entered the empty front room, he was surprised by the aroma of strong coffee but then wondered why the smell of coffee should surprise him. He could hear Mike rummaging around in his room.

"I have an idea, Mike," Tyler said, raising his voice to make sure Mike could hear.

Mike appeared in the hallway wearing his running shorts and a baggy T-shirt. He had one running shoe in each hand.

"Actually," Tyler continued, "it's something Deputy Dodge suggested. He says you have to run in Pasco. No option."

"That doesn't make any sense. Why does he care?"

"I told him your father will need to agree to what I'm going to suggest, but Dodge said your dad has no say since he's hardly ever here."

Tyler started to say something about liability or responsibility but realized that keeping his job was a longshot anyway if he and Mike went through with Dodge's suggestion.

Mike stood in the middle of the room and waited.

"I want you to take it easy this morning. Go to the track after the team's done with practice. I'll be there with a workout. You're running at Pasco."

Mike sat on the couch and let the shoe in his left hand drop.

"Did Mr. Thompson change his mind?"

"No. I'd think he'd like to, but Mr. Sorenson insists you stay suspended."

"So, now what?"

"There's a book all of the runners I knew read when I was in college. *Once a Runner*. I can never remember the author's name, John something. Parker—that's it. The main character gets kicked off his college team right before the biggest race of his life. So...he borrows the name of a runner from Finland, disguises himself somehow, and runs the race anyway."

"You want me to use someone else's name?"

"No."

"I don't get it."

"The guy in the book pretty much ruined his college career, but he got to run in the race. The race mattered more than—"

"Doing what the school wanted him to do."

"Exactly."

"So, what are you saying?"

"Here's what we do, unless you have a problem with it. You could go back to school on Monday, finish the season, win a couple of state titles, and get on with your life."

"I still don't get it."

"Or you could run at Pasco. You're already entered. They

don't know you've been suspended from school. So we go over Saturday morning as if nothing's wrong. And you run the race."

Mike was silent.

"If we do this, you'll no doubt be kicked off the track team and probably be expelled," Tyler warned. "You won't graduate on time. Maybe not at all."

"But I'll get to race?"

"Yes," Tyler said. "You'll get to race."

64

SILVERTON WAS at least five hours from Pasco, so Saturday morning, Tyler was at Mike's house before six because he wanted to get Mike to the meet by eleven-thirty. Mike leaned into the car and started to throw his bag into the back seat and was surprised to see Joyce sitting there.

"Joyce?"

"It's okay. My mom knows I'm here."

"What about your dad?"

Joyce did not answer.

"Get in, Mike," Tyler said. He seemed anxious to start the road trip that would almost assuredly end his days as a teacher. Mike tossed his bag into the back seat next to Joyce and got into the car. Tyler backed out of the driveway and headed back through town.

When they reached Everett, Tyler got onto I-5. Thirty miles of crowded freeway later, they reached Seattle. The city fascinated Mike, but the endless, manufactured landscape made him feel squeezed. They turned east onto I-90, and in another thirty miles, they were back in the Cascade

Mountains, and Mike began to relax, even though he had never been this far from home.

Tyler had been quiet, but now he began to tell Mike and Joyce tales of his own high school days when he'd made this trip once a month, driving from Tacoma to Spokane to train with the great runners in that city. Mike listened, but his mind drifted to the coming effort, though he was not nervous.

"You'll know soon," Joyce said. "We'll all know."

Tyler pulled off the freeway at the Indian John Rest Area, about twenty miles east of Ellensburg. Joyce and Tyler used the restrooms, and Mike got out and looked around at the nearby mountains. The trees here were smaller and farther apart than at home, and the little bit of underbrush was almost all brown and close to the ground. But the sparse vegetation made the rugged and imposing Sawtooth range to the north seem close enough to touch.

"Wait 'til we get closer to Pasco," Tyler said after they resumed driving. "They've got a hill the locals claim is the tallest mountain in North America without a tree on it."

When they reached the top of Manastash Ridge ten miles south of Ellensburg, the trees were gone. Sagebrush and prairie grass covered the steep hills in every direction, but little else. They rolled down off the ridge through Yakima. An hour later, they crossed the Yakima River at Richland and then the Columbia River west of Pasco.

Tyler parked next to the Pasco High gym.

"Stretch your legs," he said to Mike and Joyce. "I'll be right back."

In less than ten minutes, he returned with a manila envelope containing Mike's race number, Tyler's coach's pass, and a manager's pass for Joyce. "We'll walk to the stadium," he said. "It's only a couple of blocks."

They approached the stadium from the northeast and showed the woman at the gate their passes. She smiled and indicated a tall turnstile at the top of a steep driveway that led to the bottom of the stadium. At the far end was a flat, grassy area at the top of the deep bowl covered with colorful tents, most adorned with the logo or mascot of a specific school.

Tyler put his hand in the middle of Mike's back. "More than a thousand kids in this meet," he said. "More than a hundred schools from three or four states. Maybe even Canada."

Mike did not move.

"But none of them can run like you."

They walked around the outside of the track past the discus and shotput areas. High jumpers were warming up beneath a goalpost that had been turned sideways to make room for the javelin throwers. They climbed to the top of the steep bleachers and settled into a spot above the finish line.

"Four states?" Joyce said. "And Canada?"

"Don't matter where they're from," Tyler said. "Either they can run, or they can't."

Mike looked around, surveyed the activity on the stadium floor, and nodded.

65

TWO HOURS LATER, eleven of the twelve runners in the invitational mile sprinted away from the starting line halfway around the first turn, then jogged back and sprinted away again. Mike was not nervous because he figured everyone in the stands would be watching the local hero Jonah Hart or one of the Spokane big shots.

Mike stood alone a few yards behind the line, slowly shifting his weight from one foot to the other, staring down the track and waiting for the starter to call the runners to their marks.

Tyler had pointed Jonah out to Mike and told him to watch the Richland runner warm up. He was taller than Mike and thinner. His shaggy blond hair danced around his ears and on the back of his neck when he ran. Mike watched with interest as Jonah took a long time to warm up. Light running. Stretching. Six strides. And then finishing with a hundred-meter sprint at close to full speed. Jonah finished ten minutes before the race and jogged back and forth on the infield until the runners were told to report to the starting line.

Mike had left Tyler and Joyce in the stands about twenty minutes before race time. He'd jogged two laps around the congested infield, put on his spiked shoes, and ran two quick strides on the backstretch. Afterward, he sat on the grass with his back against a goalpost, waited, and watched Jonah jog back and forth, either unconcerned with or oblivious to Mike's presence.

He doesn't know who I am, Mike thought.

Tyler had tried to get Mike to do a longer warmup, but the length of his warmup had never seemed to have any effect on how he raced. The clerk called the runners to the starting line. Mike left his sweats in a pile at the base of the goalpost and strolled to the line.

The clerk lined up the runners, beginning at the inside of the track, and the nervous striding began. Mike was in the ninth position, with Jonah three runners over on the extreme outside. The other runners continued to dance at the line while the starter gave last-minute instructions.

"Okay, guys," the starter said. "Take one more run off the line. Then we'll go."

Again, Mike stayed at the starting line while the other runners sprinted into the turn one last time. When they returned to the line, Jonah looked over at Mike before taking his place.

"Take your marks!"

The starter's pistol roared, and the twelve runners ran hard around the first turn. Tyler was pleased to see Mike was on the outside near the middle of the pack. Jonah was right in front of Mike, also on the outside of the pack. Mike hadn't raced enough for a discussion of strategy to do much good. All Tyler said before the race was, "It's good to have a plan, but as soon as the gun goes off, someone always does something that will disrupt the plan. Pay attention and be alert." He told Mike to stay off the curb and be aware of what was happening at the front of the pack.

The pack strung out behind the lead runner, Micah Madrigal, a tall, gaunt kid from Spokane. As the field completed the first backstretch, someone outside the low fence that circled the track yelled, "Thirty, thirty-one." The pace was fast, but when Jonah began to move up on the first homestretch, Mike followed him. The first lap ended with Jonah in second place, crowding Micah's outside shoulder.

"Sixty-two, sixty-three!" a timer yelled.

The Spokane runner surged hard around the turn to start the second lap, with Jonah and Mike following two yards behind. The rest of the field was already beginning to fade.

Micah maintained the pace onto the home stretch of the second lap, but as they approached the finish line, the Spokane runner's shoulders came up, and his stride became a bit more labored. Jonah pounded into the lead ten yards from the end of the second lap, and Micah was unable to challenge him.

"Two-oh-four, two-oh-five."

Twenty yards past the line, Mike closed the narrow gap on Jonah, burst into the lead, and was three yards ahead before Jonah could respond. Jonah accelerated slightly and made up the difference by the time the two runners reached the middle of the backstretch.

In the bleachers, Tyler and Joyce stood up.

"Do you think he can keep up that pace?" Joyce said.

"We'll know soon. I guess we'll find out."

Mike continued to lead around the turn and into the home stretch for the next-to-last time. The bleachers that rose above the track were full, and everyone got to their feet as the two racers passed the finish line with one lap to go. Joyce latched on to Tyler's arm.

"Three-oh-eight, three-oh-nine."

Tyler was not interested in the time. He watched Mike as he tried to speed up around the first turn, but for the first time in his running life, Mike appeared to be struggling.

Jonah and Mike sprinted into the last lap, aware of nothing except the cold, hard, brutal fact of the race. They slammed into the backstretch for the last time, and Jonah sprinted past Mike.

Tyler put his hands over his mouth, and Joyce stood up on her seat.

"It's not over yet," she said. "Look!"

"No, it is not."

Jonah was still in the lead with half a lap to go, and Mike was five yards back. Then, in the middle of the final turn, Mike surprised Jonah for the second time. He closed the gap, and the two runners, in a glory of shared suffering, entered the homestretch side by side.

Mike slowed to a jog and ran halfway around the first turn before realizing the crowd was silent. He turned and looked back toward the finish line and saw Jonah jogging toward him. Runners were still crossing the line, and those who had finished were either bent over with their hands on their knees or flat on their backs, arms outspread, observing the ritual of suffering, a sacred rite reserved for the few willing to bear the cost.

Micah Madrigal put his hand on Mike's shoulder and pointed to the scoreboard, but an untimely glitch had caused the lights to blink off. He pointed again, and the scoreboard lights flickered back on, flashing 4:09.4 before the lights went out again.

The crowd erupted. Although he didn't quite under-stand why, Mike threw his arms in the air and quickly brought them down again. Micah grabbed him and lifted him off the ground.

"Great race, man," he said.

Mike wasn't sure what he should do, so he jogged back past the finish line, scanning the bleachers for Tyler. He couldn't find the coach, but he heard someone calling his name and saw Joyce along the low, chain-link fence surrounding the track. He jogged to where she was stand-ing, placed both hands on the fence, and leaned forward. He dropped his head and closed his eyes.

His mind went back to the night of Junior's party, to the reckless run through the mountains, and to the dark days after his ankle injury. To the long-ago night his mother left. To all the nights alone in the little house. Tall Paul and Pork dissolved into irrelevance. He wondered what had become of Dahlia. What would Mr. Thompson think?

And he said a little prayer. A prayer. For James. Joyce put her hands on each side of his face, and Mike raised his head and looked into her eyes.

Jonah came to where Mike was standing along the fence. He leaned back with his butt against the fence and stared down at his feet for a long moment. Then he turned toward Mike.

"I can't believe it," he said. "I really can't believe it." Jonah shook his head and then jogged off toward the infield with his head down.

Still leaning against the fence, Mike watched Jonah jog away toward the infield and then looked up at the score-board again.

"Mike?" Joyce said. "Mike!"

He turned back toward Joyce.

"Mike?"

"I'm glad you're here," he said.

Joyce leaned in and placed her cheek against Mike's face. She squeezed his hands and whispered, "Now you know."

Mike was confused for a moment. Then and for the first time since his mother left, he didn't wonder about anything. He was certain. He jogged back up the track in front of the packed stands as the crowd stood and clapped politely.

EPILOGUE

Tyler remembered only one thing from the day he graduated from high school. He had adopted the obligatory, maudlin attitude of his classmates when the ceremony ended: Newly minted young adults hugged and cried and promised to remain friends for life.

But then a favorite teacher had caught Tyler alone and said, "Get over it, Tyler. It's only high school. If you haven't forgotten most of these people in six months, you'll need to rethink some things."

Tyler had nodded and shrugged.

It's only high school.

Tyler thought about that teacher and the best advice he'd ever gotten as he drove from Pasco back toward Silverton. Mike had fallen asleep immediately and was spread out across the full width of the back seat. Joyce sat in the front passenger seat and stared straight ahead. Because the finish was so close, it several minutes for officials to decide Mike had won, even though both he and Jonah were given the same time—4:09.4. Joyce had said she thought that was the perfect result, but on the awards stand, while the large crowd stood and cheered, both Mike and Jonah seemed subdued.

Joyce remained quiet for the first hour of the journey away from Pasco, but as Tyler's car groaned up the first of three steep grades between Yakima and Ellensburg, she turned in the seat, leaned against the door, and asked, "Why were both boys disappointed? It was a great race."

Tyler leaned his elbow against the bottom of the steering wheel and massaged his chin with his index finger. "It's not disappointment so much."

"Then what?" Joyce said. "It seems like they both should have been happy."

Tyler eased back in the seat and returned his hand to the steering wheel.

"Something happens in a race. It's hard to understand, even for someone who's done it, and impossible for anyone who hasn't."

"But it can't be all that complicated. It's running. Everyone can run."

"It's not running, not necessarily the way most people think of it. It's profound exertion. It's discovery."

Joyce thought about that.

"Sometimes, I'll find something in the Bible that I hadn't noticed before." Joyce paused and craned her neck so she could see Mike sleeping in the back seat. "I'll go to talk to Pastor Clem about it, and he'll smile and tell me that *discovery*, that's the word he always uses, is the whole point of Bible study."

"And it's the whole point of running." Tyler squeezed the wheel and pushed himself back into the seat. "The whole point of racing. The whole point of doing anything difficult."

Joyce turned back to the front of the car and thought

about discovery for several miles. The brown hills rolled up and away from the highway. Then the car crested the last ridge, the vast expanse of the Kittitas Valley and the college town of Ellensburg spread out below them.

"Pastor Clem says to be careful, though." She continued to stare out through the windshield. The nearby peaks of the Cascade Mountains, which sliced through the horizon above the valley, were still covered with snow in mid-April. "He says, 'Joyce, you didn't discover anything new in the Bible. Whatever it was you found has always been there. You've discovered something new in yourself. But you can't take credit for that'."

Tyler didn't respond.

"I don't think Mike and that other boy, Jonah, were disappointed," Joyce said. "They were humbled."

Mike stirred. He sat up and tried to stretch, but the back seat of Tyler's smallish car didn't give him much room. He felt something digging into his backside, so he reached around and pulled the goldish Pasco Invitational medal out of his pocket. He rubbed the medal with his thumb and then tossed it into the front seat.

Joyce pulled James's cedar box out of her backpack and put the medal inside. Mike put his hand on her shoulder. Joyce leaned back into the seat toward Mike but did not turn around.

When the tired, old car approached Mike's house in the dark, they could barely make out Deputy Dodge's truck parked just off the highway.

"Well," Tyler said. "This can't be good."

"No. But maybe that is," Joyce said. She pointed to the house with her chin.

The porch light was on, and Grace sat at the top of the steps, playing with a wooden truck. Mike and Joyce got out on the passenger side and stood beside the car. Tyler shut off the engine, and Janine appeared in the open front door.

Tyler got out of the car and went immediately to Dodge's truck.

"I've had a talk with Thompson," Dodge said through the open window.

"I guess I'm fired. And Mike is expelled."

"You might be surprised, Coach. Anyway, tell Mike I'm going to Ellensburg next month to watch him win a couple of state titles."

Tyler nodded and turned back toward the house.

Joyce approached the porch, hesitated, and then sat down next to Grace at the top of the steps. Mike stepped up to the bottom of the steps and stood facing Joyce and the child.

Janine still stood at the front door. Robert was watching from the living room window to the left of the door.

"Are you back?" Mike said.

Janine covered her mouth and moved out of the doorway to the top of the steps behind Grace. "Well, I'm here...for now."

Mike started to back away, but Joyce reached up and took his hand. He stopped and looked up at his mother. Were those tears in her eyes? Joyce pulled down on his hand, and he sat on the steps.

Grace picked up the truck and handed it to Mike. "I can run really fast," she said. "Can you run fast?"

Janine crouched down behind her daughter. She reached out to put her hand on Mike's shoulder, but he leaned away, and she pulled her hand back.

"It'll be difficult, Mike," Joyce said.

Mike was silent for a long moment.

"But that's the whole point, isn't it?" Mike said.

He looked back and saw Dodge's truck pull away toward town. Tyler had not moved from the side of the road. Mike looked toward the window, but Robert had not moved. Janine stood up and stepped back. Mike stood, picked up Grace, and walked back toward Tyler.

"So, Coach. What time do we run tomorrow?"

COPYRIGHT

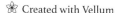

DEDICATION

I have had the good fortune to work and to know some of the best track and field and cross-country coaches in the business, and this book is dedicated to them. From Dick Bowman to Doris Heritage to Ralph Vernacchia to Phil English to Pat Tyson and others too numerous to mention.

FOLLOW BRUCE BLIZARD

Subscribe to my newsletter and get a **free eBook copy of** *A Better Place.*

This is a beautifully written novel that could appeal to young adults, but is also very appropriate for adults, especially parents. It is a great discussion starter for families. While the Christian spiritual exploration is foundational to the themes of the work, one is never "Jeremiah-ed." This novel inspires, so it does not need to preach.

   - Linda Stairet, Richland, Washington

Sign up at https://app.convertkit.com/forms/designers/2180395/edit.

COMING AUGUST 15

Right Kind of Boy

(a sorta sequel to *Always a Runner*)

Chapter 1

I was seventeen and at a point in my life when everything I thought I knew about myself was about to change. You see, every day, just as I woke up and just before my morning run, there was an insistent voice in my head. Not a dream, exactly. Maybe a nightmare.

Why are you doing this?

There are more important things.

How does this serve God?

Get up and do something for someone else.

For the Church.

Give up this running nonsense.

You are called to sacrifice.

Then the alarm clock would jangle me fully awake, and I'd roll over and sit up on the edge of my bed. I'd fumble for the invisible button on top of the clock and press it down two or three times until the jangling stopped.

My name is Jonah Hart, and I was a serious runner in those days. I mean *serious*. I ran every day. Twice a day. Training and racing and winning—and I always won—was all I ever thought about.

But I was a Christian, too, so I thought maybe the voice in my head was a warning. I was a senior in high school, almost an adult, and the voice seemed to be telling me it was time to rethink this whole running thing and move onto something more "meaningful"

So, I'd shut the alarm off and think about what The Voice was saying, though not for very long. And then, after a minute or two, after The Voice went silent, I'd stumble out of bed.

I slept in my running clothes, which my mother washed for me every day, to save time in the morning. Nylon shorts that stopped far enough above my knees to be considered immodest by some of my more Puritanical friends. Baggy t-shirt. Thin wool socks. Then I'd stand and stare out through the curtains to begin the ritual that preceded every morning run.

The sun was not up this early at this time of year, so I was glad for the yard light out back. I'd check to see if the grass was damp with either dew or rain. The thermometer on the metal brackets screwed to the exterior wall of the house outside my window told me whether I'd need a sweatshirt or could leave the gloves I'd worn all winter on the windowsill.

Every day the same. Consistency mattered.

On this particular morning the second week of April, I put on my thick-soled running shoes and noticed they were showing some wear. The tough black rubber on the outside edge of the ball of each foot was worn down to the white EVA that protected my feet and legs from the eighty-plus miles I ran every week.

I never ran on Sunday, but I'd not missed any other day since the seventh grade. I'd run ten to twelve times every week since I started high school, two to three miles at a time at first, then as much as fifteen miles a day, five days a week. Every Saturday morning I'd do a single fifteen-mile run with my teammates while Coach Easton, who coached the distance runners during track season and the cross-country team in the fall, drove ahead of us in his rusty panel van giving out water and encouragement.

I didn't mean to try to impress anyone with all this. It was just that most people didn't believe me when I told them how much I ran. I don't think it was all that hard. It's what I'd done daily since middle school. Coach Easton used to say if you do something difficult every day, it either becomes easy or eventually you don't mind that it's hard. I thought that was true when it came to running, but not so much for anything else.

Since I was also a Christian, I went to church with my family every Sunday. Except for that time in the third grade when I had my tonsils out and developed a fever that scared my parents. My father was the senior pastor at our church—Eastside Protestant Church in Richland, Washington—but my mom and dad both stayed home with me that day to make sure I was okay.

My parents were not the type of churchy Christians who would place a sick kid's fever-wracked body on the altar so the congregation could pray over him. The doctor said I needed to stay in bed until the fever broke, so Mom and Dad stayed home with me and prayed. By Tuesday the fever was gone, and we were all back in church the next Sunday. I also attended youth group every Wednesday night with Pastor Rick.

So, that was it. Running and Religion. My own adolescent brand of spiritual R and R.

I was pretty normal otherwise. I had a satisfactory social life, although, it seemed to have organized itself around running and church. I had a lot of friends, but they were almost all runners or church kids. Coach Easton said that was because those were the two things that mattered most to me. Pastor Rick said it was because running was either becoming part of my ministry, or it was keeping me from my true calling. I think they were both about half right.

I didn't know I had a ministry.

And I wasn't sure I wanted a calling.

I went to church twice a week because that's what we did. My father was the minister. My mother was the head of the Sunday school. They wanted me to do the right thing, and I tried. I never thought about being a Christian much beyond that. Church was like running; I'd done it so often and for so long, it had become automatic. It just happened. I just did it.

But then, there was this voice. It didn't say exactly the same thing every morning, but it was always some variation of the same theme.

Is this really what you should be doing?

Isn't there a better way to spend your time?

You run at least ten times a week, but you only go to church twice a week.

You need to get serious, son. There's work to be done.

God's work.

And here's the strange part. My father—you know, the minister—thought my running was great. Did I mention yet that I'd never lost a high school race? Well, almost never. I'm sure that made my father proud. He may be a minister, but he's also a human being. The last time anyone beat me had been at the state track meet when I was in the ninth grade. I led the mile for three laps, then two seniors passed me, and I finished third. Coach Easton said I had a God-given talent and a great cardio-vascular system, and I used to wonder if they were the same thing.

And if they were, whose voice had I been hearing?

So, I'd get up and put on my shoes, grab a sweatshirt from the pile in the bottom of my closet, and leave the house as quietly as I could. By the time I'd get back from my run, the whole house would smell like bacon and coffee, and Mom and my sister Naomi would be tinkering around in the kitchen. Mom grew up on a wheat-and-cattle ranch up north around Connell, so there'd be pancakes and bacon and eggs on a platter in the middle of the kitchen table. Dad would already be at the desk in his study with a huge mug of coffee, reading and making notes on a yellow pad. He'd stop when I'd come through the back door, and we'd all have breakfast together. Our family was very normal.

Except for my sister. Naomi confused people, including me.

She always dressed in black. Her favorite garment was a torn black t-shirt with the words *Ask Me About My Savior* in blood-red paint scrolled across the front. She wore heavy black makeup to school and a baggy pea coat with the collar pulled permanently up around her ears. An English teacher asked her once if she was a Goth.

"No, Mr. Parker. I'm not a Goth. I am a Christian."

Like I said, my sister confuses people.

My parents still live in the same just-big-enough house next door to the church. People in Dad's congregation called it the parsonage, but we didn't. Maybe if I thought of our house as the parsonage, I'd have taken the voice in my head more seriously. Usually, The Voice shut up after I turned off the alarm, and I wouldn't have to think about it until it started up again the next morning. But for some reason, The Voice came back during my run on this particular Monday morning, just five days before the biggest track meet of my life.

I didn't usually have to wait to cross the streets in Richland because there was almost no traffic at 6:00 a.m. But on that morning, I stopped to re-tie my shoe before crossing George Washington Way, and The Voice came back.

What in God's name are you doing out here?

You are becoming a man.

Put away childish games.

You've got a calling, and it's not running in circles to impress people.

You're a Christian. For God's sake, start acting like it.

I finished tying my shoe, and The Voice shut up, but I couldn't stop thinking about it. The Voice seemed sort of nagging, but in a passive-aggressive, non-threatening kind of way. I mean, The Voice was very reasonable. It wasn't shouting and didn't sound angry. It actually sounded a little like my dad when he talked to the youth group. You know the tone I mean...like he's really serious but doesn't want to scare or upset anyone. Kind of slow and soft and measured. Like, "You kids know all about peer pressure, and you've heard about the bad things that can happen when you make the wrong choice, so I'm not going to tell you what to do..."

Since he was really being reasonable and calm about it, the over-all effect was that he was telling us what to do, and we knew it.

That's sort of the way it was with The Voice. Like it was just reinforcing something I should already know. The Voice never said anything that didn't ring true. But it never made a compelling case for any other version of the truth, either, like it wanted me to start an argument with myself.

I am a Christian. But since I grew up in the church, I never had the Damascus Road, Come to Jesus experience like some of my Christian friends had. Or like my father had. Because of my mother. When it comes to Christianity, I'm a legacy. I was *born* into it, not *Born Again* into it. But I didn't know if that was the same as being born for it.

So, this voice was nagging at me while I was tying my shoes, and I couldn't get it out of my head until I was well into my run. I would run a half mile to Howard Amon Park, and when I reached the bike path along the river, I'd have to decide whether to turn north or south.

Either way, I'd run about three miles then turn around and repeat the same route. Then another half mile back home and just like that, six or seven miles before breakfast. Everyone thought I ran along the bike path because it was so pretty, especially with the rising sun shining off the Columbia River. But I never noticed the river or the sunrise. I ran along the bike path because it was flat, and I could really get moving on the smooth pavement.

I loved to run very fast. I never jogged. Coach Easton didn't have a lot of use for easy runs or jogging, except for warming up and cooling down or recovering from a hard race. We didn't have a lot of guys on our cross-country team because almost no one could handle the amount of hard work Coach gave us.

Not to brag, but I ran by myself because no one else could keep up, even though we had some really good guys on our team. I'd think about that as I hammered down the bike path toward Columbia Point, past the condos and the marina, past a couple of retirees out for their morning walk.

Every morning was the same, my head empty of every-thing but running. How and where are my feet striking the ground? Are my hands in the right place? Am I running too hard to finish at this pace?

And I'd think about my next race. On this Monday morning, that meant thinking about the Elite Mile at the Pasco Invitational coming up on Saturday.

#

The Pasco Invitational Track Meet is a Big Deal. Other than the state meet, it was the only other race Coach Easton ever talked about. He'd been coaching at Richland High School for...like...ever. As the day of the meet got closer, he'd tell us a different story every day about some great race from back before I was even born.

Last year just before I won the two-mile, he took me aside after the meet and told me about the 1966 Pasco Invita-tional when Rick Riley set the national record in the two-mile, coming in at 9:01. That was faster than I'd run at the time, but not by much.

The first time I met Coach Easton, I was thirteen years old and naked. As a physically un-precocious seventh grader, I didn't even know who Coach Easton was. But after a slushy, middle school cross country race around the grass playfield at the local junior high, I was shivering in the locker room, trying to get into dry clothes.

My teeth were chattering as I tried to get dressed in a toilet stall. I must have looked ridiculous because the cold had exaggerated my normal prepubescent awkwardness, and I couldn't get even one leg into my underpants. I fell over on the second try and had to catch myself on the toilet seat. I heard a soft chuckle behind me, and when I turned around, with my long pants in one hand and my underwear in the other, a man I did not recognize was leaning against the wall opposite the stall.

A strange man had followed me into the locker room and watched while I struggled with my underpants in a bathroom stall, and if I had not been naked, I probably would have tried to run away.

But the man just smiled and said, "I'm Coach Easton, the cross-country coach from up at the high school. You need some help?"

I looked down at myself and heard a loud banging on the door. The eighth graders were trying to get into the locker room. I looked toward the door, worried.

"I locked the door," Coach Easton said. "They can go get a key from their coach, or they can wait in the rain. Where are the rest of the seventh graders?"

"Everyone else just grabs their stuff and leaves," I said. "But my mom says to always put on dry clothes after I run." I thought about why I said that. "And I haven't been sick once all year."

"Well, that's good advice. Finish putting your clothes on. I'll wait a minute."

I'd warmed up enough to dress myself, which I did as fast as I could, spurred on by the high school coach's interest and by the imminent return of the eighth graders.

"Jonah, right?"

"Yes, sir." My parents insisted Naomi and I call all adults sir or ma'am whether they deserved it or not. I always did, but I don't think I ever heard Naomi call anyone sir or ma'am.

"So, you like to run, Jonah?"

I thought for a few seconds about how to answer. "I like being good at it."

Coach Easton glanced at the ceiling and laughed. "Good

for you. That's what I like to hear. Because, son, you're going to be really good. You remind me of Rick Riley."

"I don't know who that is."

"Well, when you get up to the high school, and if you work really hard, I'll tell you about Mr. Rick Riley."

There was more pounding, and Coach Easton unlocked the door, unleashing the torrent of eighth graders. I stayed close behind him so he could protect me from the rowdy deluge as we left the locker room. He patted me on the back as I headed toward the front of the building where I knew my mother would be waiting with the car.

The next morning, I got up to run before school for the first time.

#

I won the two-mile at the Pasco Invitational last year, but "only" ran 9:06. I was disappointed because I ran the first half of the race too fast and lost ten seconds over the last two laps. It seemed like a failure, even though I'd won. I've since discovered that I had a teenage athlete's typical misunderstanding of the nature of failure.

"That was brave," Coach Easton told me, "but I hope you learned something."

"Yes, sir." What he hoped was that I'd learned to run a more even pace, but I was thinking I would train so hard from then on that I wouldn't ever fail again.

After practice on the Monday before the Pasco Invitational, Coach Easton sat me down in the bleachers to go over the guys I'd be racing. He always knew each kid's best time and something about how they raced. I think he spent a lot of time on the phone with other coaches. I listened but didn't think too much about the other guys. There were some good runners out there, but remember, I hadn't lost since the ninth grade.

"There are two kids I think you need to pay special attention to," he said. "Micah Madrigal you know. He was third at state last year. He hasn't run a mile yet this season, but he ran a solo 800 in 1:53 just last week."

I liked Micah. He was a muscular kid from Spokane. He was quiet but always upbeat. When we raced, he always seemed happier about how well I'd run than he was upset about losing.

"And there's this kid from a tiny town on the west side of the mountains. Mike Beck."

"Mike Beck?" I'd never heard of him, so... "He can't be that good, Coach."

"He's come right out of nowhere. A coaching friend of mine from Snohomish said he beat everyone over there in cross country. He said this Beck kid was the best he's ever seen. Then he disappeared. Didn't finish the cross-country season."

"Then he can't be that good. I'm not worried."

Coach Easton was standing in the front aisle of the bleachers, and I was sitting three rows up, so we were eye-to-eye. He stepped up onto the bleachers, stood over me for several seconds, and then sat down beside me. He didn't say anything for a long time, and I was a little curious about what he might be thinking.

"Jonah, you're as good as any kid I've ever seen around here. But no matter how good you are, there is always someone who might beat you. And sometimes, they'll come from someplace you've never heard of."

Okay, I got the point. I'd be sure to keep this Beck kid in mind. But I still didn't think he'd be a problem.

As I approached the halfway point of my morning run, The Voice was silent, but the questions lingered. *Am I a Christian?* There was an answer, tentatively floating up to the front of my mind. And the answer was yes. But maybe not a very serious Christian, at least, not as serious as The Voice wanted me to be.

Okay, then. Next question: *Should I be out here like this every morning? Or is there something else I should be doing?*

I ran the short loop at Columbia Point and then started back. The questions continued to bounce around in my head, mixed together with the running. I was more familiar with the running half of the debate, so I decided to push hard all the way back home, at a faster pace than some decent adult runners can manage when they race.

I turned left out of the park and dashed across George Washington Way just ahead of someone's showy new pickup. The driver had to slow down quickly to keep from hitting me, and he honked his horn. My legs were heavy, and I was breathing hard. The running had slid into the back of my mind again, and the questions had returned... *Am I a serious Christian? Am I as serious about being a Christian as I am about being a runner?*

I tried to silence the confusion by running even harder for another half mile. I couldn't seem to focus on the running, though, so I slowed to a jog for the last half mile, and by the time I got home, I was breathing normally, and my legs felt light and bouncy again.

But then, suddenly and without warning, one more question joined the jumble in my brain.

Just how good is Mike Beck?

\#

Thankfully, The Voice was silent for the rest of the week. A blessing, I guess, because I really, *really* needed to concentrate on the Mile at Pasco. There was absolutely no reason that I should not win because I'd already won the two-mile there twice, and I'd run 4:10 for the mile indoors back in February.

Coach Easton didn't have much to say in the days leading up to the race. He'd already let us know that Pasco was *the* title every kid in our part of the state wanted to win. He told us the stories about past Pasco-race heroes. Rick Riley and Keith Tinnier and Willie Turner and all the rest. But the week of the meet, he went silent. It was as if he'd made his point, and now it was up to us to just get the job done.

That's why after a practice on Monday, I was surprised when he called me aside to talk about the race, or not exactly about the race, but about one particular unmentioned participant.

He walked me over to the bleachers and sat me down in the first row. Usually, he stood over us when he had something to say, but this time he sat next to me and put his arm around my shoulders. I waited, but he just stared out at the track for a long time without saying anything.

"Coach? Is anything wrong?"

He waited another long moment before he answered.

"Jonah, this race Saturday is a great opportunity for you."

"I know, Coach. I'm going to win the mile at the Pasco Invite."

He took his arm away and folded his hands.

"I expect so. Maybe."

"Maybe, Coach?"

He stood, turned, and leaned back against the low railing in front of the bleachers.

"There's not a lot any coach or athlete is ever certain about going into a big race. But given what I know about you, your character as an athlete, I'm certain you'll run the best race of your life Saturday, and that's saying something."

"Then what are we talking about, Coach?"

"Jonah, have you ever heard me say anything to you or any of the other guys about winning or losing?"

I thought about it. Winning mattered to me. A lot. I liked the post-race high-fives and the pats on the back and helping the team and making my school and the program look good. I liked that a few teachers and some kids and even people in town all thought I was a big deal. All because I'd never lost a race.

And then I realized that none of that had come from Coach Easton. He never had anything to say about my winning, only about how I'd run and how I could run even better next time.

"I hadn't thought about it, Coach. But I guess not."

"That's because if you do everything right—train correctly, prepare, run smart—then winning takes care of itself. You'll win if you're good enough."

Good enough?

"But I've done all that." I was beginning to feel uncomfortable. And just a little annoyed.

"Yes. You have. You've done an admirable job handling everything you can control. But there is one thing you can't control. Your opponents. Keep that in mind as you prepare to race Saturday."

So, there it was. And for the first time. Coach Easton was concerned about someone I would be racing against.

Mike Beck.

Made in the USA
Monee, IL
14 October 2021

79808553R00174